THE LIGHT & THE NIGHT OF THE FIREBIRD

The Light & The Night Of The Firebird

Kimberly Ann Zeidner

First Printing, 2025

This is a work of fiction. Names, characters, businesses, events and incidents are the products of the author's imagination. Any resemblance to actual persons, living or dead, or actual events is purely coincidental and not intended by the author.

To the women who over-analyze,
who speculate,
who create stories in their heads.
I wrote this down for you.

And to my sister, Kelsey, who inspired this
story.

Contents

PROLOGUE

They had been traveling through the Endless Forest for what felt like forever. But a fortnight after their journey began, the small group of fae finally reached the ancient tree they had been seeking. At the base, they began to build a small fire while chanting the words that would set the plan into motion. Then, with trembling hands, the fae opened the vessel they had been protecting all throughout their journey.

At first, a thick, black smoke rose from the flames. But suddenly, the fire died down and once it extinguished entirely, it was then that they saw the bird emerge. It spread its wings in performance, displaying vibrant shades of red, orange, and yellow so radiant, they rivaled the sun. Then the bird glided forward mere feet from their heads and disappeared into the sky.

"When King Remis' blood spills, the Firebird will return and usher us from the dark into the light."

She stands at the edge of the cliff, her long, black hair whipping around her face like the tendrils of shadows that were wrapped around her body. Somewhere in the distance, lightning cascades down through the sky and strikes. She takes one last look behind her, tears in her eyes, before raising her hands over her head and swan-diving off the precipice.

PART 1

ENTER THE FOREST

1

CHAPTER ONE

S carlet woke up with a gasp as she fell out of her bed and onto the hard, wood floor. Tangled in white sheets, she took several deep and steadying breaths to slow her erratic heartbeat and clear the buzzing in her head. No matter how used to having strange dreams and nightmares Scarlet had become, her body always had the same jarring reaction. She started to stand up just in time for two white balls of fluff to tackle her back down to the ground to give her little, wet licks on her face. Scarlet smiled at her two white foxes, Pearl and Alabaster, who had been a part of her life for as far back as she could remember. Which is why she knew that Pearl surely felt her anxiety and was trying to soothe her while Alabaster was probably just hungry and wanting to be fed.

Typical, Scarlet thought.

"Okay! Okay! I'm up!" she told them as she finally untangled herself from the sheets and her beautiful babies' affection. They stood in front of her like obedient, domesticated dogs, their icy blue eyes seemingly staring into her soul.

Scarlet wrapped herself in a soft, white robe and opened the curtains in her room to greet the morning. It was still dark out, but Scarlet could tell that it was going to be a gloomy day with clouds snuffing out the starlight in the sky. At least there was no lightning to be seen. She shivered, thinking about her dream again and the woman who jumped off the cliff. The woman seemed strangely familiar to Scarlet. She *always* seemed familiar to her. Maybe that was just what happened when you had the same dream for as far back as you could remember: the cast of characters became kin.

Scarlet tightened the drawstring around her robe and made her way down to the kitchen in search of some scraps of meat for Pearl and Alabaster. Despite the fact that the sun hadn't yet risen, the kitchen was already bustling with energy as cooks and maids scuttled about, giving Scarlet a wide berth as they passed around platters of food and prepared for the big day. Scarlet, on the other hand, was less than enthused.

"Princess! What are you doing down here?" Marta gasped as she gazed over Scarlet's appearance. "You're not dressed! And you're barefoot!" The matronly cook tsked at her.

Scarlet tucked a piece of loose hair behind her pointed ear and looked down, realizing that she had forgotten to put on shoes and then shrugged. "Pearl and Alabaster were insisting on breakfast, so I had no choice but to cater to the demanding beasts."

Marta rolled her eyes before placing a small, parchment-wrapped satchel in her hands. Marta always had a determined look about her, but today she looked somewhat weary. Troubled, but trying to hide it. "You won't be able to do this in the mansion, dear. Please promise me that you'll mind yourself and behave." Marta placed both of her hands on Scarlet's shoulders and squeezed.

Scarlet always knew that she was meant for more. A powerful firestarter with red hair as bright as flames and a fiery temperament to match, she always believed that she wasn't reaching her full potential. Maybe if she had been nurtured at a young age, she would feel more fulfilled. Maybe, she'd be more likable. But instead, her mother had died when she was a baby – something that no one ever talked about – and her father passed her off to the governess, not wanting to be bothered by a crying infant. But one day, during a fit, Scarlet accidentally set her nursery curtains on fire, frightening her governess enough to quit. A new one was hired, but she soon quit, as well, blaming Scarlet for practically killing her when she set the servant's hair on fire. Governess after governess entered the castle and soon exited, fearing Scarlet's unpredictable fire magic.

Because fae didn't discover their magic until they were around five years old, having powers as a baby was unheard of. Had Scarlet's powers manifested later in her childhood, she would have been able to control the flames within her. Instead, her magic was unruly and untamed and caused distress around the castle.

If she could have managed it, she would have, but she was just a baby.

She was just a baby and yet, despite the issue of her unpredictable magic, most found Scarlet to be disagreeable for other reasons.

She cried far more than "normal" infants.

Her eyes were disturbing, either perpetually bloodshot or with pupils that were blown so wide, they looked like portals opening within her.

She bit some of the servants so hard, she'd make them bleed.

And then there was the issue of *her* blood. It was the darkest red anyone had ever seen. In fact, it was practically black. Which started whisperings among those within the kingdom of Tellus that Scarlet was cursed – a baby born of black magic.

She never understood how anyone could think she was cursed. Unlucky, maybe. But what she *did* understand was that the rumor – likely started by one of the servants – coupled with the fire magic that ran through her veins, could be a frightening combination to anyone who didn't know her.

And most didn't.

Because her mother's death was never discussed in front of her, Scarlet often wondered if everyone blamed Scarlet's curse for the queen being taken from them too soon. She desperately wished she knew more about her mother. Even her father, who seemed to only care about himself, must have been so grief-stricken when she died, because there wasn't a single portrait of his late wife anywhere. Did *he* blame Scarlet's curse for her death?

Scarlet rolled her eyes at Marta – one of the few people in her life who didn't treat her with fear or disdain – as she placed both of *her* hands on the cook, mirroring her seriousness. "I will behave. But only because my father would sooner see me beheaded than have me sully his good name and that of his kingdom."

"Your father loves you, Scarlet," Marta replied earnestly, releasing Scarlet from her hold. No matter how sweet the old woman was or how much she wanted to protect Scarlet's feelings, even she couldn't make that lie sound believable. "Now go! Today's a big day!" she exclaimed optimistically.

A big day, indeed. For today was the day that the Phoenix Mansion would open its doors for the Endless Forest Trials.

Every ten years, hundreds of people from all over the realm traveled to Tellus to compete in the trials for a chance to win the grand prize of a wish granted by the kingdom's sorcerer. An immense honor and one her father insisted she win this year now that she was twenty-one and old enough to compete. But before the games began, the sorcerer's apprentices would need to choose the contestants. Scarlet never understood for what reason contestants were chosen. Not one book that she had ever read about the trials discussed the criteria that was used by the apprentices. It almost seemed like a random selection, but she knew there had to be more to it than dumb luck.

Scarlet thanked Marta for the food before heading back to her room where she found her two little snow foxes waiting patiently for her. She unwrapped the packet of meat and placed it in a small dish that was left next to an almost empty bowl of water. Scarlet grabbed the jug on her nightstand and poured water into the bowl.

"You two better behave while I'm gone," she told Pearl and Alabaster as if they were children who could understand and obey her. They always looked at her like they had something to say, but couldn't find the right words.

As much as Scarlet didn't want to compete in the trials, she knew it was her duty. "For the good of her kingdom." Her wish had been chosen by her father years ago: She would wish for the darkness within her to be removed. Scarlet always thought it was silly that her father believed the superstition about her. She wasn't full of darkness; she was void of love. And as Scarlet got older, the temperament that had been exhibited during her early years had weaned its way out of her. Nevertheless, her father insisted that the darkness would be her undoing and in order for her to rule one day, she needed to survive.

Ironic that it seemed the darkness had long since eaten away at both *his* humanity and sanity and yet, he was still ruling.

Regardless, Scarlet wanted more than just to survive. She wanted to live.

As if her heart could conjure exactly what it desired, there was a tap at the window and outside was Hanre. Scarlet ran to the window and quickly opened it, Pearl and Alabaster seemingly ignoring her movements entirely, continuing to chow down on their breakfast.

"What are you doing here?" she shout-whispered, pulling him into her room by the front of his tan tunic.

His sparkling blue eyes stared into hers. "I had to see you one last time before you left for the mansion... Princess," he smirked, climbing through the window. He raked his hand through his mop of blonde hair.

"*You* are going to get in trouble. You need to leave before someone sees you here," Scarlet declared, pushing him back with false effort. Hanre grabbed her hand and held it captive against his chest.

"I'll be in even more trouble if you don't win this." All of the mirth left his eyes and a look of complete sadness plagued them instead. "You can not die, Scarlet. Do you hear me?"

Ah, yes. That bit of information that Scarlet always tried to forget. The Endless Forest Trials often ended in the deaths of most of the participants. Sometimes she wondered if her father insisted on her competing just to get rid of her. But then who would take the crown when he eventually died?

Scarlet sighed. Hanre had been her first – and only – love. They had been young and felt a deep tenderness for one another, but knew that it could never last. Scarlet was to be the queen of Tellus and Hanre was to be the servant that fetched her horse. That was her fate for as long as she could remember and all she and Hanre had done was fool themselves.

There was also the small fact of him being human and her being fae. And in her father's kingdom, humans and fae didn't marry and they *definitely* didn't reproduce. Crossbreeds, she'd heard her father call the children of human-fae couples in other kingdoms. Always spitting out the word like it disgusted him. There was only one thing about human-fae relationships that concerned Scarlet: their lifespans. While few humans lived to ever see one hundred years old, most fae lived centuries, aging at a much slower rate than humans once they entered their third decade. It took approximately thirty years for a fae to fully embrace their powers and once they did, the magic would decelerate the aging process.

In another life, Hanre and I would be together and live happily ever after, Scarlet mused.

But regardless, they remained the closest of friends and Hanre was still the only one in Scarlet's life that she had ever felt truly loved her. The only one that made her feel like her thoughts mattered, despite her ignorance of the realm and the struggles faced outside the castle's gates. The only one who didn't treat her like she was carrying a contagious disease within her.

"If something happens to me, please don't forget about me," Scarlet whispered sadly to her favorite person in the world.

Hanre scoffed as he pulled her into his embrace. "I could never." He paused. "But you *will* win, Scarlet. Do you understand me? I need you to believe that you will win."

Scarlet sighed against his chest.

What could have been?

What would never be?

I'm so scared.

She couldn't help the thoughts from flooding her mind.

"There, there," Hanre whispered, taking her chin in one hand and wiping her tears away with the other. "You are a princess. You are a firestarter. You are strong and beautiful and powerful and you *will* win." His words were a mantra that Scarlet wanted to repeat until she spoke them into existence. Manifestation. She had heard that term before. She wondered how often it was successful.

Scarlet's heart felt like it would burst for how much she loved the stable boy who befriended her when she had no one. The blonde-haired boy who became her companion and was as much a part of her life as Pearl and Alabaster. How could she have darkness in her when all she felt was overwhelming love for the ones she held dear?

Scarlet tried to compose herself and appear strong. She sniffed before pulling away from Hanre and looking back into his eyes. "I know," she lied, nodding her head. "I know."

There was a knock at the door.

"You have to go," Scarlet told Hanre, looking at him so hard, as if trying to imprint his image in her brain for eternity.

Hanre leaned down and kissed her cheek. "Be good, Princess." Scarlet didn't miss that his eyes were misty as he climbed out the window. Turning towards the stables, he didn't look back.

She wiped the remaining tears from her eyes. "Come in!" she called to whoever was waiting outside of her room.

The door to the bed chamber opened and her maid, Gretta, tentatively walked inside.

"Good morning, Your Highness! I'm here to prepare your bath," she stated more cheerfully than usual.

Scarlet internally rolled her eyes, assuming Gretta's new disposition was because the maid hoped to finally be rid of her and saw the trials as her chance, even if it was only a temporary respite. Gretta's false smile briefly slipped when she saw Scarlet's reddened eyes and tear-streaked face.

A bath did sound lovely, though, so Scarlet mustered a small smile. "Very well."

* * * **

After her bath, Scarlet was summoned by her father. She made her way through the castle and couldn't help but notice how the servants lowered their heads and whispered to one another as she walked by. Scarlet tried to ignore their tittering and soon stepped into the throne room, colored light flooding in from the enormous stained-glass windows depicting different scenes from fae history, or rather, what was believed to be fae history. There was so much that was unknown about the Fates – how they created the realms and how humans first discovered the existence of the fae – but there were stories passed down from generation to generation that were believed to be the truth.

Scarlet continued walking, just giving the windows a cursory glance before she found King Remis, proudly sitting atop his throne on the raised dais.

Obviously, Scarlet thought to herself. She never saw her father in any casual capacity. He was always to be addressed in the throne room where he always sat on his gilded throne and always wore his crown, as if meeting with his subjects on Yielding Day. But she was no subject, nor was she there to pay her tithe in magic. She was his daughter and she had hoped that on such a big day for her, he could have played the role of father and not just the king.

Scarlet walked closer to him, her shoes making a clacking noise as they tapped on the expansive floor, the sound echoing throughout the room. Her eyes drifted to the three witches that stood on either side of King Remis. The Six, they were called in Tellus. Their long, midnight black locks always fell in front of their faces, practically covering their snow-white skin and milky, unfocused eyes... and they never spoke, which Scarlet thought was incredibly creepy. Quite frankly, she didn't even know if they *could* speak.

"Princess! Lovely to see you!" the king called down to her from the dais, his booming voice bouncing off of the walls and echoing throughout the space. His lips curled into a sneer, causing Scarlet's stomach to churn as she walked closer.

The throne room was the epitome of opulence with sparkling, white marble floors, red curtains adorned with gold filigree and a throne that was so large, it was almost laughable. Not "almost;" it really was ridiculously oversized.

"Your Majesty," she replied with a polite curtsy. The king loved formality and she was there to please him during his summons.

"I called you here today to wish you well during your trials." He smiled down at her, but there was no love in the act. In fact, there was nothing but disdain in his cold, beady eyes.

"Thank you, Your Majesty," Scarlet answered with a nod, keeping her gaze lowered to the floor. There was actually a spot that needed to be shined, but she would never dare say anything, lest a servant be punished. And the punishments never matched the crimes. "I hope to make the kingdom proud."

"Hope?!" he bellowed at her and she audibly swallowed, immediately noting her mistake. "You better do more than hope, girl." It was a threat. And she expected nothing less. "Need I remind you what is at stake here? You *will* win these trials. There is no other option. Do you understand me?"

Scarlet clasped her hands in front of her and squeezed them together almost painfully, desperate to cease their shaking. Fates, he was awful and always unnerved her.

"Yes, Your Majesty." Scarlet decided to keep her responses shorter for fear of angering him any further. He had never caused her any physical harm, but the emotional pain was enough to instill the fear in her.

The king's aggression was one of the many reasons for the townsfolk's unhappiness in the kingdom. Scarlet had been isolated from everyone outside the castle gates, the king claiming that it was what was best for royal heirs – to keep them and the bloodline safe – , but Scarlet knew the truth: It was so that she would be completely ignorant to the state the kingdom was in. Hanre would often tell her stories about children starving on the streets. Of humans getting caught stealing loaves of bread and their unjust penalty of a public execution. Hanre said it was so the king could remind everyone what happens to thieves. But the reality was, these were just poor folks trying to keep their families fed. When, meanwhile, Scarlet and her father sat in the lap of luxury with all of the wealth anyone could ask for. Would it be such a hardship for the king to invest in his people? In the town? Why was he so set on keeping them impoverished? Hanre had explained to her that with control comes vast power. And Scarlet knew that her father was always hungry for more. By withholding the bread, the king made it so that the poor would do anything just to get some crumbs.

Which was why every Yielding Day, any fae with magical abilities had to pay a tithe to the king in exchange for a small amount of coin. The Six would extract a portion of each fae's magic and transfer it to her father. The consequence for refusal? Death. It seemed so wrong, especially since Scarlet was never forced to give away any of her magic, but what could she do? She could never stop her father.

The Endless Forest Trials were supposed to be a way to appease the citizens of Tellus. Without knowing how the sorcerer's apprentices chose contestants to compete, it gave everyone, whether fae or human, rich or poor, an opportunity to win a wish. It seemed ridiculous to Scarlet that she could potentially take that from someone who needed it far more than she did. But these were all things she would change when she eventually became queen.

"Your magic... it's strong? You've been practicing your wielding?"

"Yes, Your Majesty." While Scarlet had been using her fire magic since it manifested as a baby, all fae had inherent magic. They were faster than humans and had enhanced senses. Their minor wounds healed quickly and they could perform basic spells like moving small objects. But then there was magic that was gifted by the Fates, like Scarlet's fire magic, and was chosen based on fated destinies. Scarlet always figured that if her magic was tied to her fate, it was important to harness its power to the utmost of her abilities. After so many years of using it, Scarlet's fire magic was as much a part of her as her arms and legs. It was something that she could control now without much thought.

With a wave of his hand, the king dismissed her. "Then I will see you soon... daughter." He spat the word like there was acid in his mouth.

A chill ran up Scarlet's spine as she exited the throne room, the clacking of her shoes faster than when she entered, and made her way back to her quarters to gather her belongings before heading to the Phoenix Mansion.

2

CHAPTER TWO

Scarlet stood within the wrought-iron gates of the Phoenix Mansion, a tan and brown valise filled with some clothes and toiletries in hand. She had packed enough for a fortnight, the accounts of past trials stating that the duration of their time at the mansion never lasted longer than that. Now all she needed was a little good fortune to get past the selection process and then she would do whatever it took to win the trials, make her wish and be done with this nonsense of her darkness once and for all.

A layer of fog covered the grounds of the mansion giving Scarlet an ominous feeling. There was a buzz around her as the crowd began to recognize the Princess of Tellus standing among them. While most had likely never seen her in person, Scarlet had seen the portraits that were painted of her to hang in public buildings. Glancing around, Scarlet guessed there had to be at least one hundred fae and humans surrounding her, hoping to get selected. The murmurs and pointing continued, but the crowd's attention quickly shifted away from her as the three sorcerer's apprentices exited the mansion and stepped outside to face them all.

"Welcome to Selection Day for this decade's Endless Forest Trials," one of the apprentices announced to the crowd. "My name is Francois and today myself, along with Gebert and Marcus will be conducting the selection of contestants. There is nothing you need to do. Please remain silent and still as we make our way through the crowd."

With that, Francois, Gebert and Marcus, dressed in brown, burlap robes, made their way down the mansion's steps, their hoods covering much of their faces. They started weaving their way through the mass of hopefuls and the thought of the burlap's harsh fibers rubbing against skin made Scarlet scratch herself absentmindedly. Meanwhile, everyone stood like statues as the apprentices simply glanced at some and studied others, scrutinizing over things like the details of their faces or the feel of their skin. This part unnerved Scarlet. She very much felt like cattle being sized up for the slaughter. Little by little, several fae and a couple of humans were selected and made their way to the front steps of the mansion. Most looked happy or relieved. Scarlet wasn't sure she'd feel either emotion.

Scarlet could feel Marcus' presence at her back as he made his way through the remainder of the crowd. There was an energy that radiated off of him that made Scarlet feel even more uncomfortable, if that was even possible. She couldn't tell if it was just her nerves making her feel that way or if it was something else. Slowly, he approached Scarlet and looked at her curiously, his head cocked to one side.

"Firebird…" he breathed, in awe. Marcus stood in front of Scarlet, wonderment glittering in his eyes.

Scarlet felt like she was going to pass out. Breathing normally suddenly became hard. Sensing her distress, her fire magic made its way to the surface of her skin, but she knew it wouldn't ignite without her direct intention. That's how it had worked for as long as she could remember. Her body would get hot, but until she called to her magic, it would lie simmering on the surface like an army waiting for its commander's signal to charge.

Nearby folks started to stare and whisper. For a brief moment, Scarlet felt like she was a child again. The whispers. The confusion. The shame. Her magic continued to dance along her skin, practically asking permission to be released.

Francois and Gebert came around to stand with Marcus. "Do you really think?" Francois questioned, his face as much in awe as Marcus'.

"She is the answer," Marcus stated as he took both hands and wrapped them tightly around Scarlet's forearms. Alarmed, Scarlet stood with wide, unblinking eyes. "After all this time!"

"I… um… I don't think…" Scarlet rambled nervously. She didn't know what or who this Firebird was, but she was sure it wasn't a reference to her.

Scarlet was quickly ushered by Marcus, Gebert and Francois up to the front steps where the trial contestants all stood, now looking at her with the same intense curiosity the apprentices had. Did any of them know who or what the Firebird was? She noticed a small, fae female with brassy auburn hair and warm brown eyes staring at her, but when they made eye contact, both quickly turned their heads away from one another.

Scarlet was still in too much shock. Not only was she actually selected to compete, not only did she actually have a chance of winning... but they thought she was someone or something called the Firebird. There was so much to take in at that moment. For a brief instant, Scarlet thought of her father, wondering what he would make of this moment. Would he be proud or disgusted? Scarlet assumed the latter and then shook off the thought.

"We are pleased to announce that we have selected our ten chosen ones for this year's Endless Forest Trials!" Marcus declared. "Thank you all for coming! We hope to see you again in ten years!" And with that, the crowd applauded with very little vigor and slowly started to disperse, making their way outside of the mansion's grounds and back to their everyday lives. Ominously, the gate creaked closed behind them.

The apprentices turned to face the contestants. "You may all head inside to settle into your assigned rooms. There you will find everything you will need to make your stay more comfortable while you compete," Marcus announced. "Dinner will be served in the Great Hall promptly at sun down." And with that, all three apprentices turned and entered the mansion as the contestants shuffled quietly behind them.

Scarlet glanced over at the small fae she had previously noticed outside. The female was staring back at her with wide eyes as they began filing into line.

"Do you think we'll be assigned to our own rooms or that we'll have to share with other contestants?" she asked.

Scarlet shifted uncomfortably on her feet. "Uh... I'm... I'm not sure. I hadn't given it much thought, but I suppose we'll find out soon enough."

The female nodded as if Scarlet had given her something extraordinarily deep to consider. "Hm. I'm Tory, by the way," she stated as she boldly put her small hand out for Scarlet to shake.

"Scarlet," she replied, taking Tory's hand tentatively.

"You're the Princess of Tellus. I heard the apprentices call you the Firebird." Tory looked at Scarlet inquisitively, as if expecting an answer to a question that was never asked.

"I am the princess and, yes, I heard the same," was Scarlet's retort. "Although I have to be honest, I don't know who or what the Firebird references. I mean, I am a firestarter, but I've never heard of a Firebird. Is it because of my hair? It can't be. That's silly," she rambled nervously. Scarlet chastised herself for her last remark. Obviously her hair wouldn't cause such a reaction, but this attention was feeling an awful lot like the attention she received as a child from her governesses and it was making her increasingly uncomfortable.

Mentally getting herself back on track, Scarlet continued. "I know there has to be more. They looked... stunned? And the crowd seemed... I don't know... concerned? To be honest, I'm really not sure what to make of it. I'm just trying to get through all of this." Scarlet took a deep breath, her shoulders sagging after she exhaled.

Tory continued to stare at Scarlet with those eyes that said so much more than she was saying aloud. It was as if she knew something that Scarlet didn't. And that she was trying to determine if Scarlet's naivete was just that or a clever deception. "How old are you?" she asked.

"Twenty-one," Scarlet replied. "How old are you?"

"I'm twenty-eight, although sometimes I feel like I'm one hundred and twenty-eight." Tory paused. "Do you think you'll win?" she asked, somewhat matter-of-factly.

Scarlet was taken aback. "Do you?" she inquired.

"I think I can. I've been analyzing the trials from past years... I've trained physically and mentally, using my magic. I feel very much prepared, so I think I have a fighting chance. Pun intended, of course." Tory folded her arms in front of her. She looked formidable despite being rather petite. Tory had an air about her that somehow demanded respect while the easy way she spoke could lull someone into trusting her. She had a strong, determined jaw and perfectly arched brows that gave her an almost hardened look, but her soft eyes and full, rosy cheeks contrasted her sharper features.

"What kind of magic do you have?" Scarlet asked, genuinely curious. The more she knew, the more she could potentially use to her advantage in the competition.

"I have the power of eidetic evocation. Basically, I can remember anything I see or hear and with precise clarity. It comes in handy when needing to solve puzzles." Tory grinned.

Scarlet paused for a moment before asking, "Do you recall ever hearing anything about the Firebird?"

Tory looked up towards the ceiling of the mansion and squinted before she shook her head slowly, as if racking her brain for information. "I know that phoenixes are birds known to be reborn and rise from their own ashes. They represent renewal and immortality. Obviously we are in the Phoenix Mansion, so I imagine that there has to be a connection there, but if there is one, I've never heard of it before."

At that moment, the line brought them to a table where another petite female stood. Her pale complexion and ebony black hair gave her a somewhat ghostly appearance, which made Scarlet feel apprehensive.

"Names?" she questioned in a deep voice that did not match her appearance. Her quill was poised over a book, ready to record them into the history books of the trials.

Both replied their names in unison.

"Well, isn't that something?" the creepy lady declared as she narrowed her eyes at us. "I'm going to have you two share a room. Suite Thirteen. Up the stairs, down the hall and to your left." She held out a tarnished, bronze key with an elaborate bow at one end and three teeth at the other. "Dinner starts at sun down. We expect all of the contestants to dine together this evening for the welcome message, but meals will generally not be expected to be taken at set times."

Scarlet looked at Tory who reached out and took the key.

"What's your name?" Scarlet asked, slightly narrowing her eyes. There was something about this female that was setting her on edge and making her fire magic tingle at her fingertips.

"That's none of your business!" she replied in a snarky tone, practically sneering at Scarlet.

Scarlet shook her head, trying to shake off the bad vibes she felt from this stranger who refused to divulge something as simple as her name when, meanwhile, everyone within the mansion seemed to know something about her that she didn't even know.

Going against her better judgement, she asked, "Why did the apprentices call me 'Firebird'?"

The woman simply clicked her tongue at her in disapproval as Tory gently grabbed Scarlet by the elbow and ushered her away.

"Don't bother," Tory whispered. "That's the sorcerer's assistant. No one knows who she is or where she came from, only that she 'welcomes,'" Tory said with finger quotes, "the contestants upon arrival with an unparalleled warmth." She laughed at her own sarcasm which made Scarlet smile. Tory was an odd bird, but she seemed nice enough. She was at least trying to be friendly, which was more than Scarlet could say for most of the fae she came across in her life within the castle.

"Shall we?" Tory asked as she held up the ancient-looking key and motioned towards the old, wooden stairs.

They started walking when they were approached by the most attractive human man Scarlet had ever seen. Rich, chocolate brown hair framed a chiseled face with twinkling brown eyes that sparkled like hessonite. He had an athletic build that made her wonder what he looked like without his tunic on. His sleeves were rolled up to his elbows, showing off elaborate tattoos swirled along his forearms.

"Hi, ladies," he said in a charismatic tone. "I'm Beaumont DaFoe, but my friends call me Beau. And since I think we're all about to get a lot closer, you can call me Beau, too." And then he grinned and winked. His grin was as wicked as it was beautiful with teeth so straight and white they made Scarlet swipe her tongue across her own, jealously wondering how he got his so impossibly perfect.

Growing up, Scarlet often had to find solitary activities and developed an affinity for painting. She mostly painted flowers or bowls of fruit... things she could easily obtain in the castle for inspiration. But as soon as Scarlet laid eyes on Beau, she felt the deep desire to paint him.

"I'm Tory and this is Scarlet." Tory replied, completely unaffected by this beautiful man in front of them.

"Firebird," Beau tipped his head in greeting.

"I really wish everyone would stop calling me that," Scarlet mumbled under her breath.

"What was that?" Beau asked, perfect brows furrowed in confusion.

"I just said that I wished everyone would stop calling me 'Firebird' without an explanation." If Scarlet was honest with herself, she was not only annoyed with being kept in the dark, but with the fact that she was becoming the center of attention again. She knew that some attention was to be expected, given that she was Tellus royalty, but she didn't want to be made a spectacle of. And this was quickly starting to feel like a spectacle.

"You don't know the story of the Firebird?" Both Scarlet and Tory shook their heads. "Where are you from?"

"Well, here, actually," Scarlet replied. "Tellus."

"She's the *Princess* of Tellus!" Tory clarified.

"Princess, huh? And you've never heard about the prophecy? The Endless Forest is literally part of your kingdom and you don't know its history?" It wasn't an accusation, but sounded more like he was utterly dumbstruck. "Well, allow me to be the one to enlighten you! But first, maybe we should settle into our rooms?" Beau pointed a thumb towards the stairs.

"That's probably a good idea," Tory replied, seemingly anxious to get into our suite.

"After you," Beau motioned with a wave of his hand.

As the trio headed up the stairs that creaked far more than Scarlet was comfortable with, she asked Beau what room he was assigned to. She didn't know what to feel when she realized he would be in the room next door to them. Was she happy? Relieved? There was an emotion bubbling up inside of her that she couldn't quite put her finger on. It felt like butterflies were fluttering in her stomach and it made her feel strange and a little light-headed.

After a few moments of settling into their rooms, Beau joined Scarlet and Tory back in their suite and sat on Scarlet's bed. It also creaked under his weight and she couldn't stop her mind from wandering to thoughts of him *in* her bed – hair disheveled and chest glistening with sweat as she straddled him...

"Are you listening?" his voice cut through her thoughts.

"Erm... what?" she asked as her cheeks reddened. The reality was, outside of Hanre, Scarlet had very little experience with the opposite sex. She was mostly surrounded by other females within the castle, so Beau's presence on her bed was slightly unsettling. And those damn butterflies were making it so much worse!

Beau smiled. "I was telling you about the prophecy, but you seemed to have spaced out for a minute there." He paused, seemingly waiting to ensure she was paying attention this time. "Anyway, as I was saying..."

Tory smirked from where she was sitting on her bed. Scarlet couldn't figure Tory out yet. She seemed nice enough, but there were moments where something dark bubbled up from within her. Was she friend or foe? Scarlet realized she would have to be cautious around her new roommate until she figured her out.

"Hello?" A head with impossibly white hair popped into their doorway from the hall.

"Hello," Tory said, eyes locked on the stranger's blue ones as she sat up straighter. "Who are you?"

A body suddenly joined the head as he strolled into the room. "I'm Ricky." He turned to Beau. "I think we're sharing the suite next door."

Beau smiled and reached his hand out to shake Ricky's. "Oh, hey! I'm Beau. Nice to meet you! You just met Tory and that's our dear Princess of Tellus, Scarlet." She waved meekly. "We were just talking about the prophecy of the Firebird. Do you know it?"

Ricky shook his head and it looked like he narrowed his eyes at Scarlet. He had a beautiful face – just as handsome as Beau's – but while Beau's looks were wild and disarming, Ricky's face was what she imagined the hero of every story to look like. Utterly charming! And yet, despite reminding Scarlet of the white knight in shining armor that she read about in fairytales, the way Ricky looked at her made the hair on her arms stand up straight.

"Legend has it that, like, two hundred or so years ago there was a war between the Light and Dark Kingdoms. The details are very unclear, but it's known that the king of the Dark Kingdom was obsessed with power and sought to take over all of the Light Kingdom. The king and queen of the Light Kingdom tried to put an end to his tyranny, but they disappeared. And it's said that the Light Kingdom is frozen in time until the prophecy comes to pass. The prophecy was that the Firebird would rise and usher in a new era in the Light Kingdom, uniting it with the Dark Kingdom. They say that the Light Kingdom, frozen in time, has disappeared from existence, but meanwhile, no one knows which of our current kingdoms is the Dark Kingdom..." Beau paused and looked hesitantly at Scarlet. "Many believe that with the... um... unrest in Tellus, that we're *in* the Dark Kingdom. There are others who believe that it could be a neighboring kingdom like Spirare or Gelu. It's also possible that the Dark Kingdom was of another realm and has already fallen or that it's frozen, as well. There are some older fae who claim that

Tellus *is* the Dark Kingdom referenced and that Fiah was the Light Kingdom, now winked out of existence. But depending on who you talk to or what texts you read, the story will be different."

Tory and Ricky stared intently at Beau as he finished his story, but Scarlet's uneasiness caused her to stare down at her feet. She hated that her kingdom's subjects were so unhappy that their unrest was a known fact amongst others. And the source of their unhappiness was her father.

"So no one knows exactly what happened to the King and Queen of the Light Kingdom?" Tory asked.

Beau shook his head, "Not that anyone has shared with me. I've heard that other kingdoms have intentionally wiped the prophecy from their records to protect the Light Kingdom." He shrugged. "If you ask me, someone knows the truth."

"And so the apprentices believe that I'm the Firebird? How do I rise? And how could I save a potentially non-existent, frozen kingdom?" Scarlet asked, the questions continuing to add up in her mind. She wondered if her father knew anything about this prophecy. Based on Beau's estimated timeline, her father would have been alive – on the younger side of the fae lifespan, but definitely alive – when this took place.

Beau shrugged. "I don't know; I'm just telling the story as I know it, Princess."

"On that note," Tory said as she jumped off her bed, "We have to clean up and head down for the dinner festivities." She began ushering Beau and Ricky out the door and Scarlet caught the slight tilt to Tory's mouth as she put her hands on Ricky. "It's been lovely to meet your acquaintance, gentlemen, but out with you!" And with that, she closed the door behind them, leaning against it to face Scarlet. "They were awfully chatty." She rolled her eyes and shook her head, but the smile remained.

Scarlet smirked. "They seemed nice." Especially Beau. There was something about him that made her feel weak in the knees.

"Scarlet, this is a *competition!* Get your head in the game! They're both the enemy!" Tory yelled at her, pointing at the door.

Scarlet considered this for a moment. "But what about you? Are you my enemy?" The words left her mouth before she could stop them.

"I'm whatever I need to be to win."

3

CHAPTER THREE

Scarlet and Tory got out of their casual tunics and leather pants and dressed in attire more appropriate for a formal dinner – Tory in a long, black, velvet dress and Scarlet in long-sleeve, blue silk one that was loose-fitting and draped just below her knees. They headed down to the Great Hall where they were immediately greeted by Beau and Ricky, both of whom were looking quite handsome in black tunics and matching pants. They each had their hair slicked back, giving them a very refined and almost regal appearance. The ballroom was beautiful, albeit a bit old. Wooden beams adorned the vaulted ceiling and three stunning chandeliers hung down, but the curtains that cascaded along the windows looked a bit dusty. Two long tables were filled with dishes ranging from roast turkey and grilled fish to roasted root vegetables, creamy mashed potatoes, soft-looking rolls, and trays and trays of luscious cakes and pastries. Several carafes of wine adorned the table, as well.

"At least we'll be eating good tonight!" Beau declared as he pulled out a chair for Scarlet. Ricky glanced over at Tory and did the same for her. A bit surprised, both females took their offered seats and settled in.

Little by little, the rest of the contestants, some fae and some human, started to take seats, as well, at the table and make small talk with one another. After a short period of time, the sorcerer's apprentices filed in, followed by the creepy, dark-haired female from when they first checked in. They all stood at the head table as Marcus received everyone.

"I would like to welcome you all, once again, to the Endless Forest Trials! Each trial is designed to test your will, strength and heart. Heed my warning, not everyone will survive these tests. We know that you did not make the decision to come here lightly, but the reward is the greatest in not just the kingdom, but all of the realm! A wish granted by the all-powerful sorcerer! Anything you can dream up will be yours as long as it doesn't threaten the balance. If, of course, you persevere and win..."

The ballroom started to rumble with excitement from the contestants, but Marcus' last words made Scarlet's skin crawl. Even the way he said them felt ominous.

Do they all not realize that most of them will die? Scarlet wondered of her counterparts. *Especially the humans.* They made a choice to be here. She was forced to do so. Scarlet knew in her heart that she would never willingly come here. Even if she had been granted the opportunity to choose her own wish, there was nothing that would make her *choose* to compete in such a cruel game.

Scarlet leaned in towards Tory. "What does he mean that the wish can't threaten the balance?"

"You can't wish for something that would change the general course of things. For example, I can't wish to be Queen of Tellus because your father is the king. In order for me to be Queen, I'd have to marry your father or both the king and his heir would have to die. But I can wish to be rich. Does that make sense?"

Scarlet wasn't really sure, but she nodded, nonetheless. She wanted to ask Tory what her wish was, but knew that wishes tended to be deeply personal and not often shared with others.

"Tomorrow will start the first of the three trials. Be prepared for anything," Marcus continued as he looked around the room, making eye contact with each contestant.

"How could we ever be prepared for *anything?*" Tory leaned in and whispered to Scarlet. "It's impossible to have enough knowledge of something to prepare for every outcome. I would know."

Scarlet just shook her head, somewhat in disbelief of what she was about to take on.

"Remember, magic is allowed, so use the strengths you have as either fae or human to come out successful on the other side."

Scarlet whispered to Tory again, "Why would humans even want to participate in this? They're so much weaker than us. What chance do they have?"

Marcus took a look around the room before holding up a golden goblet and solemnly saying, "Good luck to you all and may the Endless Forest bring you to your ultimate wish." He took a sip of his drink as everyone in the ballroom followed his lead, raising their goblets in a toast, of sorts. But to Scarlet, it didn't feel like a celebration.

Tory finally replied. "The human's wish is usually the biggest motivator. In past trials, the records show that the few humans who either won or shared their wish had a sick or dying relative and their wish was to heal them – to save them. Sometimes strength of heart wins over fae abilities."

Scarlet considered this as everyone at the head table sat down and began eating. The contestants followed their example and began serving themselves from the platters of food laid out before them. How any of them had appetites, Scarlet didn't know. Some were anxiously chattering away while others sat in stunned silence.

One of the contestants got up from his seat and made his way over to where Scarlet sat, standing behind her. "Hello, all!" he exclaimed as he addressed the small group. "I just wanted to come by and wish you luck."

This was one of the humans who had been selected. Scarlet eyed him, wondering what his motivation for entering the trials could possibly be. He seemed... happy. Unlike how someone would look if they had a relative with a fatal illness. Then again, Beau was human and seemingly happy and she knew nothing about his motivations for being there. Maybe this general cheerfulness was all a facade. A way to lull the fae into feeling that the humans were non-threatening.

"I'm Charlie, by the way," he went on. "While I obviously want to win, I see no reason why we have to kill each other in the process. So just know, I'm not your enemy here." He held up his hands to show his vulnerability.

Beau and Ricky nodded along as Charlie spoke and Scarlet had to admit that the "deadly" part of the trials was really the worst part of it. Sure, the games were set up to sometimes be dangerous, but according to what she had read, most of the time, it was the contestants that took one another out. Scarlet, like Charlie, had no intentions of being that type of contestant.

After a few kind words shared between the group and Charlie, he walked back to his dinner. Or rather, he stumbled back. It was almost like he turned and initially forgot to pick up his feet. Tory said that she needed some air, so Ricky escorted her outside to the gardens. That left Scarlet with Beau, who was smirking at her in between bites of food and sips of wine. That stupid smirk made Scarlet feel giddy, but she pushed those feelings down and shoveled some more vegetables in her mouth.

"Do they not serve you carrots in that fancy castle of yours, Princess?" Beau chided her.

Scarlet cringed and then took a giant gulp of wine to get her food down. "Sorry," she replied meekly. "I'm just a little nervous."

Beau was clearly fighting for his life not to smirk again and was failing miserably. Scarlet's toes curled in her shoes.

"Nervous for the trials or..."

Scarlet pulled back. "Or what?"

Beau shook his head. "Never mind."

Scarlet, not being one for conflict, put her head down went back to eating her food. She wondered if Beau thought he was making her nervous. He was – or rather, his smile was – but she didn't want him knowing that.

"It's just – "

Scarlet looked up with wide eyes as Beau clearly changed his mind and decided to pursue this further. Trying to calm her nerves, Scarlet took another sip of wine.

"Everyone knows that the Princess of Tellus has been tucked away in the palace her whole life. One has to wonder how much experience she has with... the opposite sex."

Scarlet choked on the last sip she had taken and nearly spewed wine all over Beau. She was mortified, but also felt indignant. How dare he discuss something of this matter so casually? Or at all!

Scarlet embraced the diplomatic side of her before she spoke again. "Not that it's any of your business, but I have not been as secluded as some may believe."

Beau pressed his lips together and nodded. Why did he look so amused? "Interesting," he stated.

Scarlet wanted to wipe that smirk off his face, but before she could say anything further, her head started to softly buzz. She glanced around the room – looking for what, she didn't know – but before she could process what was happening, everything went hazy and dark.

* * * * *

Scarlet woke up in the Endless Forest, sunlight streaming through the trees and onto her face. Her head was killing her and she quickly realized that either the food or wine had been drugged. A sleeping potion. And one potent enough to knock her out until the next day. It was then that Scarlet realized why Tory had needed air and why Charlie had stumbled. They must have been feeling the effects much quicker than anyone else had. Scarlet sat up and noticed that she was still wearing her dress from the night before. She flexed her fingers, feeling the familiar warmth that surged through her veins – her fire magic was ready to obey her command, if necessary. The heat of it was comforting, like an old friend, although she knew better than to grow too confident. She supposed every contestant was dangerous in their own right, for the will to win and live could make anyone lethal.

"Good," she said aloud. "Now to figure out what in the Fates' Hel is going on."

She heard a rustling behind her and with a gasp, turned to face the interloper. Beau was standing there, much to Scarlet's relief.

"Beau!" she exclaimed. "Are you all right?"

Beau slowly walked closer towards her, nursing his aching head. He looked slightly disheveled, but still handsome in his evening clothes. "Scarlet? What's going on?"

"We were drugged. I think the trials have started."

Scarlet heard another sound behind her and quickly turned around. The forest was alive with the hum of hidden creatures and the rustle of leaves. Thick trees towered over

Scarlet and Beau, casting long shadows as the air shimmered with a tension so heavy, it made her skin prickle. The trial really had begun. But what was the game?

Scarlet backed up against a large oak, watching as the other eight contestants started to join them.

Wait, no.

There weren't eight other contestants. Scarlet counted again in her head. There were only seven others gathered there.

"Someone is missing!" Scarlet announced as everyone looked around to determine who.

"It's Charlie! Charlie isn't here!" declared a fae male with blonde hair and a scar going across his left cheek. Scarlet remembered him introducing himself last night as Rouge.

Suddenly, a shirtless Charlie stumbled out from behind a tree. He had a shocked and weary look on his face, but when Scarlet scanned him over, all she noticed was that he was holding a piece of parchment.

No, not holding.

The parchment was *nailed* to Charlie's body with a dagger, his blood dripping onto the grass around him and coating it in viscous red.

"Oh, Fates! Are any of the fae here healers?" Scarlet shouted as she ran up to Charlie and he collapsed in her arms. He was so small. Why had Scarlet not noticed the previous evening how small he was? "Who did this to you?" she asked as she lowered them both to the ground. His eyes were staring deeply into hers, but he did not respond. "Is anyone a healer?" she cried again, more urgently.

"Shaelyte is," Scarlet heard a voice say.

Beau reached Scarlet and Charlie and kneeled down in the grass to read the parchment.

"Find the heart of the forest, retrieve the relic and return to the starting point. The only rule is to survive," Beau read and then redirected his disbelieving gaze to Charlie.

Charlie who had been so kind. Who had wanted to make it clear to everyone that he wasn't their enemy. But clearly, he had an enemy of his own. Or three, as Scarlet looked down and saw Charlie holding up three fingers.

"App – " he tried to get out, but the rest died on his lips.

The apprentices?

Scarlet looked around, noticing that the healer still hadn't come forward.

"Which one of you is Shaelyte?" Tory asked, her cheeks looking flushed with anger.

There was a moment of silence before Shaelyte raised her hand with a look of annoyance on her face.

"Heal him!" Tory and Scarlet screamed in unison. Charlie moaned in Scarlet's arms as Tory approached Shaelyte. Scarlet noticed that, despite her stature, Tory was a force to be reckoned with as she encroached upon Shaelyte's space.

"What's your problem?" Tory shouted as she took her hands and used them to shove Shaelyte's shoulders. Scarlet was shocked at Tory's sudden aggression, but filed the information away for later.

Shaelyte caught her balance and rolled her eyes. "My *problem* is that the only rule of the game is '*survive.*' This is a competition and only one of us can win it."

Scarlet's eyes widened as Ricky walked up to Tory and stood at her side. "Are you serious right now?" Ricky asked with animosity dripping from his voice. "He's a human *boy! Heal him!*" he roared.

Maybe Scarlet had initially misjudged Ricky.

Shaelyte rolled her eyes again as if this all was just a meager nuisance to her.

Charlie's heartbeat started to slow and his breathing became ragged. Why would the sorcerer's apprentices do this to him? He wasn't even given a chance! "We're losing him! Someone help!" Scarlet screamed, her voice shaking. She looked helplessly at Beau, tears welling up in her eyes and then rolling down her cheeks, falling on the poor boy's face below her. Was she really about to watch Charlie die?

Beau got up and joined Tory and Ricky. "If you don't heal him, mark my words, I *will* kill you!"

Shaelyte, looking unimpressed, sighed before turning and walking deeper into the forest. Eight sets of eyes watched in shock as the healer walked away. Charlie then closed his eyes before taking his last breath and Scarlet felt her heart shatter into a million pieces.

4

CHAPTER FOUR

S carlet, Tory, Ricky and Beau stayed behind to bury Charlie while the remaining four contestants took off in the direction that Shaelyte had gone: Into the heart of the forest to find where the relic was hidden.

"I just don't understand why they would do this to him," Scarlet sniffed as she wiped tears from her eyes and stared down at the fresh grave. She had considered asking the group if she should use her magic to cremate Charlie's body, but with so many trees around them, a large fire didn't seem like a good idea. "It feels so inhumane."

"Well, they're not human," Beau said. "Are they?"

The foursome looked quizzical. *Were* the sorcerer's apprentices human? Scarlet had never questioned it before. And their long, disheveled hair and hoods always covered their ears.

"We need to get a move on to find this relic," Ricky stated. "Are we all in agreement that we're officially a team? From this point forward, we do what we have to do to win, but we don't betray one another?" He looked from fae to human to fae and they all nodded their acceptance.

"Are we sure the heart of the forest is the center where everyone was headed?" Tory asked skeptically.

Scarlet looked at her, realizing that Tory, self-declared Master of Memories and Puzzles, was possibly onto something that no one else had previously considered. "Go on..." she cued her new teammate.

Tory thought for a moment before speaking again. "Well, everyone always assumes that the heart of something is the center; the core. But what if – " she cut herself off and shook her head as if trying to shake the thought out of it.

"No," Ricky said, affectionately squeezing Tory's arm in a way that made Scarlet's heartstrings tug. She remembered how Tory had reacted to Ricky when they first met and how Ricky jumped at the chance to keep her company outside last night. Was something going on between the two of them? So soon? "What were you going to say?" he urged.

"What if this spot right here is the heart? Figuratively speaking, of course. I don't think the apprentices would be so obvious about the heart of the forest being the center. It's too easy. And why kill Charlie without even giving him a chance? It's just too cruel. But so was Shaelyte not healing him. *We* are the ones that stood up to her. *We* are the heart. So what if where we're standing is already the heart of the forest? No one would come to that conclusion immediately."

Scarlet, Beau and Ricky stared at Tory, unbelievingly. No one spoke for quite some time until Ricky blew out a breath and broke the silence.

"You're a genius!" he shouted, hugging Tory and lifting her feet off the ground like she weighed nothing. Tory looked slightly alarmed, but once Ricky placed her back on her feet, she tentatively hugged him back. She looked incredibly uncomfortable with affection, but not against it entirely.

"Okay, okay. So if Tory is right, and I'm not saying you're not," Beau added quickly. "What is the relic and where is it?" he asked, looking around aimlessly.

The group quietly started to spread out and look in all directions as if accepting Tory's premise to be the truth. Scarlet didn't know what they were looking for, but had a feeling that if there was something to be found amongst them, they *would* find it. It was smart that they had decided to band together. An individual searching for an unknown relic had less of a chance of finding it compared to four. Plus, it was nice that they had quickly developed this friendship despite the circumstances surrounding them. It seemed that something was growing between Ricky and Tory. Beau was definitely intriguing to her. The only other human Scarlet had really ever known was Hanre and other than being mortal, the two didn't seem to have much in common. Whereas Hanre was Scarlet's comfort, Beau was an unknown danger that excited her, if she was being honest with herself.

Don't fall for the competition, silly girl, Scarlet chastised herself. *Even if they're attractive and declare themselves allies.* She hated to admit it to herself, but Beau had gotten under her skin last night with his assumption of her inexperience. Yes, she and Hanre had once been in love, but it was sweet and innocent. It wasn't the desire that inspired epic love stories. And if nothing else, Scarlet yearned to be desired like that. Which was why Beau's assessment had burrowed inside her and hit bone-deep. What would it be like to be desired like that? It hurt Scarlet's heart that she didn't know. She craved to feel that one day.

Lost in her thoughts, Scarlet tripped on a tree root and fell over. She hadn't noticed Beau nearby, but he was suddenly in front of her, catching Scarlet before she hit the ground.

She blinked at him, wide-eyed. "Thanks," she whispered almost inaudibly. She could feel the flush of her cheeks and quickly stood up and away from Beau's strong, well-defined arms. What did he do to get arms that large and toned?

Focus, Scarlet! She scolded herself.

"Anytime, Princess." He flashed her that crazy-beautiful smile and then the bastard *winked* at her again. "I'm always available to save a damsel in distress."

Scarlet winced at his words. "I am *not* a damsel in distress! I'm the damn Fi – "

Did she really almost just call herself the Firebird? Beau's lip turned up into a snarky half-smile. He gazed into her eyes for what felt like a lifetime before shaking himself out of whatever thoughts he was having. When he looked down at his feet, his eyes went wide.

"No, you're definitely not a damsel in distress!" he excitedly told her. "You're our salvation! Look!" He pointed at the ground where Scarlet saw an X carved at the base of a very large and very old tree.

Ricky and Tory joined them to see what Beau was pointing at. Both of their eyes went wide before a grin tugged at Ricky's mouth.

"X marks the spot?" he asked while looking suggestively at Tory.

Tory smiled and nodded her head enthusiastically. "Let's start digging!"

Using the same sharp, flat stones they had used to dig Charlie's grave, they began digging at the base of the tree. It took a while, but they eventually heard a distinctive clinking sound about a foot and a half below ground. The group abandoned their shovels and started using their hands to carefully dig around whatever was buried underground. After a few minutes, Scarlet held up what looked like an old, red vessel adorned with gold filigree and a large X carved into the center.

"Another X?" she inquired, scrunching her nose.

Tory had that look again that Scarlet had quickly come to learn was her recalling a memory and pondering on it.

"In some cultures, an X is considered a rune. It represents giving and receiving and the balance between the two. It also represents sacrifice, which… is essentially the balance between giving and receiving."

They all looked to one another, not sure what to make of the information Tory had given them. Charlie had been sacrificed, had he not? Or was he murdered? Apprentices or not, Charlie's death didn't feel like a sacrifice; it felt like a cold-blooded killing.

"So now we have to return to the starting point, but this is where we all woke up, so isn't it already the starting point?" Ricky asked, looking to Tory for guidance. Clearly he had determined that she was the brains of this operation.

"Or it refers to the starting point of the trials? Back to the mansion?" Tory looked at Ricky and then to Scarlet and Beau, all of whom nodded.

"It's worth a shot," Beau said. "You've been right so far and it's really the only thing that makes sense."

Tory and Ricky turned to walk towards the mansion as Beau held a dirty hand out to Scarlet, who was still crouched down on the ground with the vessel, her hands just as crusted with dirt as his. She took his outstretched hand and then bent down to pick the relic back up.

"Ow!" she yelped as she pulled her finger away. There was a broken piece of the vessel that Scarlet had cut her finger on. Her dark blood now broke the surface of her skin, flowing freely.

"Are you all right?" Beau asked as he took her hand and looked down at her finger. An alarmed expression crossed his face before he spoke again. "Is your blood... *black*?"

Scarlet quickly pulled her hand away, feeling ashamed, although she knew she shouldn't. "It's not black. It's just a really dark red. It's always been like that. Plus it's mixing with the dirt. It's going to get infected."

"Okay! Okay!" Beau exclaimed, putting both of his hands up in surrender. His previous look of alarm was now gone, replaced by what Scarlet acknowledged was a careful mask of arrogance to cover his fear. "Come on, Princess, let's get you back to the mansion and clean that finger up."

They followed behind Tory and Ricky who were now quite a bit out in front of them. Scarlet knew she should have felt relieved to be making it out of the first trial with no more than a cut that had already closed up, but she had a bad feeling that she couldn't shake.

* * * * *

When the foursome approached the gates of the mansion, Tory quickly turned to face all of them. "We have to all be holding onto the vessel as we go inside!"

Ricky looked at her, nodding. "Okay," he agreed. He obviously trusted her judgment. Scarlet realized that she did, as well. "But why?" Ricky asked.

"According to the parchment, the winner is whoever finds the heart of the forest, retrieves the relic and brings it back to the starting point. If Scarlet is the only one holding it when we enter, she will be the only winner," Tory explained.

"Yeah, okay, but we all still survived, so who cares if Scarlet wins this round?" Beau asked.

Suddenly, Ricky closed his eyes and nodded as if understanding before Tory spoke again. "Because the only rule is to survive. If only Scarlet is holding the relic, there's nothing to say that we can't be killed after she's declared the winner. But if we all win, we *all* survive and move onto the next trial."

Tory enthusiastically shook her head. "That's what I was thinking! The apprentices can be tricky with their rules. It's documented from past trials that I read about. Plus... well, Charlie. We can't take any chances."

"Okay, so are we all in agreement then?" Beau asked, looking around the group, making eye contact with each one of them to confirm.

Scarlet held out the vessel and they all placed their hands on it as, together, they walked through the gates of the Phoenix Mansion and up the steps to where the three sorcerer's apprentices stood.

"Congratulations!" Marcus shouted. "It looks like this trial has *four* winners! How... unique..." he declared, narrowing his eyes at the group.

Scarlet couldn't help to feel he didn't seem happy with what they had done. Which made her further wonder about the apprentices. Why was she only now questioning their motives?

Francois snapped his fingers and suddenly, the other contestants were all standing inside the gates, looking out of sorts. It was then that Scarlet realized that the apprentices were definitely not human. She had always assumed the sorcerer used his magic to construct the trials, but with that snap of fingers, Scarlet now knew she had been wrong.

"We have our winners," Marcus said, still seemingly annoyed as he wrinkled his nose at the word 'winners.' "Everyone can come back inside. Dinner will be served at sun down."

Tory was the first to enter the mansion, followed by Ricky. As Scarlet started to walk through the door, she heard a snapping sound and then a collective gasp. When she turned around, Shaelyte's body was a crumbled heap on the ground, her neck bent at an impossible angle... And Beau stood over her.

"I told you I'd kill you," he snarled before turning back around, pushing past Scarlet and heading up the stairs to his room.

Scarlet couldn't move, still staring at Shaelyte's unmoving body in disbelief. When had Beau left her side? How had a human snapped the neck of a fae?

Beau wasn't human.

5

CHAPTER FIVE

Scarlet marched up the stairs and threw the door open to Beau's room. Once inside, she slammed the door shut with such force that it rattled the walls. Beau turned and gaped at her, a look of utter confusion spread across his face.

His stupid, lying, *fae* face.

"How did you do it?" she snarled as she approached Beau, fire dancing at her fingertips.

Beau furrowed his brow and looked at her like she was crazy before turning away and flopping onto his bed. He folded his hands under his head, as if this were a casual conversation. "Do what?"

Exasperated, Scarlet cried, "Kill Shaelyte! I saw you! You were right next to me! There's no way a human could make it down those steps that quickly!"

He lifted his head ever so slightly to release his hands and ran his fingers through his hair, the movement bringing attention to his very rounded, very *human* ears. "Princess, I don't know what you think you saw, but I wasn't standing next to you. Or rather, I hadn't been for a while. Once the apprentices called the other contestants back, I walked down the steps towards Shaelyte."

Scarlet blinked a few times, questioning if she had remembered everything properly. *Had* Beau been next to her? She had been so sure, but now she couldn't remember.

"Okay, fine, but you're human! How did you snap her neck so easily?" The flames at Scarlet's fingertips were still there, but smaller than they had been when she first barged into Beau's room.

The bastard smiled at her like she was a simple child. "Babe… Have you seen my arms?" And then he *flexed*!

Fates above!

Scarlet stood in front of him, speechless and stupefied.

Something is severely wrong with me, she thought. She could practically feel herself drooling and wanting to pounce on him.

Beau stood up and walked towards Scarlet like he was stalking his prey. With nowhere to go, Scarlet backed away from him until the wall stopped her progress. Beau caged her in with his tattooed arms as Scarlet's eyes widened and her breathing became labored. He smelled like citrus and sandalwood and leather and Scarlet found herself fighting the urge to lean in closer.

"Remember this," Beau demanded, his lips just an inch from Scarlet's face. He then moved and whispered in her ear, the sound like melted caramel, "I always keep my promises."

He promised to kill Shaelyte and he did.

Beau then reached his arm towards the bookshelf and grabbed something wrapped in cloth. He pushed it towards Scarlet. "Keep this on you at all times." And with that, he stalked away, went into his bathing chamber and closed the door.

Scarlet, still feeling lightheaded, slowly unwrapped the parcel. Inside was a dagger. She held it in front of her and stared at it before looking back up at the closed bathing chamber door. She could hear water running and the rustling of clothing. Why had he given her this dagger? She had magic and he didn't. What would she need it for?

Then she thought of the apprentices that she now knew were fae and not humans using potions. The apprentices that stabbed a human boy for sport. What were they not capable of? And were the apprentices now angry with Scarlet and her friends for bending their rules?

If Scarlet wanted to stay alive and protect her new-found friends, she needed every advantage available to her. She wrapped the dagger back up and lifted her dress, grateful for the loose fit, before placing the parcel against her stomach and using the waistband of her undergarments to hold it in place. She stood for a moment, eyes drifting back to the bathing chamber door before shaking her head and leaving Beau's room.

* * * * *

She stood at the edge of the cliff, her long, black hair whipping around her face. She looked down at the ground, her feet standing on top of an X that had been etched into the dirt. There was a sound in the distance. She took one last look behind her, tears in her eyes, before raising her hands over her head and swan-diving off the precipice.

Scarlet gasped for air as she awoke and immediately brought a ball of fire to her palm for light and comfort. She heard blankets rustling in the bed beside hers as Tory woke.

"Are you all right?" she asked, her voice sounding like she was still half asleep.

Scarlet nodded wearily. "Just a dream I have from time to time."

"You have reoccurring dreams?" Tory asked, looking intrigued.

Scarlet nodded again. "Yes. Well, it's just the one. It was a little different this time, though."

Tory sat up in bed and rubbed the sleep from her eyes as she faced Scarlet. "Tell me about it."

Scarlet hesitated. She had never told anyone about this dream. There was something about it that always felt too real to her, even when she was awake. "Well, there's someone... a female... with dark hair standing at the edge of a cliff. She looks sad and then she jumps off. That's usually when I wake up. But this time, before she jumped, I saw that she was standing on an X. She *sacrificed* herself on an X."

Tory looked at Scarlet sympathetically. "Scarlet, reoccurring dreams usually mean you're dealing with some unresolved issue in your life. Now, I can't help you with that part, but as far as the X and the sacrifice, it's likely that you just dreamed that part because of what happened today. Especially since it was the one part of the dream that was different."

Even though what Tory said made complete sense, Scarlet wasn't entirely convinced. Regardless, she replied, "Yeah, I guess you're right. I'm so sorry I woke you up."

"That's all right!" Tory exclaimed. "I have strange dreams, too, so I understand." She paused and Scarlet felt like she could see the cogs working in Tory's mind.

"What do you dream about?" Scarlet asked, genuinely curious.

"Different things," Tory began, "but what makes them strange is how real they feel. Like they're not dreams, but memories. Except that can't be true, because if they were memories, I would remember them..." Tory trailed off and looked as if she was lost in thought, trying to reach for something that had once belonged to her, but was now gone.

"Can I ask you something?" Tory questioned.

They had both just divulged deeply personal things to each other. What was another insight into Scarlet's thoughts? If she was being honest with herself, she felt like she was one of the maids she would sometimes see in the castle. They were always chittering together in hushed tones. Likely sharing secrets. Being normal. "Sure," she replied. "Of course."

Tory leaned in, wide-eyed with excitement, "What do you think about Ricky?"

Scarlet could swear Tory was about to giggle! She smiled warmly. "I think he definitely likes you."

Tory smiled back, a big, toothy grin. In the short time that Scarlet had known Tory, the last thing she would expect from the wildly intelligent and somewhat reserved fae was giddiness. Tory always seemed so reserved that this conversation and her actions felt so out of place. Like Tory was two different people.

"I'm guessing you have some sort of feelings for him, too?" Scarlet inquired. The answer was evident, but Tory was the closest thing to a girl friend that Scarlet had ever had and she was enjoying this new relationship and exploring all of its nuances.

"I do. Or, at least I'm starting to," Tory said and then paused, considering her next words. "For what it's worth, I think Beau is attracted to you."

Scarlet was taken aback. Sure, Beau had a naturally effusive personality, but he was like that with everyone, wasn't he? Of course Tory didn't know anything about the dagger that was currently hidden underneath Scarlet's pillow...

"Do you not feel anything for him?" Tory asked, looking concerned. "I really thought there was a spark there."

It was then Scarlet realized her own brow was furrowed and she was frowning. Scarlet shook her head, "No, it's not that. I was just thinking. I mean, yes, I think he's very attractive. And disarmingly charming. But I hadn't given it too much thought. Honestly, we don't really know if we'll make it out of this experience alive..." Scarlet trailed off seeing the crestfallen look on Tory's face. "Oh, Tory, I'm sorry. I didn't mean... Well... It's just..." She was rambling. She didn't know what to say to make her previous statement any less true.

Tory waved her hand and shook her head, "No, you're right. I don't know what I was thinking. I shouldn't be feeling anything other than determination at such an important time. I need to stay focused on the goal. The wish." Tory tucked herself back into bed and closed her eyes. "Good night, Scarlet."

She had been dismissed.

Scarlet felt like someone had punched her in the stomach. She had upset her one friend and although she hadn't meant to, she still wasn't used to these interactions and how to behave or what to say. Her father, the one person who should have been her rock, was never there for her. He never taught her the ways of polite society and relations. But she should have known better than to let the inside thoughts out.

"Good night, Tory," Scarlet sighed before placing her head back down on her pillow and spending the next few hours staring at the ceiling. She was determined to do better next time.

* * * * *

The next morning, when Scarlet woke up, Tory was already gone. Taking a deep breath, she got up and stepped into their bathing chamber to clean up before getting dressed in a tunic and loose-fitting pants and heading down for breakfast. It still felt strange to not have Pearl and Alabaster around to feed and care for before starting her day. Scarlet wondered if they were okay. She knew that Marta and Hanre would be taking good care of them, but she missed them nonetheless.

This is probably how mothers feel when they're away from their children, she thought absentmindedly.

There would be no trial that day, so Scarlet wondered what was in store for her and the rest of the group as she entered the Great Hall for breakfast. The remaining contestants were all gathered around the table enjoying plates of eggs, bacon, croissants and fruit as if nothing terrible had happened the previous day.

"Hi," Scarlet said tentatively as she took a seat next to Tory.

"Hi," Tory replied back.

Scarlet leaned in and lowered her voice, "Listen, Tory, I'm really sorry – "

"There's no need to apologize," Tory cut her off. "I overreacted. You were correct in what you said and I appreciate your candidness." She gave Scarlet a close-lipped smile. It wasn't the toothy grin of the fae she got a glimpse of the previous night, but it was a relief to see, nonetheless.

"Morning, Firebird!" Beau exclaimed from across the table. "You look well-rested."

"I tossed and turned all night," Scarlet replied blandly as she reached for an apple.

Beau smirked. "I would have loved to have tossed you and turned you all night!"

Ricky audibly choked on his croissant.

"Sorry, buddy," Beau said as he patted Ricky on the back until he cleared his throat.

"So what is on the agenda for today?" Tory asked, clearly trying to change the subject. She shoved a fork-full of eggs into her mouth and looked around the table.

"Yeah, what happens when we're not competing?" Scarlet asked.

"Oh, you know... strategizing, building alliances... the usual war tactics," Beau rattled on.

"We haven't really done a good job of learning about the other contestants," the one amongst them with memory magic suddenly realized, perusing the room. Scarlet wondered what Tory could learn about the contestants that she could use later to their advantage.

"Speak for yourself!" Beau exclaimed. "That's Miranda over there." He pointed to a blonde human with glasses that were way too big for her face. "Really nice girl."

Something in Scarlet's stomach sank.

"Not really my type," Beau continued, "but we talked about what happened to Charlie and the poor thing is terrified now."

"Maybe she needs a weapon to keep her safe," Scarlet drawled, picking at her fingernail while staring down at the table.

Beau glanced at her, but didn't say anything. His silence felt deafening.

"That over there is Faygar. He's from a tribe of fae warriors that reside in the woods of Spirare. He has traveled here every ten years for the past three decades and was finally chosen. He says it's a great honor to his tribe." Beau continued around the room, now looking at a beautiful fae female with honey-blonde hair and eyes that matched. She was very tiny and very delicate-looking. "That's Jettevieve. Turns out, she's actually good friends with a fae I dated a few years ago."

Again, that sinking feeling overwhelmed Scarlet's insides. It felt awful and unsettling.

What is wrong with me? She wondered. Sure, Beau was attractive. And smart. And kind.

"Oh, Fates," she groaned, realizing she really did have feelings for Beau. Three heads suddenly whipped towards her. "Oh, I'm sorry to interrupt," she said to Beau. "My head is just killing me," she lied as she grabbed her head to make her story more convincing.

"I have some herbs in our room that would alleviate any pain," Ricky offered.

"Oh... thanks," Scarlet replied, waving him off. "I'll be okay." She looked at Beau. "Please continue. I'm so sorry." She was mortified. And still, that awful feeling thinking about Beau with another fae wouldn't go away.

Scarlet remembered after she and Hanre came to their senses and ended their short-lived relationship that Hanre dated a local girl from the village. She was very pretty in that innocent way village girls tended to be and Scarlet had been jealous. At the time, it felt like such a silly thing that Scarlet, the Princess of Tellus, was jealous of a peasant. But deep down, there was a part of her that was happy for her best friend. If she couldn't make him happy, he deserved someone that would.

This jealousy she now felt thinking about Beau's past and future relationships was nothing compared to what she felt towards Hanre's girlfriend. She couldn't stop thinking that Jettevieve had a friend just as tiny as her that Beau enjoyed "tossing and turning with all night." The thought was making her sick.

"I'm sorry," she said again. "I actually think I underestimated this headache. I'm going to go back to my room. I'll see you all later," Scarlet told her friends.

"Do you want me to go back with you?" Tory asked earnestly.

Scarlet shook her head. "No, I'm okay. I just need to lie down a bit longer."

She headed back to her room and threw herself onto the bed, placing her face into her pillow and screaming into it. Scarlet was literally risking her life to be here and needed to concentrate, but instead, was swooning over *another* human man! She was like a lovesick child that never learned.

Groaning, she placed her hands under her pillow and tentatively touched the dagger that was underneath, still wrapped like a parcel. Beau had told her to keep it on her at all times. Surely, he hadn't meant at breakfast. Then again, she didn't know what to expect. Fates' Hel! She didn't even know what she was supposed to be doing with her time when they weren't competing. Beau was treating these trials like they were all at war and she was... pining over Beau.

"Ugh," she groaned again.

There was a knock at the door and before Scarlet could respond, Beau peeked his head in. "Can I come in?" he asked.

Scarlet sat up in her bed and nodded. "Of course."

Beau walked in and wandered around the space for a moment. He looked lost in thought... and a little shy? Finally, he pointed to her bed. "May I?"

Scarlet nodded again before Beau sat down at the edge of her bed, his weight shifting the wooden frame and causing it to groan. It was the only sound in the room for what felt like an eternity. Finally, Scarlet broke the silence.

"I owe you an apology." She paused. "And two thank yous."

With a furrowed brow, he looked at her curiously, but didn't speak.

"I'm sorry that I verbally attacked you and accused you of being a liar."

Beau snorted, but Scarlet could tell he wasn't really angry. She went on, "I want to thank you for giving me your dagger, but also, for... avenging? Avenging Charlie. In the way that you could, at least."

Beau braced his hands on his knees and dropped his head, nodding slowly. "I knew there would be deaths, but I didn't think they would be so senseless. Had Charlie died fighting, I could respect that. But he wasn't even given a chance. And Shaelyte – " he said the last words through gritted teeth. "She could have given him that chance. At the very least, she could have taken away his pain."

Without realizing she had started doing it, Scarlet found herself gently rubbing Beau's back, trying to soothe him. Her eyes went wide looking at her hands and she quickly pulled them away.

He turned to her and, for once, there was no trace of a smirk or suggestive eyes. Beau was genuinely sad.

"Let's talk about something else," he said as his voice cracked a little. "If you win, what do you plan to wish for?" He shifted so that he was further onto the bed, his back up against the wall that the bed was placed against and Scarlet felt like his gaze was boring into her. She was taken aback that he asked about her wish. Beau seemed to want to get to know her, but how much was she willing to divulge about herself? She definitely didn't want to tell him about the darkness inside of her and scare Beau off. She seated herself so that she could comfortably look at Beau while they conversed and mentally prepared for giving him the truth with some omissions.

"Well, it's more my father's wish than mine, if I'm being honest."

Beau raised a curious brow.

"He wants me to wish to be the best queen I can when the time comes."

Beau was still staring at her, his lips pursed in confusion. "So your wish is to be the best queen that you can be? Not to point out the obvious, but you can never be more than what's possible for you."

"What do you mean?" Scarlet asked, blinking at him and feeling a little dejected.

"Take a glass for example. I can't fill it with more water than it can hold. So if I wished the glass could hold the most water possible, it could still only hold what it's capable of. You don't need to wish to be the best queen you can be. You just have to do things that will make that possible." Beau smiled and folded his arms over his chest, looking quite proud of himself. "Wish granted! Give me the next one!"

Scarlet gaped at him. On the surface, he was right, of course, but he didn't have all of the details. Scarlet made a mental note to make sure she practiced the wording for if the time came to have her wish granted. "Well, I would have obviously worded it differently. Like, I would wish to be the best queen ever. My father just wants to make sure that Tellus has the type of leader it deserves."

Beau got quiet and looked like he wanted to say something, but was holding himself back. Was it because it sounded ridiculous that her father would want what's best for Tellus when it didn't seem as if he cared about the citizens at all?

Beau leaned forward. "But if you *could* have another wish – a wish of your own – what would it be?" His eyes twinkled as he waited for her response.

Scarlet put her thumb to her mouth and nervously chewed the nail. She couldn't help but notice Beau's gaze drop to her lips and she quickly pulled her finger away. It was a terrible habit, anyway.

"I never really gave it much thought," she admitted. If she was being completely honest with herself, she wanted two things: to serve the citizens of Tellus so that they were happy and to find happiness herself. "Happiness," she whispered, almost inaudibly.

"What was that?" Beau asked.

Scarlet shook her head. "Enough about me! What about your wish?" She was very interested to learn what motivated this human to come to the trials and since he just opened the door, now was the perfect opportunity to figure him out.

Beau sighed. "I know it's not fair to ask you and then when you ask me, I can't fully answer."

In actuality, although it did frustrate her, Scarlet felt a little bit better about not fully disclosing her own wish.

"But my wish affects someone else. She lost someone she really cared about and she needs them back."

Scarlet's heart sank. Beau said "she." A she who was so important to him that he was literally risking his life to make a wish on *her* behalf.

He must have seen the somber look that spread across Scarlet's face because he immediately amended, "It's not like that. She's like a mother to me."

Oh.

"I thought you can't wish for something that changes the course of things. I would think bringing someone back from the dead qualifies as 'changing the course.'" Scarlet pointed out.

Beau smiled. "Her child isn't dead, Scarlet. She was separated from her and can't get her back. But I can change that." His determined look told Scarlet he was fiercely loyal to those he cared about and Scarlet couldn't help but wonder what it would be like to be cared for by Beau.

"So both of us are making wishes for others, huh?" Scarlet huffed a laugh. "I wonder what that says about us."

Solemnly, Beau took her hand and Scarlet's heart fluttered. "I think it says we're empathetic. Sometimes, there's no greater burden." He kissed the top of her hand and then squeezed it before releasing it, causing Scarlet's breath to catch. "For what it's worth, I think you will be an excellent queen if the time ever comes."

"What do you mean 'if'?" Scarlet inquired. Her father *would* die one day and she would be crowned queen. It wasn't necessarily going to be any time soon, but it was inevitable.

Beau's eyes widened like he just realized what he said – as if his 'if' was a slip of the tongue. Or as if he was surprised about something.

"I just meant that… I mean… you… you *do* know your father is invincible, right?"

Scarlet laughed. Sure, her father was powerful and sure, he had The Six to protect him. But invincible?

Beau squeezed her arms and shook her from her thoughts. "Sorry, it was just something I had heard. I obviously misspoke."

Scarlet nodded her head a little too fast and erratically. Why did Beau's statement not sound as crazy as she initially thought?

"Hey, want to go find Ricky and Tory?" Beau asked. He was clearly trying to change the subject and distract Scarlet from her thoughts.

But Scarlet didn't want to be distracted from her thoughts. She liked that Beau challenged her and made her question what she thought she knew. The days of being sheltered were in her past. It was time to start acting like the queen she would wish to be.

* * * * *

Over the following days, Scarlet and Beau fell into a quiet rhythm to what could only be described as friendship with the possibility of more. Although she didn't voice it to Beau, Scarlet knew their time together was potentially limited and since feelings developed quickly, they could crush her if these trials ended badly. They were taking things as slow as possible under the unusual circumstances of being together daily in such tight quarters.

Each morning, Scarlet and Tory would wake up and meet Beau and Ricky for breakfast in the Great Hall. Although Tory didn't say much, Scarlet could tell feelings were growing between her and Ricky. They often stole glances at one another or found excuses for gentle touches. But Scarlet could tell Tory was still bothered by what she had said about their reality and was treading these waters with Ricky carefully.

After breakfast, Beau would take Scarlet to the gardens behind the mansion to walk and talk. It was in these moments Scarlet would learn the most about Beau and when she would open up about her hopes and dreams. She shared with Beau her desire to change Tellus for the better – starting with eliminating Yielding Day. Once she was queen, there would be no reason for magic to be taken from her subjects. Scarlet wanted to be a fair and just ruler who led a kingdom known for peace and love.

Beau always listened carefully, practically hanging on her every word, but he always looked a little sad when she talked about becoming queen. Scarlet hadn't forgotten what he had said about her father and his alleged invincibility. She would try to press him further about it, but conveniently, there would always be a beautiful, red flower he just had to pick for her hair or a bird's nest with a mama feeding her babies.

Scarlet learned a lot about Beau, as well. She could tell there was much about his life he held back from her, but he was very open about things like his childhood or what he wanted for his life after the trials. Scarlet assumed he had some official position that required secrecy and that it was the reason for him being less willing to talk about the present than he was the past and future. Or maybe it had something to do with the woman he said filled a matronly role in his life. He never talked about her or her child, which made Scarlet suspicious.

After their garden walk, they would join Tory and Ricky for lunch and were surprised to discover one day that the apprentices kept some puzzles and games in a coat closet. Sometimes the other contestants would come play with them to pass the time, but no one was attempting any further alliances. While Tory won most of the puzzle games, they all agreed the greatest puzzle of all was where the apprentices went when there were no trials. Not a single one had been seen since the first trial ended. Even at dinner, they were absent and while someone was likely bringing food to them, Ricky joked that they probably don't eat. Either option sounded like a possibility to Scarlet who didn't trust them after Charlie had been killed.

At the end of every dinner, Beau would escort Scarlet up to her room and give her a chaste kiss on the cheek.

One day, Beau suggested that instead of going to the gardens, that they head up to Scarlet's room to talk. The garden walks had become something Scarlet looked forward to every day, but the reason they were so appealing was because she could feel herself falling for Beau more and more with each passing day. The more she got to know him, the more she liked. So whether they were in the gardens or in her room, Scarlet didn't care as long as they were together.

They were sitting on Scarlet's bed when Beau looked into her eyes reverently – as if he were searching for an answer to a question in his head. "You are so unexpected," he said with a sigh, shaking his head slowly from side to side like he was in disbelief.

Her breath caught and she could have sworn her heart stopped for a split second. Was Beau really feeling the same things she was feeling? Suddenly, Scarlet felt like a million butterflies fluttered in her stomach.

Beau continued to look at her, his twinkling brown eyes seemingly staring into her soul. He leaned in and Scarlet felt as if they were magnets being drawn to each other. She couldn't resist this pull. She closed her eyes and their lips brushed gently against one another's. Suddenly, there was a spark and they both pulled away, alarmed.

"What just happened?" Beau asked, clearly just as shocked as Scarlet was.

Scarlet touched her lips, confused. "I think my magic... ignited. On its own."

Beau narrowed his eyes and looked at her thoughtfully. "Has that ever happened before?" he asked.

Scarlet, still touching her lips, replied, "No. No, it hasn't. Did I just lose control?"

A smile that was as disarming as he was stretched across Beau's face, teeth on full display. "I think you did." And then he grabbed her face and kissed her with a ferocity like nothing she had ever experienced before. Scarlet felt both lost and found. Beau's tongue swept across her lips and she moaned as he slipped inside her.

Scarlet's body was on fire. Not the literal kind she was used to. This was a burning deep inside of her that allowed her magic to dance underneath her skin. She felt its seductive crackle and never wanted it to stop. If Beau was the kindling to her fire, then she would happily burn for all of eternity.

Beau pulled back before peppering kisses along the length of her neck. He paused for a moment before pressing his forehead against hers.

"You are going to be my undoing," he told her, practically breathless.

Scarlet was trying so hard to get oxygen back into her brain while also trying to look alluring. She didn't want Beau to stop. For this to be the end. She wanted a beginning.

Suddenly, the door swung open and Tory and Ricky's heads popped in.

"We're going out!" they declared excitedly, both of their eyes wide when they realized what they had walked in on.

Scarlet covered her face in embarrassment as Beau threw his head back and let out an annoyed groan.

"Sorry..." Ricky sheepishly uttered.

Beau got up and offered Scarlet his hand, helping her off of the bed. "Let's go then," he said.

6

CHAPTER SIX

The foursome headed into the town, which was only a short distance from the mansion. As they walked, Tory told them about how the forest had once been much larger, but a significant portion of it had been torn down to build the homes and shops in Tellus. Once they were out of the forest, life outside of the competition existed and it took Scarlet by surprise. She had been outside the castle gates so infrequently that she was never able to truly appreciate the town and the bustling energy within it. There were some fae, mostly courtiers, who strolled about, going in and out of shops followed closely behind by servants who carried large boxes in their struggling arms.

Scarlet saw a small and very dirty human boy with a stack of papers running from home to home. He would roll up a few pieces of paper at a time and secure them with twine before throwing the bundle at each doorstep and then would run to the next as fast as his legs would take him. His cheeks were sunken in and Scarlet wondered when the last time he ate was. She looked around to see if there was a bakery nearby so she could at least buy him some bread. That's when she saw a female fruit vendor, calling to passersby about the deals she was offering, swatting flies away from her face as she did so. Much of the fruit looked rotted, to Scarlet's dismay, and she quickly realized that the fruit delivered to the castle was always perfectly fresh. It seemed the folks within the town were offered the leftovers.

She also observed the blacksmith inside the forge, the sweat glistening on his skin evident even through the window Scarlet peered through. He was forging weapons that would likely be used the next time her father decided to attack another unsuspecting kingdom.

These were all hard working folks in the town, trying to make their way in the realm. And her father wasn't even trying to make their lives any easier. Instead, he was taking the magic from the fae who served him.

Scarlet couldn't help herself from stealing a quick glance at Beau before she decided to purchase some food for the boy. If she was quick, she could catch up to him. She smiled shyly when she caught Beau already looking her way.

"I'll be right back!" she exclaimed as they were about to turn into a local tavern.

"Where are you going? Do you want me to come with you?" Beau asked.

Scarlet shook her head and ran off. She popped into the bakery and bought a few loaves of bread and some sugary biscuits. It wasn't much, but it was better than nothing. At least it wasn't more than the boy could carry. She chased after him and handed off the baked goods, the boy's face filling with so much joy.

"Thank ye, ma'am!" he exclaimed when she told him to bring some home to his family.

When Scarlet made it back to the tavern, she noticed it was small and pretty packed for the early afternoon. It seemed that most were there to drown their sorrows, as no one smiled or laughed. The place was nicer than Scarlet expected, although there was a tangy scent in the air that made her crinkle her nose. Scarlet noticed that both human and fae were indulging in the mead and wine the tavern provided and all seemed to be watching her group as they found an empty table. Scarlet could hear the hushed conversations, pointing out that they were some of the Endless Trials contestants.

"For you!" a barmaid declared as she placed four frosty mugs in front of Scarlet and her friends. "Contestants drink free!"

Tory's eyes went wide as she looked at Scarlet.

"That's incredibly kind, thank you," Ricky said with a nod to the barmaid.

Scarlet stared at her mug before taking a tentative sip, the effervescence tickling her throat. Beau watched her curiously before smirking.

"Have you ever tasted mead, Princess?" he teased, placing his hand on her thigh and gently squeezing it.

"Of course I have!" she yelped, alarmed at how Beau's big hand on her made her feel so alive. "I mean, not more than a few sips at a ball or at a special dinner hosted by my father for the visiting nobles," she went on. Scarlet turned to Tory. "Have you?"

Tory nodded. "I've had a few, but I definitely don't think it's a good idea to dull our senses too much. We have no idea what the trials still have in store for us and drinking too much mead is known to cause some less than desirable side effects."

Beau leaned into Scarlet, his hand still on her leg as his thumb began to trace circles along her inner thigh. "I'm only interested in the desirable ones."

Scarlet felt her heart beat quicken and her core pulse. A blush spread across her cheeks. Seeing the tint of pink stain, Beau kissed her cheek.

"Keep it in your pants, Beau," Ricky jokingly warned. "Unless you want to share with Tory and me what we walked in on a little while ago." He took a swig from his mug and wagged his eyebrows at Beau.

Tory sunk her elbow effectively into Ricky's side and he nearly spit his mead across the table. Scarlet's blush deepened, but Beau just smiled and shrugged.

"A gentleman never kisses and tells," he said simply. His smile immediately widened as he leaned across the table, placing a fist under his chin. "But I'm no gentleman, so let me tell you all about it!"

It was Scarlet's turn to elbow someone, but Beau grabbed her arm before she could make contact.

Damn his quick reflexes!

"Okay, so, I think we need to get serious," Beau stated solemnly. "Let's talk strengths and weaknesses."

Scarlet, Tory and Ricky nodded.

"Tory was spectacularly helpful in that last trial! I mean, truly, without you, who knows what would have happened," Beau said, turning to Tory. Scarlet saw she was beaming, but also noticed Ricky was beaming equally hard. Scarlet hoped Tory wouldn't push him away after what she foolishly said the other night about them possibly not making it out of the trials alive. They both deserved to be happy.

"Scarlet has her fire magic, which I think can definitely come in handy at some point. How exactly does it work?" Beau asked.

"Well," Scarlet began. It was hard to explain something that was just simply a part of her. "If I feel any kind of heightened emotions, my magic sort of comes to the surface. Like, I can feel it along my skin. Most of the time, it just kind of simmers there. But if I feel like there's danger, I can call to it and create fire. Something as small as sparks at my fingertips, a ball in the palm of my hand or... if really necessary, a surge of fire directed towards an enemy. Mind you, I've never used it when I was in any real danger. I had a trainer at the castle who worked with me from the time I was little, helping me hone the skill. I think my father was hoping he could use me as a weapon one day."

They all listened to her intently, but she noticed that Beau was studying her. She looked at him curiously, but before she could ask what he was thinking, he looked at Ricky. "Do you want to tell them about your magic?"

Ricky nodded. It was the first time his magic had been mentioned in front of Scarlet since they all met. She wanted to kick herself for not asking him sooner, but because she had been so sheltered her whole life, she had the worst social skills. It was such an obvious thing to have talked about on the day they met, but one thing or another had stopped her from inquiring.

"I have conjuration magic. It's definitely not as cool as flames, but it can be a neat party trick!" Ricky told them as he flicked his wrist, an apple appearing in his hand.

"That's more than a 'neat party trick!'" Scarlet exclaimed, her eyes wide with excitement. "I mean, is there anything you *can't* conjure? Are there any limitations?"

Ricky shook his head. "Not that I know of. Anything I've ever attempted, I've succeeded at."

Scarlet was impressed. Ricky's abilities meant that he could conjure weapons, if need be. Realizing this made Scarlet feel grateful they had created their alliance early on. She silently thanked the Fates for getting her past her first impression of Ricky.

"Well," Beau said, snapping Scarlet out of her thoughts. "I'm obviously the useless one in this group, but I vow to you all that I will do everything in my power to protect you. I may be a human, but I'm strong and healthy and can hold my own in a fight."

Scarlet put her hand over the one Beau had resting on the table. "You're not useless," she remarked. She had seen how his emotions gave him an advantage over all of them. He had been the one who approached her and Tory on the first day, which inevitably led to their alliance. He had been the one to avenge Charlie after such an injustice. He had been the one who cared enough to give Scarlet the dagger to protect herself. Something she hadn't had the wherewithal to even consider needing! And he had been the one to make the effort to get to know the other contestants. Information was power.

"Your sympathy is a strength that I think a lot of us fae lack, whether intentionally or unintentionally. I can only speak for myself, but I'm starting to see how there are so many things I was sheltered from at the castle and it made me never question anything. Never see anything for more than what it was. *You* use your emotions in a way that allows you to see a bigger picture. I'm so grateful for that." As Scarlet stopped speaking, her eyes instantly went wide, realizing how ridiculous she must have sounded. Beau *just* kissed her and now she was practically writing poetry about him! She groaned internally. Beau was looking at her with an expression she couldn't read. He looked as if he were trying to solve a riddle.

How embarrassing! Scarlet thought. *He probably thinks I'm professing my love for him!* She wanted to crawl into a hole and never come out.

Beau smiled softly at her as Tory replied confidently, "You're absolutely right, Scarlet! Beau, you are far from useless! You're a piece to a puzzle that's just waiting to be put together, I just know it!"

Scarlet couldn't stop herself from smiling at her friend, but she was feeling so many conflicting emotions. Scarlet promised herself that no matter what happened during the remaining trials, she would fight to protect this new family of hers. She was terrified of what was still in store for them, but she knew this group was worth fighting for.

* * * * *

Scarlet woke up in the Endless Forest again. She was quicker this time to realize the second trial had begun. She took a deep breath and waited a few moments, hoping the rest of the contestants would emerge like last time.

After they had left the tavern, the group headed back to the Phoenix Mansion and spent the day strategizing. In the evening, Scarlet, Tory and Ricky had dinner in the Great Hall. Beau said he was tired – humans being much more susceptible to the effects of mead – and took a plate of food up with him to his room. Scarlet avoided the wine at dinner, having already indulged in the mead, but the next thing she knew, she blacked out and was back outside, deeper within the forest.

Truly alone for the first time in a few days, Scarlet took advantage of the peace and quiet. She took another deep breath to get fresh air into her lungs. Somewhere high above her, birds chirped their songs in the trees. She could also hear water running in the distance. A river maybe? Or a brook? A few leaves from the tree above her drifted down towards the ground, some landing in her hair. She pulled one off, admiring how the red was almost a perfect match to her locks.

When was the last time I felt appreciation for these simple things around me? Scarlet wondered. Her experience in the town and sudden admission at the tavern made her realize there was so much to the realm she was ignorant of. Scarlet had always believed she was meant to do more with her life than "just" be the Princess of Tellus and now she was seeing that she needed to learn everything she could about her kingdom – the land, and the fae, and humans... all of it – if she was going to make a difference.

While the beauty surrounding her was something she wanted to take longer to feel gratitude for, she felt an overwhelming sense that something wasn't right. Where was Beau? And Tory and Ricky? Why was it *so* quiet?

It was then that Scarlet heard a rustling in the tall plants behind her. She stood up and set out to investigate, but not before sparking a few flames at her fingertips, just in case.

"Hello?" she called out. "Is anyone there?" She inched closer to the plant – which was clearly moving – as someone attempted to hide themself.

She ceased advancing any further and began to shout out another "hello," but before she could finish the word, someone jumped out at her.

No, not someone. Some*thing.*

It was a creature the size of a human, but that was where the similarities ended. The creature's head was devoid of eyes. Where its nose and mouth should have been, gaping holes replaced them. Its skin seemed like it was barely holding on to its bones, giving the visual effect that it was melting off.

Scarlet screamed while also trying to process what she was seeing. If she survived this encounter, she'd need to warn her friends. As the terrified sound left her mouth, shadows as black as night erupted from the creature's mouth and quickly made their way towards Scarlet.

She turned to run and sprinted as far as she could, but very quickly tripped over a thick tree root and stumbled to the ground, hitting her head. She scrambled to get back onto her feet, but a wave of dizziness hit her, making it too difficult for her to continue running. The creature's shadows were quickly approaching Scarlet, but suddenly, running didn't seem to matter as the shadows abruptly stopped their chase and began to retreat. The creature tipped its head to the side, looking like it was assessing her, despite not having eyes. It stood immobile as blood dripped from Scarlet's head onto her arm. She touched her fingers to her forehead and felt the gash that was inflicted when she fell. She could hear her heart was pounding out of her chest, but still, the creature just stood, shadows nearly gone.

Wait, it wasn't her heart that was pounding to that particular beat. It was hooves.

She quickly turned around, momentarily forgetting her fear of the creature in front of her, and that's when she saw Beau riding towards her on a pegasus! The creature hadn't been assessing *her*; it had somehow sensed the freakin' pegasus!

Beau rode past her at an incredible speed before deftly withdrawing a sword from a scabbard at his side.

Where did he get a sword from? She wondered, then shook her head in disbelief. *Never mind that! Where did he get a* pegasus?

Beau took his sword and sliced it through the neck of the shadow creature, its head toppling to the ground with a thud, followed shortly by its body.

"Fates' Hel, Scarlet! What were you doing?" he yelled at her.

She couldn't understand why he was angry at her, but then she saw the look on his face. His anger was wrought out of fear. Beau jumped down from his *pegasus* – she wasn't going to get over that – and made his way towards her, gently gripping her face in the palms of his hands. He looked her over, assessing her injury. When his finger brushed the cut on her forehead, Scarlet hissed.

"You really need to stop tripping," Beau said, reminding her of when she briefly stumbled during the first trial. "You're going to need to get that looked at," he informed her.

"It's just a scratch. It's already healing," she attempted to assure him, trying to brush his hands away from her. "And I can't help that the forest is so… rooty!"

"It's a scratch and a bump which potentially means head trauma that your fae abilities might not be able to heal," he argued before looking at her incredulously and exclaiming, "*Rooty?*" Sighing, Beau ushered Scarlet towards the pegasus that was grazing nearby. It was a sight to see with its snow-white coat that had a pearly, iridescent quality to it and large feathery wings to match. Each wing had to be at least as big as Scarlet. "Come on. We need to find Tory and Ricky."

Scarlet allowed Beau to lift her onto the pegasus' saddled back, the pegasus not even seeming fazed, let alone concerned. "I have some questions first."

He looked up at her before climbing up behind her, his hard body pressed to her back. "And those would be?"

She turned over her shoulder to look at him. "Well, for starters, you have a pegasus."

"That wasn't a question," he remarked, a smirk turning his lips up in one corner.

Scarlet shook her head and sighed. "*How* did you get a pegasus?" she clarified as the pegasus started a slow trot. She wondered if Ricky had the ability to conjure a winged horse.

"When I woke up, she was standing over me, beating her wings. Scared the shit out of me, actually."

"She?"

"Yes, she's a she. And she was kind enough to allow me to ride her and so I set off to find you. Which I did. Along with that... thing." Beau snarled.

Scarlet realized then just how truly sheltered she had been her whole life. Being kept mainly within the grounds of her castle and with no more than a couple of relationships, Scarlet was completely ignorant to the outside world. A world with pegasuses and deadly shadow creatures that would haunt her nightmares.

"Any idea what it was?" Scarlet asked.

"Not a clue, but I'm wondering if this trial has something to do with mythical creatures. That's why we need to find Tory. She'll know more about what we just saw."

Scarlet nodded. Her head was really starting to hurt, but she didn't want to say anything to Beau. They had bigger things to deal with at the moment. She allowed herself to sink into his heat for a moment and relish in the hardness of his chest, his strong arm tight around her waist. She thought she felt Beau tense briefly, but her mind quickly refocused as the pegasus picked up the pace. Scarlet felt like she was being jostled around a bit, so she tried to adjust her seating. Beau huffed into the shell of her ear, his breath warm and giving her those butterflies she was getting so used to around him.

"What?" she asked, still trying to reposition herself. Beau's sword was pressing into her backside and she squirmed a little more. "Can you readjust your sword?"

Beau erupted into laughter, disturbing some of the birds in a nearby tree. "That's not my sword, Princess." His deep tone sent an alluring chill through Scarlet.

Scarlet turned to look at him, but he just pulled her closer to him. "Stop moving or this trial is going to turn into something else entirely very quickly."

Liquid heat shot through Scarlet's core. Only moments before, she was being attacked by a horrifying shadow creature and now she was thinking about the things Beau could do to her in the shadows of the forest. She suddenly realized that she was stroking his tattooed forearm.

"Scarlet..." Beau warned, his voice low with a sultry warning. "It's taking everything in my power not to have my way with you against a tree right now. If you don't want that, then you need to stop touching me like that."

Scarlet's eyes went wide and she froze. But she *did* want that.

"What if –"

"No," he cut her off. "Not like this. When I claim you, it will be in a proper bed."

Her eyes went wide again. "When?" she managed to squeak out, her heart hammering in her chest so hard, she thought it would burst.

Beau lowered his head once more to the shell of Scarlet's ear. "Yes, when. And I've already told you, I always keep my promises."

Scarlet turned her head, hoping to be able to reach Beau's lips, but before anything could happen, she felt a tingling sensation spread throughout her whole body. It wasn't the same as the tingles she felt when thinking of Beau taking her against a tree. This felt more like passing out, but her brain didn't feel foggy.

"What's – " She suddenly landed on the ground with Beau falling on top of her. "Happening?" Scarlet searched Beau's confused face while taking a moment to appreciate the solid weight of him on her and wondering what it *would* feel like if they were in a bed right now.

"Hi, guys!" she heard Tory exclaim, jolting Scarlet out of her reverie. Beau rolled off of her and Scarlet quickly got to her feet where she saw Tory waving at them, Ricky, thankfully, right by her side.

"Did you just – ?"

Ricky cut Beau off before he could finish his sentence. "Conjure you? Yes."

"That *is* a neat trick!" Scarlet exclaimed before realizing that the pegasus was gone. "We had a pegasus! Can you conjure her, too?"

"Oh, sure... conjuring a full size fae and an adult human man weren't enough! Now I have to conjure a freakin' pegasus!" Ricky exclaimed, throwing his hands up with exasperation.

Scarlet thought he was only half-joking so she looked at him sweetly, fluttering her eyelashes, and asked, "Pretty please?"

Ricky sighed. "Only because you're the Princess of Tellus." He winked at her in a friendly manner before the pegasus appeared in front of her.

"How do you do it?" Scarlet asked, genuinely curious about the logistics behind it. With her fire magic, it was always something she could feel inside of her, but it was fire and it was hers. How did Ricky summon objects to him? Especially objects he was unfamiliar with?

"It's all based on my feelings," Ricky explained. "Like, when I conjured the apple... I wanted an apple, so I thought about what it would feel like to get to eat one. I thought about the waxy texture in my hand and the feel of my teeth breaking the surface of its skin, the juices filling my mouth... and then the apple appeared! With you two just now, I thought about how I really wanted us to be together again and I thought about what you both look like and the sounds of your voices and then you were here!"

Scarlet nodded along as Ricky spoke. "So how did you find the pegasus?"

"It's a little more abstract, but I looked at how you were smiling at me and how it made me feel and so I was able to conjure the thing that created that desire from you. Does that make sense?"

Scarlet nodded again. "It does. I wanted the pegasus so badly and you could feel that from me. It's a very special form of magic, Ricky."

He smiled and then clapped his hands together. "Well, with all of that out of the way, Scarlet, what happened to you?" He pointed to her forehead.

Scarlet touched the wound and could feel that the abrasion had already closed up, her skin feeling smooth under her fingers, but her forehead was still bruised. "I was attacked by a creature!"

Beau burst out laughing and everyone looked at him, confused. He put his hands up in defense.

"I'm sorry! I'm sorry!" he exclaimed, trying to catch his breath. "She *was* attacked by a creature and we have a lot to talk about, but Scarlet's injury was not inflicted by the creature, but rather... the *rooty* forest."

Tory and Ricky turned back to Scarlet whose lips were pulled into a straight line as she narrowed her eyes at Beau. "I tripped, okay?!"

"While you were being attacked by some creature? Are you all right? What happened? Where is it now?" Questions were just falling out of Tory's mouth and it made Scarlet smile again.

"It was some horrid-looking thing with no eyes and holes for a mouth and nose. And it had shadows that were able to chase me. Who knows what would have happened if Beau hadn't shown up! It froze in terror and then Beau took his head off with his sword!" She paused. "Where *did* you get that sword?"

Beau grinned, obviously pleased with whatever his answer was about to be. "I was testing a theory. During the last trial, we were transported here with all of our clothes on. It made me wonder if anything that is on us or that we're touching at the time comes with us. So I ate in my room last night so that I could have my sword on me before the drugs took effect. Looks like my theory was right!"

Beau gave Scarlet a quick, pointed look that made her realize that moving forward, she'd have to keep her dagger on her at all times.

"Okay, so let's recap," Ricky declared. "We can bring things with us to the trials. There was a shadow creature that's now dead, but we don't know if there are any more of them. And we have a pegasus. Do we have any idea what the actual trial is?"

Suddenly, the hairs on the back of Scarlet's neck stood up. As if on cue, day suddenly became night and the ground beneath their feet trembled. An unsettling screech pierced the air. Scarlet turned and saw the pegasus standing on its hind legs, flapping its wings. Then the trees groaned as something massive shifted in the darkness, the air thick with the scent of damp earth and something far worse.

Beau drew his sword and pulled Scarlet to his side in a fluid motion as the ground around them cracked open.

From the depths of the realm, more shadow creatures emerged.

Tory gasped, stumbling back. "Scarlet, you were right! They *are* horrid!"

Scarlet's heart pounded in her chest, but she drew on the fire within her. Flames flickered to life in the palms of her hands.

One of the creatures lunged at Tory, its shadows snapping out like whips. She ducked just in time and, hoping she wouldn't burn the forest down, Scarlet thrust her hands forward, releasing a burst of flames straight at the creature's sagging chest. The creature's shadows recoiled as its body ignited and turned to dust, Scarlet's flames dying in the air. Was it Scarlet's imagination or did it "look" at her just like she thought the last one had?

Beau slashed his sword, the blade cutting through one of the other creatures as the pegasus, holding one by the neck, tossed its head from side to side, breaking the creature's spine.

Ricky, on the other hand, was conjuring rocks and throwing them with precision at the oncoming creatures. A large rock shot out like a bullet, slamming into one creature's head, sending it crashing to the ground. He summoned more sharp stones, launching them at the advancing creatures. "Tory, behind you!"

Tory whipped around just as a creature lunged at her. Ricky roared as Tory was tackled to the ground. Fortunately, Beau was nearby and was able to stab the creature with a shallow thrust through its back.

"Tory, are you okay?" he asked, quickly helping her to her feet.

Tory nodded, breathing heavily.

"We need to take them down faster," Scarlet said, stepping forward. "They won't stop coming until we defeat them all."

Beau grimaced, wiping blood from his face. "Let's do it, then. Together."

Scarlet and Beau moved side by side, each a perfect counterpoint to the other – her fire blinding and searing, his sword cutting with deadly precision. Ricky, more calculated, summoned a chain of rocks that wrapped around one of the creatures' limbs, pulling it to the ground. With a snap, he conjured a large blade into his hands to finish it off.

As the creatures staggered back, Scarlet stepped into the fray once more. She focused on her magic, amplifying the fire in her palms. Her heart raced as she let out a breath, sending a massive torrent of flames sweeping across the forest floor. The creatures howled, their bodies writhing and burning along with several trees, but there wasn't any time to focus on that.

"We're not done yet!" Tory shouted, eyes wide in horror as another wave of creatures emerged from the dark. The pegasus joined her at her side, wings spread, as if trying to protect her.

"Everyone, stand back!" Scarlet commanded. She held out both hands, and this time, the fire within her surged like a storm. Flames spiraled around her, forming a vortex of molten energy that rose higher and higher, engulfing the creatures. The heat was unbearable, the fire swirling with such force it seemed to twist the very air.

With one final push, Scarlet screamed as she released the magic in a concentrated blast, a surge of fire that obliterated the last of the creatures in a brilliant explosion of light and heat, turning the creatures to ash.

The forest crackled as trees continued to burn. But suddenly, Scarlet felt a few drops of water land on her head. She looked up and a torrent of rain fell from the sky, dousing the flames. She turned to Ricky who was breathing heavily, but with a smile on his face.

"Your doing, I presume?" Scarlet said while pointing to the sky.

Ricky nodded

"That is *so* neat!" she said with a big, but tired, smile.

"I could say the same to you!" he replied. "Nice work!"

"Is... is it over?" Tory asked weakly. With what little strength she had left, she still was able to gently stroke the pegasus' fur, as if reassuring them both that they were all okay.

Beau wiped the sweat from his brow, his chest rising and falling rapidly. "I think so."

They sat in silence for a moment, the only sounds coming from their heavy pants and rain droplets falling through the trees and onto the ground. The flames finally all died down, leaving the forest mostly intact.

"Do you hear that buzzing?" Tory asked, looking around.

Before she could reply, Scarlet suddenly heard it, too. The droning almost sounded like it was in her own head, but then she felt tingles all over her body again.

The next thing she knew, she was standing inside the mansion in front of the sorcerer's apprentices. Scarlet quickly looked around and saw her friends were by her side, but the pegasus was gone.

"Congratulations, again, you four," Gebert said. "With somewhat minimal damage," he glared at Scarlet, "you were able to defeat the shadowborgs and complete the trial. You may go back to your rooms."

Beau didn't wait for another invitation as he grabbed Scarlet's hand and ran for the stairs.

7

CHAPTER SEVEN

Scarlet woke up alone.

After the trial, Beau had raced her up to his room where they spent several hours just holding each other and taking the opportunity for the occasional kiss. At some point, Ricky had come by to let them know he was going to give them some privacy and stay with Tory. In all honesty, Scarlet was hoping he was also staying with her to bring some comfort to her. Ricky also let them know that Miranda had almost been killed by one of the shadowborgs during the trial. Rouge saved her, but both were badly injured. They were going to make it, but needed to rest.

With only one trial remaining, there were still eight of them left to compete. Scarlet wasn't sure how she felt about that as she got out of Beau's bed and peeked into the bathing chamber to see if he was there. When she saw that he wasn't, she made her way into the hall. She was about to enter her room when she heard Beau's voice, barely a whisper, around the corner. She then heard what sounded like a body being pushed against the wall and then a female gasp.

Scarlet made her way towards Beau and whoever he was with, fear clutching her heart. She knew that if she saw Beau being romantic with anyone, she wouldn't be able to take it. Tentatively, she peered around the corner.

For a moment, she couldn't process what she was seeing. It looked like Beau was kissing Jettevieve's neck and Scarlet's heart sank. But then she saw that Jettevieve's eyes were glazed over and her limbs looked limp.

Scarlet gasped and quickly covered her mouth just as Beau looked up, blood dripping from his *fangs* as he made eye contact with Scarlet. She started to run and heard Beau snarl behind her, as well as a thumping sound, which she imagined was Jettevieve's body hitting the floor.

She raced for her room, her fire magic igniting at her fingertips. She couldn't use it inside the mansion. Not without risking the whole place burning down. Scarlet continued running for her room, not sure if she was hoping that Tory and Ricky would be inside to help her or if the room would be empty and they would be spared. What Scarlet did know was that she needed to get to her dagger. Beau's dagger. Why hadn't she kept it on her like he told her to?

With Beau right on her feet, she threw open the door and tried to quickly close it. Beau slammed his hand out onto the door, stopping it. Tory and Ricky weren't there, but her dagger was right inside her nightstand. She opened the drawer, but Beau grabbed her by the waist and pushed her up against the wall. She shrieked, but Beau covered her mouth, dulling the sound.

"Let me explain," he pleaded through gritted teeth. "If I take my hand away, do you swear that you won't scream again?"

Scarlet nodded and as promised, Beau removed his hand from her mouth.

"What are you?" Scarlet asked through shallow breaths, tears welling in her eyes. "Are you a vampire?"

Beau gave her a soft smile, no longer looking like the vicious killer she had just caught in the hallway, and shook his head. "No, Scarlet, I'm not a vampire. I'm a macarong. Do you know what that is?"

It was Scarlet's turn to shake her head, dissenting.

"A macarong is similar to a vampire in that we're made, not born. A fae has to take their last breath and a macarong who hasn't used their one immortal ember has to give it to them in order to turn them into a macarong."

Scarlet just stared. She had never heard of a macarong or immortal embers. It was like Beau was speaking another language.

He went on. "I don't drink blood for sustenance; only to kill, if necessary. And what you just saw was necessary. She *threatened you,* Scarlet!" He snarled again and Scarlet flinched.

Beau took a calming breath before continuing. "My blood can't heal an injured human or fae like a vampire's can, according to legends. I'm just a fae who touched death and was given this new life instead."

Scarlet considered what Beau was telling her before asking, "You almost died?"

Beau nodded. "I did die. But only for a second. And then I was saved by a dear friend of mine."

"I'm sorry," Scarlet whispered, not making eye contact with him. She was so scared and hurt and couldn't help but wonder if the macarong shared a certain ability with vampires. Fearfully, she asked, "Can a macarong compel someone like a vampire?"

Beau studied her face and slowly assessed her like a predator sizing up its prey. "Scarlet, everything you felt for me was real. Macarong do not have the power of compulsion. I swear it."

Scarlet swallowed her sobs. Part of her was relieved, but another part felt like she was being ripped apart from the inside out.

"Why?" she cried out of desperation. She couldn't help the tears from spilling from her eyes. She had known that Beau wasn't human and yet, she had believed his lies.

Beau didn't need her to clarify what she was asking. "Your father hired me to kill you during the trials," Beau replied, no emotion lacing his words.

Scarlet gasped. "He *what*?" she shrieked, feeling delirious. He wouldn't. He was her father. But he was also the same male that sent her to the trials knowing that it could mean her death.

Beau took a deep breath before continuing. "I received word from a messenger that the king had a deal for me. When I arrived at your palace, he told me that he needed to kill his evil daughter. He explained that there was darkness in her... you... that would lead to the fall of his kingdom. He needed to ensure that whatever the outcome of the contestant selection or the trials, that you wouldn't return. He was aware of my glamouring abilities and knew that you wouldn't see it coming if I disguised myself as a weak human."

A sob escaped Scarlet. She couldn't believe the words she was hearing, but somewhere deep inside her, she knew that there was truth to them.

"What was in it for you?" she asked, anger and resentment in her tone.

"A high ranking position within his army," Beau replied flatly. "But Scarlet," he reached for her face, but she turned away. Grabbing her chin in his large hand, he turned her so that he could look her in the eyes. "When I saw how much what the apprentices did to that boy, Charlie, in the woods affected you, I knew that you couldn't have any darkness in you. There's nothing but light there."

"But after we found the relic and you saw my blood, you looked suspicious of me," Scarlet countered.

"I couldn't deny what I saw and there was a moment - a *moment* - where I questioned my judgement. But I know, Scarlet, I *know* that you are good. It's your father that's evil."

"You lied to me," she said, her voice weary.

"And for that, I couldn't be more sorry," Beau replied earnestly. "But that is why I gave you the dagger. I think that there are others here who could harm you and I wanted to do everything in my power to protect you."

"But they called me the Firebird," she whispered, barely audible.

Beau nodded. "I know. And I think you are the Firebird," he replied, brushing her untamed, red hair away from her face. "I think you're the savior that rises to save the Light Kingdom. And I think that your father would do anything to stop you." He searched her eyes as if waiting for her to understand. When she didn't speak, Beau went on. "Remember the day we met when I told you about the prophecy?"

Scarlet nodded her head slowly.

"I told you that it's believed that Tellus is the Dark Kingdom. If that's true, that would mean that your father could be the king that sought to destroy the Light Kingdom. Scarlet, don't you see? Your father is trying to find the Light Kingdom to rule it as his own! And *you* are the thing that could get in his way!"

He waited again. Waited for a response. Waited for some sign that she was still with him. And then, with a deathly calm, she said three words.

"I *hate* you."

Beau pulled away from her as if he had been burned by her fire.

"You are a traitor and a murderer. You betrayed my father. You lied to me. You *keep* lying to me!" she screamed, covering her ears and shaking her head.

Despite everything, Beau tentatively approached Scarlet and gently wrapped his arms around her as she began to sob. "He's my father," she cried, devastation wrapping around her like a cocoon.

Beau tightened his embrace, "I know, Scarlet. I know."

"Please leave," she whispered.

Beau let go of her and slowly backed up. "Are you sure?" he asked.

Scarlet nodded.

"Okay," he replied, gingerly walking towards the door. "But Scarlet?"

She looked up at him and sniffed.

"Jettevieve said that she needed to kill the Firebird. You're not safe. Keep the dagger on you, okay?"

She nodded before Beau turned and walked out the door. Scarlet locked it behind him.

* * * * *

Scarlet stayed locked up in her room all day, not even going down to the Great Hall for meals. Tory came back to check on her at some point, but Scarlet lied and told her that she had another headache. She wasn't ready to talk about Beau. She didn't even know what she'd say if she was ready.

The Endless Forest Trials had been the catalyst in Scarlet's life. Never had she been more aware of how naive she was. Her limited life experiences had caused her to lack any real understanding of the world around her. And, apparently, the world around her was either lying to her, trying to kill her, or both.

Scarlet barely slept that night. She dreamed of the black-haired female, standing on the rune and then diving off of the cliff. The only variation this time was that when she looked back, she said, "Death is my gift," before heading towards her death.

Beau had lied to her. Her father was potentially trying to kill her and she could deny it all she wanted, but part of her believed that everything Beau said was true. Speculation, quite possibly, but there was something there. And now, the mysterious fae from her dreams was telling her that death was her gift. *Who* was she and what did it mean?

Sleep-deprived and agitated, Scarlet made her way down to the Great Hall for breakfast. She immediately saw Tory and Ricky sitting at the table, with the noticeable absence of Beau. Where was he? He always had breakfast with them.

"Rough night?" Ricky asked, looking Scarlet up and down.

"The roughest," she replied, shoving a croissant in her mouth in hopes of not having to elaborate.

"You were talking in your sleep," Tory told her, chewing on a chocolate-filled pastry.

"I was?" Scarlet mumbled, mouth still full. "What did I say?"

"You kept saying that death was your gift," Tory replied flatly. "Do you remember dreaming about anything?"

"Just the same dream I told you about. But this time, she said 'death is my gift' before jumping. I guess I was just repeating that while I slept."

Tory eyed her somewhat suspiciously, although Scarlet couldn't figure out why. "Yeah, that must be it."

"Where is Beau?" Scarlet asked as casually as possible.

Ricky shrugged. "No clue. He wasn't in our room when I woke up. I figured he was with you."

"Should we be concerned?" Scarlet asked cautiously.

"I don't think so," Ricky told her. "He's probably just off reading somewhere."

Scarlet looked at Ricky incredulously. "Why would you think that?"

Ricky stared at her for a moment before replying, "Because he reads a lot. He's usually in our room reading a different book or scroll at night after you go to bed."

Scarlet was shocked. She had never seen Beau read anything. But then again, up until yesterday, she thought Beau was human, so what did she really know about him?

"If you'll excuse me," Scarlet said as she stood up from the table. "I'm going to look for him, just to be sure."

Tory and Ricky nodded before Scarlet turned and headed back upstairs. She was so caught up in her thoughts that she ran directly into Beau in the hallway, causing him to drop his books.

His *books*.

"I'm so sorry!" Scarlet exclaimed as she bent down to pick them up.

"It's all right," she heard Beau say as she saw the covers and their titles.

Prophecies of the Old World and *The History of Tellus*.

"Where did you get these?" Scarlet asked.

Beau blinked a few times before smiling. "The library?"

"There's a *library* here?" Scarlet shouted incredulously.

"You really aren't very observant, are you?" Immediately, a pained look spread across Beau's face. "I'm sorry! I shouldn't have – I mean, after the other night – I didn't mean to imply – "

Scarlet waved him off. Despite her stomach being twisted into knots, she didn't want to be upset with him anymore. Maybe it was just her naivete, but Beau did seem to always be trying to protect her. And he was clearly trying to do research and find sufficient evidence to support his claims. The least she could do was be civil towards him until she could learn more about Beau's past and what her father was up to.

Scarlet handed the books back to Beau and wordlessly, they went back into his room. There was some unspoken agreement between them. An understanding. She couldn't forget, but she could forgive. And, so, they spent the next few hours, pouring over the ancient texts.

8

CHAPTER EIGHT

"So are vampires real?" While Beau did the majority of the reading, Scarlet peppered him with questions. If she was going to completely forgive him, she needed to know everything.

"I have no proof that they are, but I also don't have proof that they're not," he told her.

"And the macarong... Tell me more about them."

Beau put his book down on the bed next to him so that it rested between his legs and Scarlet's. "The macarong are considered an abomination amongst the fae. We believe that the immortal embers are a blessing from the Fates, but most fae consider the act of giving an ember to save a life an unnatural feat against the Fates. Taking a soul away from them."

"But what *is* an immortal ember?"

"You know how you've said that you can feel your fire inside you, waiting to be called? That's kind of how I felt about the ember. It was something inside me, like a ball of energy in my chest. Many years ago, I used my ember to save a fae who was important to me. They had been injured – a fatal wound – and so I transferred the energy from my ember into them."

Scarlet took a moment to process everything. She wanted to know who Beau saved, but he was being so open with her that she didn't want to dig into the one thing he seemed to not want to share. It didn't escape Scarlet that this fae who was important enough to him to give up his ember for was referred to as "they" instead of the likely "she."

"How did my father discover your glamouring abilities?" Scarlet asked instead of irrationally asking, "Who was she?"

"I was being careless and using it at the market to entertain some kids by glamouring myself into different animals. One of the king's spies saw me." Beau shrugged.

"How does a glamour work?"

"Think of it as a magical spell that I put on myself so that anyone who sees me only sees what I want them to."

"Can you look different to different people? Like, when I saw your rounded, human ears, could others see them pointed at the same time?"

Beau shook his head. "No. Whatever I change about myself is seen the same by everyone. So to answer what I know is going to be your next questions, Tory and Ricky also thought that I was human. Well, they still do think that. I don't think we should tell them the truth yet. Not until we all make it out of here alive."

"Why?" Scarlet asked, leafing through her book. "Don't you trust them?"

"With your life? No."

She glanced up and met Beau's gaze. She didn't want to still have feelings for him, but when he said things like that, it was hard not to.

"Scarlet. Your *father* wants you dead. Jettevieve also believed that you being the Firebird meant something bad for Tellus. Do I believe that Tory and Ricky are also involved with the king? No. But I'm not taking any chances. Not with you."

Forget. Forget. Scarlet kept reminding herself that she had forgiven Beau and she so desperately wanted to forget that he had lied to her. Here he was, trying to protect her – and quite literally killing for her – but she didn't know if she could trust him.

She knew that her father never loved her – she had always felt that way. She knew that the apprentices believed she was the Firebird. She knew that there was a prophecy that said that the Firebird would rise and save a kingdom and that it was likely that her father believed this and wanted her dead. She also knew that there was so much she didn't know – so much that she had been sheltered from – like the fact that there were creatures called macarong. And if these creatures existed in other kingdoms and she never knew about them, what else didn't she know?

"I'm still mad at you," she finally said under her breath.

Beau nodded. "I know."

He looked sad and something in Scarlet broke at the sight of him. Maybe she wouldn't forget – couldn't. And maybe she wasn't ready to trust him. But she *could* let him know what it meant to her that he seemed to always be trying to keep her safe.

Scarlet leaned in and kissed him. It was a tentative kiss and she could feel Beau tense, but she could also feel the spark. She reached up and gently traced the point of Beau's ear. There was a split second where she thought she felt him tremble and then the next thing she knew, she was pressed against the wall, Beau kissing her deeply.

"I thought I had lost you forever," he said against her lips and then kissed her again. "Scarlet, I am *so* sorry. I will never be able to apologize enough for lying to you. But please know, my intentions were good."

Feeling blissfully lost in Beau's kiss, Scarlet hummed her response. Maybe she was being foolish for allowing Beau back into her life so quickly, but she was tired of chastising herself. Tired of the lies and the deaths. In this moment, Scarlet just wanted to feel alive. She just wanted to forget.

"Tell me this is okay," he whispered as Scarlet tried to catch her breath. She nodded, but that wasn't good enough for Beau. "No, you have to say it," he practically growled.

She wanted to say no to the beautiful liar, but everything in her body said yes. "I want this," Scarlet whispered. "I want you."

He leaned into her, pressing her even harder into the wall, the evidence of his arousal firm against her.

"Are you still mad at me for lying to you?" He ground into her harder, making her moan.

Scarlet arched, trying to shamelessly generate more friction between them before she narrowed her eyes at him.

"Oh, I hate you," she practically moaned, the words feeling false on her lips. She knew she was as much of a liar as Beau.

Beau's lip tipped up at one side, mischief dancing in his eyes. "Keep telling yourself that, Princess." He then lifted her off of her feet and the traitorous things wrapped around his waist. He placed her on the table beside his bed and pulled away before taking off his tunic. Scarlet couldn't help the flush that colored her cheeks. Beau was chiseled to perfection. His sculpted muscles flexed as Scarlet perused his body, dim light dancing off of him and leading her gaze down to the V-shape that led to...

"Patience," he chuckled as he peeled Scarlet's tunic over her head. His hands grazed down the side of her body until he reached the waistband of her pants. He looked back up at her as if asking for permission.

She nodded her approval at him before he dropped to his knees and pulled her pants down and off of her at a tortuous speed. Before she knew it, he was standing again, ripping his pants off so fast, a startling contrast to how fast he had removed hers.

Her mouth went dry when she looked down at his cock that was now standing at attention, free of the fabric prison it had wanted so desperately to get out of.

Beau reached down between Scarlet's legs and moaned when he felt how wet she was.

"I guess you're not as mad at me as you say, huh?" he laughed before lining himself up at her entrance. Scarlet tensed in anticipation. Beau smiled as he wrapped one arm around her back and placed his other hand at the crook of her hip so that his thumb pressed down on the bundle of nerves at her apex. Her eyes went wide and she gasped before Beau used her surprise to glide into her.

The delicious fullness made Scarlet's head swim. Beau pulled back before thrusting back into her, a breathy moan escaping before she could hold it back.

"You feel so good," Beau told Scarlet, his voice sounding almost strained. "Tell me how much you hate me again," he said as he pulled out of her almost fully.

"I – " he slammed back into her before she could finish her sentence, her eyes rolling to the back of her head as the table banged against the wall.

He continued thrusting in and out of her, picking up the pace as his thumb played with her. Scarlet reached around and grabbed Beau's ass as he flexed in her palms. She arched back, all of the sensations building. She writhed against the desk, trying to pull Beau closer to her. She felt Beau widen his stance between her legs, his thrusts becoming quicker and more shallow. He then bent his head and took one of Scarlet's nipples into her mouth, sucking before gently biting down.

It was all too much. Scarlet unraveled as her vision went black and her core clenched against Beau's cock. A few more thrusts and Beau was roaring his release before collapsing against Scarlet, both of his hands against the wall, caging her in. She remembered being in a similar position not too long ago when Beau had given her the dagger.

"Fuck... That was amazing. *You're* amazing," he sighed against the shell of Scarlet's ear. Her blood was still pumping so hard that she could hear the pulse of it.

"It's about time!" she heard Tory exclaim, her voice muffled through the wall.

Scarlet's jaw practically unhinged, her eyes wide with panic and embarrassment.

"We're happy for you guys!" came Ricky's voice.

Scarlet covered her mouth as Beau laughed. "Sorry!" he shouted back before kissing Scarlet's forehead. The act somehow feeling more intimate than what they had just done.

"It's all good! But I use that table, so if you could wipe it down..." Ricky yelled back.

Scarlet was mortified, but also felt... beautiful? Empowered? Desired.

For so long and to so many, she was the girl that others shied away from. The abomination associated with evil. But with Beau, she was simply Scarlet.

9

CHAPTER NINE

A few days went by and there still had been no final trial. It was almost as if the apprentices were intentionally trying to get the contestants to let down their guards. Feeling restless one evening, Scarlet and Tory decided to go back to the tavern. "Females only," they had told Beau and Ricky.

As soon as they got their frosty mugs of mead, Tory leaned in, eyes gleaming. It was evident what she wanted to talk about.

"So, Beau," she said bluntly.

Scarlet took a sip of her mead, the bubbles immediately tickling her throat. She smiled. "Beau."

"It was inevitable," Tory declared. "I remember the way you two looked at each other when you first met."

Scarlet giggled. "Of course you do! You have memory magic!" she laughed.

Tory grinned and nodded. "Yes, but even without it, it would be something memorable. I mean, you were practically drooling!"

Scarlet gave Tory a scandalized look. "I was not!" she exclaimed, gently slapping Tory's hand. She suddenly pulled back, alarmed.

"What's wrong?" Tory asked.

"You're very hot."

Tory gave her a sideways glance. "What do you mean?"

Scarlet reached over and grabbed Tory's hand, holding it in hers. "Your skin. It's very warm," she stated, sliding her hand up Tory's arm. "Are you feeling all right?"

"I'm fine," she assured Scarlet. "This is my normal body temperature. It has been for as long as I can remember. Which, as you know, is for forever." She smiled at Scarlet, who slowly pulled her hands away.

"Oh," Scarlet simply said, feeling a little embarrassed. Tory was always so reserved and she felt bad about touching her when she obviously valued her personal space.

"Just try to keep your hands off me. I don't need Beau getting jealous." Tory winked at Scarlet who relaxed in her seat. "Plus, I don't think Ricky would like to share."

"Are you guys finally...?" Scarlet trailed off.

"We're going to explore our feelings for one another," Tory replied. She stated it simply, almost with no emotion, but Scarlet could see the smile pulling at her lips. "We both agreed that we need to make it out of this last trial before we take things any further and then we'll see where this takes us."

"But there's a possibility of an 'us' for you. That's all that matters." Scarlet was happy for her friend. She took a long swig from her mug and couldn't help to think about how much her life had changed in such a short amount of time. Scarlet had desperately not wanted to come to the Phoenix Mansion to participate in the Endless Forest Trials, but in doing so, she found friends and a... beau in Beau? But she also discovered that her whole life had been a lie. Maybe it was about time she followed her heart and stayed on the path that kept her with Tory, Beau and Ricky.

"When do you think we'll finally get called to the last trial?" Tory asked, pulling Scarlet out of her thoughts.

"I don't know, but I'm desperate for this all to be over. And when it is, I was hoping to keep you in my life."

"Friends forever?" Tory implored.

Scarlet smiled. "Yeah. That sounds nice."

* * * * *

Beau walked in and found Scarlet in her bathing chamber, trying to get into the bath while fully dressed.

"What are you doing?" he asked, grabbing her by the waist before she stepped into the empty tub.

Scarlet giggled. "I want to take a bath!" she declared. "I miss baths." She hiccupped and then buried her face into Beau's chest. "You smell good."

Beau started to laugh. "Are you drunk?"

Scarlet hiccupped again. "I'm not drunk! I'm...I'm..." she trailed off.

"You're what?" Beau asked, his voice a husky whisper.

Scarlet wrapped her arms around his neck and kissed him before quickly pulling back, eyes sparkling. "Take me to bed!" she demanded.

Beau eyed her wearily. "I'm not in the habit of bedding inebriated females."

Scarlet scrunched her face. "I really didn't drink that much. I just feel good." She shrugged before balancing on one foot and then bringing her finger to the tip of her nose. "See?" Scarlet asked as she placed her hand on Beau's chest. She stepped into his warmth so that she was flush against him and sighed. While she wasn't anywhere near out of control, she knew that the mead was fueling her brazenness. And she liked it. "And I know that you can make me feel even better."

Scarlet felt Beau's heart rate accelerate. He stood entirely still for a moment, as if contemplating, before scooping Scarlet up in his arms and taking her to her bed. He carefully placed her down and removed her tunic before she lay back, resting her head comfortably on her pillow. She smiled up at him as he loosened his tunic from his pants and lifted it over his head.

"If you hate me in the morning," he warned her while removing her pants, "just remember that I was taking orders from the princess." He winked at her. She loved that damn wink.

Beau climbed into Scarlet's bed and on top of her. She wrapped her legs around him before lifting her head to kiss him again. This time, the kiss was not quick, but rather, a slow exploration of one another. Scarlet could already feel Beau's hardness between her legs and shamelessly tilted her hips to hit an angle that made her whimper. The sound seemingly spurring Beau on. He kissed her with abandon and when she reached for the waistband of his pants, he moaned into her mouth.

"Want me to take those off?" he asked her.

Scarlet nodded.

"Your wish is my command, Princess."

His cock soon sprung free and Scarlet couldn't stop herself from reaching for it. As soon as she made contact, her hand closing around the velvet-wrapped steel, Beau moaned, his head tipping back.

Scarlet stroked him gloriously slowly, watching him start to unravel, before she lined him up at her entrance.

"Tell me this is what you want," Beau demanded. He was so good about always wanting her consent, even when Scarlet could tell he was trying so hard to restrain himself. She smiled and nodded at him.

"Thank the Fates," he ground out as he sheathed himself inside of her.

Beau pumped in and out of her, so slowly that Scarlet's eyes rolled to the back of her head. He trailed a line of kisses along her throat and she couldn't help but feel a thrill of desire thinking about him sinking his teeth into her.

He chuckled against her neck. "Are you sure?" he asked, pulling out of her to the tip before sliding back in.

Scarlet looked up at him and then propped herself up on her elbows, momentarily stopping Beau. "Can you read my mind?" she asked.

Beau chuckled again. "No, but I have heightened senses. I can smell your desire intensify when I show your neck any special attention."

"Oh, Fates!" Scarlet groaned, covering her face in shame.

Beau pulled her hands away from her. "Stop," he said. "I like that what I am excites you. It's something I've struggled with for so long."

Scarlet could feel Beau still hard inside her, the realization quickly diminishing her shame. She kissed him as she pushed him onto his back. Straddling him, she placed her hands on his chest and started to ride his cock. "Do it," she said.

Without skipping a beat, Beau sat up, Scarlet still sliding up and down his length. He brushed her hair off of her shoulder and gently wrapped his hand around the back of her neck. He placed a reverent kiss on her neck before slowly sinking his teeth into her supple skin.

For a moment, neither of them moved. He waited, ready to stop if she told him to, but instead, she weaved her fingers through his hair and gripped it.

"Oh, Fates, don't stop," she sighed, a breathy moan escaping her. That was all Beau needed to hear before he started to draw her blood into him while thrusting into her from underneath where she still straddled him.

The feeling was euphoric. The contrasting sensations of pleasure and pain were so intoxicating, Scarlet felt like she was going to erupt. She was so close. So close to her release as Beau continued to suck on her neck.

He unlatched his fangs from her before licking at her wound, the sensation of his warm tongue almost too much for her to bear. He then whispered in her ear, "Come for me."

And then she exploded, Beau coaxing her through her release until he chased her over the edge.

Trying to catch her breath while stars still danced in her vision, Scarlet tumbled onto the bed on her back. She had no words for what just happened between them. Her chest heaved up and down as she placed the back of her hand to her forehead.

"What the Hel was that?"

Beau grinned and laid down next to her, wrapping an arm under and around Scarlet and pulling her into his side. She repositioned her head so that it was atop his chest. She could hear his heart beating just as fast as hers.

"That, my dear princess, was one of the benefits of being with a macarong."

Scarlet still couldn't wrap her head around all that she was feeling. She was in no way an expert on the act of sex, but this felt like it had somehow transcended what sex usually was.

"I don't understand," she admitted to him.

He gave her a gentle smile. "Our fangs... they... have a sort of venom." Scarlet tried to pull away to look at him, but he just hugged her closer. "Our venom has euphoric properties. All of the things that you were feeling became heightened. The alcohol in your system also probably helped." He chuckled softly.

"Are there any negative side effects to having your venom in me?" she asked, her voice barely above a whisper.

"Scarlet." Beau said her name almost like an admonishment. He was now the one to pull away from her, propping himself up on his elbows and looking at her in surprise. "Do you really think that I would have done that to you? You of all people?" he asked.

Scarlet felt ashamed. No, she didn't think that, but up until a few days ago, she also didn't think that her father was trying to kill her. But she knew that in order for her to move forward in her life, she had to get out of her head.

"No," she admitted. "No, I don't really think so." Scarlet saw the unsure look on Beau's face and felt awful for putting it there. They just had this beautiful experience and she had ruined it. "Beau, I'm sorry." She placed her hands around his face and looked him deeply in the eyes. "I'm so sorry."

Beau didn't push her away. Instead, he reached up and held both of her hands in place with his own. "I would never hurt you. And I will *always* protect you," he told her earnestly.

She nodded, tears filling her eyes. She tried to pull away, but Beau gripped her hands tighter.

"Don't cry," he told her.

She sniffed. "I'm not crying. I'm just drunk."

"Liar," Beau declared as he leaned in to kiss Scarlet's forehead, her eyelids fluttering before drifting closed. Embracing her, they lay back down and Beau nestled Scarlet's body against his own. "I will protect you. I swear it."

They laid in peaceful silence for a few moments before Beau got out of bed and gathered their clothing, handing Scarlet hers along with the dagger she had left on the nightstand. "Trust me," he said as he got himself dressed and then got back into bed with her. Beau pulled Scarlet towards him so that her back was flush against his chest.

Scarlet started to drift off, but not before she sighed and breathily asked, "Beau, if you could have a second wish, what would you wish for?"

"You," he replied, but Scarlet had already fallen asleep.

That night, wrapped in Beau's embrace, she dreamed of the female on the cliff. But this time, instead of crying before she jumped, she smiled, fangs peeking out from her lips, before she dove into the darkness.

10

CHAPTER TEN

B eau was gone.

Or Scarlet was. She woke up, but couldn't see anything and was overly aware of Beau's missing warmth.

Where am I? Scarlet wondered. She was cold and the air felt damp. She quickly realized that she was on the ground, which was also cold and damp. Crawling around until she found a wall, Scarlet realized that she was in a cave. Using her hands to follow along the cave wall, she made her way to the entrance and immediately saw that a thick layer of snow was covering the ground. As she stepped out of the cave, she saw the clouds that adorned the ominous grey sky. Icicles dripped from leafless trees, one dislodging in front of her.

She groaned. She didn't come all of this way to be taken out by a piece of ice. Still cold, Scarlet used her fire magic to warm herself.

Walking around, Scarlet was sure that she was in the Endless Forest, but she wasn't sure how it became winter overnight. Or rather, she understood how, but not why. If the trial was to avoid freezing to death, she'd surely win. Ricky also stood a chance, being able to conjure warm clothes.

Suddenly, Scarlet's hand dropped to her side and she let out a breath of relief. Beau's insistence on them getting dressed before falling asleep paid off, as her dagger was safe and sound, secured to her body by the waistband of her pants.

As she walked deeper into the forest, she saw something attached to a tree. Another parchment. She got closer, thankful that it was tacked onto a tree this time and not a person. She pulled it down to be able to read it better.

The Darkest Blood is the biggest threat.

Pierce the heart and save the kingdom yet!

Scarlet didn't know what it meant, but she couldn't help thinking about her own blood. She was grateful for the dagger at her side in the event that a creature's heart needed to be pierced.

Suddenly, the sky changed from grey to a hazy blue, the sun's rays feeling incredibly hot on Scarlet's skin. She looked around and saw that the snow around her was melting.

What in the Fates' Hel is going on? She wondered as she stopped her fire magic from coursing through her. The air was so warm, it was almost stifling.

"Scarlet!"

Scarlet turned to see Tory running at her, water splashing up from her feet.

"Oh, thank the Fates I found you!" she exclaimed, sweat beading on her nose and forehead.

"Tory, are you okay?" Scarlet asked.

"Yes, I'm fine!" she exclaimed. "I found this parchment!" Tory held up the same message that Scarlet still held in her hand.

"I have one, too." She brought her piece next to Tory's to confirm that they were identical.

"I also have one," Ricky's voice declared as he emerged from behind a tree. Tory ran and leapt into his arms.

One by one, each of the remaining contestants, Miranda, Faygar and Rouge, joined Scarlet, Tory and Ricky. Beau was the last to unite with the group. He embraced Scarlet and whispered in her ear, "Stay close to me."

Scarlet nodded. Her eyes were filled with concern and determination. This was it. This was what they were all gathered for. The moment they had all been waiting for.

The ground shook with a force great enough to knock Rouge off of her feet. The contestants all looked around and found the source: An ancient stone archway emerging from the ground. Once the archway was fully uncovered, the ground stopped shaking. Their faces were all grim as they studied the massive erection.

"Do we walk through it?" Miranda asked, pushing her glasses back up her nose.

"We'll do it together," Tory said, her voice steadier than Scarlet felt.

Faygar glanced between the archway and Scarlet, eyeing her nervously. He was a warrior and yet, Scarlet got the feeling that she was somehow making him feel uneasy. Her eyes hardened as she drew her attention away from Faygar and she looked at the arch.

It was time. She could feel the heat emitting from the arch, the air growing thicker and hotter.

"Let's go," Scarlet said, steeling herself as she grabbed Tory's hand in her left and Beau's hand in her right. The remaining contestants all held hands in solidarity as they stepped forward into the archway.

The moment they crossed the threshold, the temperature changed dramatically. Scarlet immediately felt that her body was freezing again. She looked up at Beau whose lips looked like they were about to turn blue. When she turned to her left, she saw that Tory looked less cold than Beau, but was shivering slightly. Scarlet sent fire through her hands and into Beau and Tory's bodies at the same moment that clothes fell to the ground in front of them. Scarlet looked towards Ricky who shrugged.

"Thank you," Miranda said. She was the only human left among them, Scarlet remembered.

They all put their new coats and gloves on, Scarlet forgoing the gloves in case she needed her magic again. But no sooner were they all bundled up, a ring of fire erupted around them.

Beau flinched, pulling Scarlet closer to him. "Scarlet..." he began, but his voice was lost in the sound of crackling flames. The fire was alive, as if it had a mind of its own, swirling around her in a maddening dance.

"Everyone stay back!" Rouge yelled.

"What's going on?" Miranda yelped, quickly trying to pull her coat off.

"They're trying to drive us mad!" Ricky exclaimed. "These extreme temperatures! Fire and ice!"

Scarlet turned to Tory who looked lost in thought. "Fire and ice. Fire and ice," she mumbled under her breath. "Dark and light... Dark and light?"

"Tory, what are you thinking?" Scarlet asked, but before Tory could answer, the flames died down and the sky turned dark.

"Dark and light." Tory was still rambling, trying to figure something out.

An icy wind whipped around as the ground froze. Snow started falling from the sky at a rapid pace. Before Scarlet could try to snap Tory out of her trance, there was a blast of heat that sent all of them sprawling backwards. Scarlet flew back, hitting her head. She laid on the ground for a moment to let the wave of dizziness pass, but then heard screaming. A female screaming.

Scarlet's stomach dropped. "*Tory?*" she yelled as she sat up, searching for her friend. Searching for where the shrieking was coming from.

Scarlet sobbed when she saw Tory just a few feet away from her, holding her head where she also must have hit it. Scarlet's relief was short-lived when she saw Miranda – on fire.

"*No!*" Scarlet screamed, but it was too late. Miranda's body was nothing more than charred skin and bones on the ground, the flames engulfing what was left of her.

Scarlet could see Beau past the fire. He was propped up on his elbows, a look of sadness on his face. None of them knew Miranda well, but Scarlet could feel the loss and knew that Beau was feeling the same.

Ricky approached Tory, helping her to her feet. Before he could come to Scarlet's side next, the weather turned frigid again, the blast of cold hitting her like a slap. Still sprawled on the ground and feeling dizzy, Scarlet laid her head back down on the ground and took a deep breath. She watched the snow drift down towards her and saw as the icicles once again started to form on the tree branches. She was getting so frustrated. What was the point of this? Were the apprentices just going to keep driving them crazy until each either combusted or froze to death?

Scarlet blinked as another icicle dislodged and stabbed her in the arm. "Ow!" she yelped, quickly sitting up despite her head swimming. She cupped her forearm where the shard of ice had penetrated her skin.

"Are you okay?" Ricky asked as he knelt beside her, grabbing her uninjured arm to bring her to a stand.

"Yeah, but these icicles are sharp as knives," she said as she pulled her hand away, blood dripping at a steady rate out of her arm and staining the snow. Scarlet inspected the wound and then turned her gaze to Ricky who was staring at the blood-stained snow.

The black, blood-stained snow.

"The Darkest Blood is the biggest threat," Ricky recited. *"Pierce the heart and save the kingdom yet."*

"Ricky," Scarlet started to say as Ricky conjured a dagger.

"It's you," he seethed, looking possessed. "All along."

Scarlet's eyes went wide as Ricky pulled his dagger back. Time suddenly felt incredibly slow while still moving too fast. She heard Beau scream, but the sound was muffled in her ears. Out of the corner of her eye, she thought he was running towards her, the pumping of his arms and the gait of his stride indicating such, but it was as if he was running in slow motion. He wasn't closing the gap between them fast enough. Tory was screaming as she ran towards Ricky with outstretched arms. Scarlet tried to reach for her dagger, but in the blink of an eye, Ricky's pierced her chest.

There were more screams. Beau's. Tory's. But Scarlet couldn't scream. All she could do was stare into Ricky's cold and emotionless gaze as she dropped to her knees and then crumbled to the ground.

Scarlet had heard that your life flashes before you as you journey towards death, and it did. Scarlet saw her early years within the castle. Days laughing with Hanre. With Pearl and Alabaster. Of painting the landscape from her room. And then she saw Beau. Really saw Beau as he looked down at her, tears falling from his eyes. Scarlet tried to reach up. To brush the tears from his beautiful face. But her arms felt too heavy. He really was beautiful. She wished that she had painted him while she had the chance.

Scarlet's eyes drifted close and the darkness welcomed her like an old friend.

PART 2

SAVING FIAH

11

CHAPTER ELEVEN

S carlet was dead.

Tory looked at Ricky, horrified at what he'd done. Horrified and... something else. Something felt different.

"Ricky, what did you do?" Tory shrieked. Suddenly, the room felt like it was spinning, so she slowly lowered herself to the ground.

"Astoria, are you okay?" Ricky gasped, running to Tory's side. "Do you know what's happening?"

Laying on the floor, Tory blinked up at Ricky. "Why did you just call me Astoria?"

But she didn't get an answer before everything faded to black.

* * * * *

Tory opened her eyes and immediately realized that she was no longer part of the trials. Propping herself up on her elbows, she looked around. She was still in the Endless Forest, but the contestants were all gone. Hoping to clear the fog, she rubbed her eyes with the heels of her palms before hearing the sound of footsteps in the distance. Footsteps and chanting. She slowly stood up, intent on investigating.

The last thing she remembered was being in the middle of a trial. She remembered Scarlet getting injured and bleeding black. And she remembered Ricky's face before he took his dagger and sent it through Scarlet's chest.

She also remembered Ricky calling her Astoria. No one had ever called her that. She had always simply been Tory. But hearing the name made her feel a sense of rightness within her.

Tory quickly found the source of the chanting. It was a small group of men wearing simple brown robes, just like the ones that the apprentices always wore. She watched as they reached a tree and began gathering nearby twigs to build a fire. Tory squinted her eyes and that's when she realized that Marcus, Francois and Gebert were among the group. The chanting became louder as they opened a vessel. Thick, black smoke rose from the flames. But soon, the fire died down and once it extinguished entirely, it was then that Tory saw the bright red, orange, and yellow bird emerge.

Suddenly, there was a flash that caused Tory to close her eyes. When she opened them, she was no longer standing in the forest – she was flying above it!

Tory as a bird took in the sight of the tree tops and clouds. She flew for quite some time before she saw smoke in the distance. She kept flying towards the smoke until she reached a city. A city that looked as if it had once been considered great with beautiful homes and thriving businesses.

A city with people who tried to take care of one another. A city that had once been loved, but was now up in flames.

Flames and chaos as soldiers destroyed what Tory knew was once something important. And in the middle of the destruction was Scarlet pointing a sword up at her.

* * * * *

"Alaric!" I yelled, as I was brought back to reality. "I remember!"

Alaric was still seated beside me and although he looked different than I was used to seeing him, my soul recognized his the same way his recognized mine. He smiled at me. "So do I."

Slowly, everything started coming back to me. The pain. The sadness. Everything that brought us here. And everything that still needed to be done. I looked around and realized that everyone was gone. Beau, the other contestants... and Scarlet's body.

I sat up and stared into my husband's glimmering eyes.

"It's been a long time, Astoria. Or should I say, my queen?"

I smiled sadly back at him and wrapped my arms around his neck. "I'm not sure if I'm ready to be queen. I barely got to say goodbye to her."

"I know, Astoria. I know," Alaric whispered as he stroked by back. "But we're together now. We can finally put an end to all of this and save our kingdom."

"There's so much that I still don't understand."

"We'll figure it all out together. You and me. Just like it always was... before. You're the key to ending his destruction, Astoria."

I couldn't deny the truth. I was the key to ending all of this. I just didn't entirely understand how.

"Welcome back, Princess Astoria. Or should I call you Queen Astoria now?" A female's voice broke up my reunion with my husband. When I turned, I was staring at a ghostly figure that was all too familiar to me.

"Erina," I said, acknowledging not the so-called "sorcerer's assistant," but the damn sorceress herself! She was the one that orchestrated the whole debacle leading up to my soul getting put inside the phoenix. She's the one that told my mother that it was the only way to save the kingdom.

"Why make yourself the sorcerer's assistant in these games?"

A smile spread across the sorceress' face. "Sometimes it is pleasurable to take on a minor role and watch the Fates' plans play out."

"What was the point of all of this, Erina?" Alaric asked through gritted teeth. He had never been fond of the sorceress and her magic tricks, as he liked to call them. He always knew they came at a cost. "Why did I have to kill Scarlet?"

"Those are questions that I can't fully answer for you, Princeling. I create the spells, but the Fates create the plans."

"Will Scarlet be reborn now that the spell has been broken?" I asked earnestly. I really had become fond of her. She was such a sweet girl who had been dealt a bad hand.

Erina shook her head. "No, Your Majesty. The Fates had other plans for her."

My heart sank. I had felt such a kinship to Scarlet. Even now, knowing who her father was and how he had impacted my life and my loved ones', I still felt a connection to her. She didn't deserve to have to die.

"Why did you kill Charlie?" I asked. "He was just a boy."

Erina gave me a knowing smile. "No one is ever 'just' anyone, Your Majesty. You should know that better than anyone. Everyone serves their purpose in plans of the Fates."

I sighed, quickly growing angry. "You know what I mean, Erina! He was an innocent!"

"I can assure you, Your Majesty, that he was far from innocent. That boy's soul was dark as sin. He had already committed unfathomable atrocities at such a young age. My apprentices may have overstepped – "

Alaric snapped. "What do you mean 'may have over-stepped'?"

Erina looked thoughtful for a moment, clearly trying to present this to us in a way that wouldn't cause more anger. She looked at me, "They shouldn't have disrupted the balance of the Fates. It was for the greater good, but regardless, I will mete out an appropriate punishment once we're back in Fiah."

Home... Fiah... Our kingdom was a peaceful place. We believed that all lives mattered, whether human, fae or other – everyone deserved a happy and peaceful existence. I didn't know what Charlie had done, but killing unjustly would not be tolerated. I resigned myself to deal with their actions personally when we returned home.

"Tell us everything we need to know so that we can finally end this," I demanded.

"What do you remember?"

Alaric growled. "Stop playing games with us, Erina!"

Nonplussed, Erina rolled her eyes. "All of your memories will slowly start coming back to you, but Remis was using black magic. He wanted to be indestructible in the event that there was ever an attack on Tellus. He wanted to rule forever – to live forever – regardless of the cost. But you can't use black magic without consequences. He was going mad. And the madder he grew, the more dangerous he was becoming. Your mother, Fates rest her soul, was tipped off that Remis was planning to invade and conquer Fiah."

"Who tipped her off?" I asked, needing to know as much as possible of potential allies.

"I can't tell you that," Erina answered.

"Can't or won't?" Alaric growled again.

Erina ignored him and continued. "Your mother came to me, asking for my help. She knew that Fiah's small army was no match for Remis' black magic, so I provided her with a solution: Fiah would be frozen in time and hidden from the realm. It would look as if it no longer existed – wiped from the map and from existence – but its people would remain safe."

"Are they? Safe?" I asked with so much hope in my voice.

"They are, Your Majesty. As are your true forms."

Our true forms, I repeated back to myself. *Our real bodies.* I remembered that part of the spell. In order to put my soul into the Firebird to be reborn, my body needed to be kept safe so that I could return to it later. From what I could see looking at Alaric, it seemed that we were reborn into similar bodies, but with enough differences that we would be unrecognizable to anyone other than each other. His hair was lighter and his eyes a different shade of blue. The slope of his nose varied slightly from the one I was so familiar with. And his lips were less full than the ones I was used to.

"Every spell requires a key of sorts. Something that will bring things back to the way they were. I made you the key and put your soul in the Firebird for safekeeping. The phoenix symbolizes rebirth and transformation and you, my queen, will usher in Fiah's renaissance."

"But the Fates require balance," I stated sadly, remembering my mother's words.

Erina nodded solemnly. "They do. And so for you to live, your mother sacrificed herself."

"The balance between receiving and giving," Alaric said, reminding me of the first trial.

Tears shed from my eyes and I quickly tried to wipe them away. She had made her choice. She did what was best for her kingdom. But knowing that didn't make me miss her any less.

"For what it is worth," Erina began, "I am sorry for your loss. Yrsula was a good friend to me. If there had been another way, I would have led her down that path. But there is no denying the Fates and the sacrifices they require to maintain balance."

There was a moment of silence before Alaric spoke again. "And me? Why have I lived multiple lifetimes? What's my part in all of this?"

My mother had told me that Alaric would be kept safe. I didn't know that he would be reborn, as well.

Erina's eyes that usually looked at Alaric with disdain, softened a bit. "You are Astoria's mate. The Fates have bound your souls together in every lifetime. Honestly, we didn't expect for you to be part of all of this, Prince Alaric. Your presence is as much of a surprise to us as it is to you. It seems that the Fates always keep us on our toes." She chuckled.

Alaric smiled at me and I couldn't help but smile back. My mate. How long had it been since our mating bond snapped into place? Since we knew that we never wanted to spend a moment without the other, inevitably leading to our marriage and him soon becoming the crowned King Consort?

"So now what?" I asked, feeling grateful that our bond kept us together, but also still feeling lost. I looked down at my hand and drew on my magic, bringing a ball of fire to the palm of my hand. For almost two hundred years I had been without my real magic.

Erina gave me a devious grin. "Now, Queen Astoria, we go home."

12

CHAPTER TWELVE

How do you find a lost fae kingdom?
    With magic and a pegasus, of course.

After talking with Erina some more and chastising the Fates for the irony of choosing Tory's magic as memory magic when she (I?) couldn't actually remember who she (I?) really was, the apprentices joined us. I was told that they had given Faygar and Rouge a memory-wiping potion and sent them home. They would remember competing, but not the details of the trials; just that they lost.

Marcus gave me the vessel that we had dug up in the first trial – the vessel that had once contained my soul before putting it into the Firebird – and told me that we needed to take it with us to uncloak Fiah. They also told us that there was no sign of Beau and that Scarlet's body was still missing.

I felt so sorry for Beau. He was probably devastated and took Scarlet's body back to her father to lay her to rest. I still didn't feel right about Scarlet's involvement in all of this.

"Why did it have to be Scarlet?" I asked Erina again as she brought me to Priscilla, my beautiful royal pegasus. Scarlet had adored Priscilla when she first saw her. Who wouldn't? I recalled Prissy trying to shield me from the shadowborgs during the second trial and it brought a smile to my face to know that even if I didn't recognize my gorgeous baby, she had somehow still recognized something in me. I stroked her mane as she nuzzled my hand. "Hi, Prissy," I whispered before Erina answered me.

"Your Majesty, I sincerely apologize, but unfortunately, I can not tell you that. The Fates still have their plans and we can not intervene. There are things that you still must discover on your own. As a sorceress, I can only intervene in an effort to maintain the balance. The Fates do not share their plans with me, but my magic requires that for every spell cast, there is a counterbalance that keeps their plans steady."

I grimaced at her. What wasn't she telling me? Scarlet was dead, wasn't she? I saw Alaric put his dagger through her chest. "Alaric *did* kill her, though? Right?"

Erina nodded her head. "He did, Your Majesty."

"You don't have to keep calling me 'Your Majesty,' Erina. I haven't been crowned yet." I climbed onto Priscilla's back and she whinnied, happily flapping her wings.

"Your coronation is a mere formality. Once we get back to Fiah, we will arrange it immediately."

"Ready to go?" Alaric asked, stepping next to Erina, the apprentices right behind him.

I nodded, but before Alaric could mount Priscilla, Erina stopped him. Under her breath, she spoke some words and waved a hand over Alaric and then me. When I looked down at Alaric, he looked like himself again.

"Just a little magic to ensure you're recognizable until we can get you back into your bodies," Erina stated. "A glamour."

I smiled from atop Priscilla's back. Alaric joined me, wrapping his arm protectively around my waist. On top of Priscilla with my mate so close, I couldn't help but feel a rightness inside of me. It has been so long since I felt like myself. I still didn't really understand how my past lives affected my present. Was I Tory? Or was Tory a part of me? I had caught a glimpse of my reflection in a river earlier and while I looked different, if I looked close enough, I actually saw features from all of my past selves. And I still had knowledge and memories from my past lives. I had families and friends and even relationships. What did all of that mean now?

While I knew there were still things that I needed to discover and learn about this different version of myself, I was content to live in the moment with the love of my life and to plan a future with him. A future that involved us retrieving our bodies, taking back our kingdom and defeating the evil king once and for all.

Priscilla took off into the sky, followed by Erina and the apprentices on their griffins. While I loved the majesty of a pegasus, the griffins always fascinated me with their heads and wings of eagles and the bodies of lions. They were such frighteningly beautiful creatures. Perfect for beings like Erina and the apprentices who were frightening in their own way.

Alaric, still wrapped around me, used his thumb to stroke my side. He nestled his face in the crook of my neck and gently placed a kiss there. The intimacy sent a chill down my spine while a warmth pooled at my core.

"I love you," Alaric whispered in my ear as my body relaxed into his. "I know there is much we need to discuss, but I just want you to know that regardless of who I have been, where I have gone, or what I have done, I have loved you and will continue to love you, Astoria. Even after my last day in this world, I will wait for you in the After Realm."

I took a deep breath and sunk even deeper into Alaric's warmth. There *was* a lot we needed to talk about. But I believed how much my mate loved me because I could feel how much I loved him. It was never something that I could put entirely into words.

I remembered when I first saw Alaric. Fiah was celebrating Solstice Eve and while the castle would be hosting a ball on the evening of Solstice for the royals and courtiers, I knew that there would be celebrations being held all over the kingdom on the eve before the longest night of the year. I had ventured into town to enjoy the revelry. I strolled through the market to pick up a few trinkets, making sure to give extra coins to the shop owners in hopes that it would help spread some additional joy. There was music playing and bawdy voices coming from a tavern, so I headed inside and took a seat, watching as fae dressed in their holiday best came in for a mug of mead and to dance and toast and be merry. I watched them wistfully – the sight was so beautiful that it tugged at my heart. Fiah was such a peaceful kingdom and I always loved seeing my mother's subjects find happiness in being able to live so harmoniously.

I felt my attention pull to something across the tavern. A small tug that drew my attention away from the revelers and towards the bar where a handsome fae male wearing a black cloak sat, flashing a dazzling smile at me. His skin was a warm bronze and he had hair that was as white as snow and as sparkling as his grin.

He gestured for me to join him and as much as I wanted to play coy and uninterested, the pull was demanding that I follow it towards this male.

"Have we met before?" I asked as he pulled a seat out for me.

I hadn't yet sat before he laughed, "Definitely not!"

I crinkled my nose at him. "What's so funny about that?" I asked, taking an alarmed step back. An almost painful step, for the pull was trying to draw me closer to the fae that was seemingly mocking me.

"Do you feel it?" he asked, looking deep into my eyes, searching for something unknown to me.

He reached out and tentatively took my shaking hand and I immediately felt a spark followed by a warm sensation up my arm and into my chest.

"Feel what?" I rasped, my throat suddenly feeling incredibly dry. I didn't want to give him the satisfaction of knowing that I felt something, too, but my traitorous body was quickly giving me away.

"It's the pull of the mating bond," he laughed again as his hand presumptuously traveled up my arm and back down again, prickling my skin with goosebumps. "You can't tell me that you don't feel it." He placed his other hand over my heart and it practically leapt out of my chest. There was no way he couldn't feel *that*.

Without realizing what I was doing, I placed my free hand over his heart and my eyes widened when I realized that both were beating in time with one another. I wanted to pull away, but I couldn't move. My feet felt like they were rooted to the ground.

But he was right. My mother had told me bedtime stories while growing up of the fortunate fae who felt an undeniable pull of their soul towards their soul's mate. A bond gifted by the Fates themselves. So rare that most fae only knew about it through fairytales.

But in that moment, I knew the truth. This was my mate. And I didn't even know what to call him.

"What's your name?" I asked almost inaudibly.

He smiled softly. "I'm Alaric."

I looked him over, studying his face before traveling down his body. His attire was nearly covered by his cloak. Nearly. It was then that I saw the insignia of the kingdom of Gelu embroidered in silver on his tunic.

I pulled back, as much as the bond would allow me to. "You're Prince Alaric!" I exclaimed. With the mating bond already being so rare, what were the chances of royals becoming mates?

"That I am!" he confirmed, his dazzling smile returning to its home on his face. "It'd say that it's a pleasure to make your acquaintance, Princess Astoria, but since the Fates have declared us mates, I think we're beyond the pleasantries of mere acquaintances."

He must have seen the look of confusion on my face because he nodded towards the door of the tavern and said, "Your royal escorts. I saw them enter shortly after feeling the pull towards you."

Handsome and smart. I had never been more pleased with the Fates.

"What are you doing in Fiah?" I inquired, butterflies fluttering in my stomach.

"Well, as I'm sure you know, your mother sends invitations to your Solstice festivities each year to all of the kingdoms."

I nodded. While my mother knew that each kingdom had their own customs for celebrating the longest night of the year, she always invited the royal families of each kingdom, saying that it was better to send an invite and have it declined than not send an invite and have someone feel badly. Bad relations led to difficult politics and my mother wanted peace to continue for Fiah more than anything.

She even invited the King and Queen of Tellus, a kingdom that was becoming increasingly difficult to deal with, despite the fact that the queen was my aunt.

I was suddenly pulled out of my reverie and back to the present. Alaric's grip on my waist tightened.

"What's wrong?" he asked, startled.

"Who was Scarlet's mother?" I turned my head to look at Alaric who I watched have the same realization that I just had. With so much going on, we had not even thought about the connection.

Scarlet was my cousin.

13

CHAPTER THIRTEEN

E rina!" I yelled as I jumped off of Priscilla and stalked towards the sorceress who was still sitting on her griffin. We made an unplanned stop on a deserted piece of land due to my epiphany and subsequent rage.

"Yes, Your Majesty?"

"Scarlet was my *cousin*?!"

I had to give it to Erina... she barely flinched. But it was enough for me to realize that she had at least *some* semblance of a conscience. Fates, help me.

"Yes, Your Majesty. She was."

Through gritted teeth, I asked her to explain. My fists were balled up so hard, I could feel my nails digging into my skin. I looked down at them and saw small, white crescents imprinted into my palms. Alaric tried to grab one of my hands, but I shook him off. I was too angry, but I wanted to feel it. I needed to feel it. And I wanted to bathe in this rage.

Scarlet – who was killed because of some bull shit sorcery rule – was my cousin.

Erina took a deep breath. "Scarlet was born many decades after your soul was put into the Firebird." As if that reply was answer enough.

I swear, my teeth were about to crack. "That doesn't explain much," I ground out.

"While your mother's sacrifice created the balance of keeping your soul safe for lifetimes, there needed to be a balance in *restoring* you. The Fates require balance in all magic, Your Majesty. Scarlet was the balance."

"Fuck you, Erina," I spat with vehemence.

This time she definitely flinched. It was the first time I had ever seen Erina react and if I wasn't so angry, the appalled look on her face would have made me laugh.

"Astoria…" Alaric's voice warned.

"Oh, fuck you, too, Alaric! You can't stand Erina. You never could." I sunk down to the ground and rubbed my face with my numb hands, instantly regretting the venomous words that had just left my mouth. "I'm sorry, my love, that was out of line."

Alaric joined me on the ground and put his arms around me, pulling me into his chest.

"Astoria, I'm so sorry that I killed your cousin," he said with so much earnestness that I didn't know what was more painful to hear – the words or the way they were said.

And then I cried. I cried for Scarlet and I cried for my mother and I cried for myself and the lives of those that I had lost. Sobs racked my body, but Alaric continued to hold onto me. I placed my hands on his chest to try to ground myself. Listening to the beat of his heart and hearing the in sync beat of mine pulse in my ears began to soothe me. I took a calming breath and tried to remember details of my past lives to concentrate on something other than my rage.

In one of my lives, I had a sister who was only a year and a half younger than me. We were inseparable. Our favorite thing to do together was to catch fish in the pond with our bare hands. They would splash us as we brought them out of the water and then we'd kiss their puckered lips and release them back into the pond.

In another life, I had a dog – a corgi. His name was Jasper and he was my best friend... my soul dog. Wherever I went, Jasper followed with his short, little legs. Sometimes we'd play a game where I would pretend that I couldn't see him and would call his name. He'd look at me, confused, until he would finally lick my face and I'd laugh, hugging him to assure him that I could see him.

There was also Derrick. Derrick was my boyfriend in a different, human life. Or a life where I believed that I was human. I was so drawn to his ruggedness, but he was also incredibly thoughtful and kind. I remember feeling deep down in my soul that Derrick and I would get married one day and have a hoard of adorable children.

"Wait." I pulled away from Alaric. "We were together in another life?" I searched his face. "Were you Derrick?"

He smiled softly and kissed my forehead. "Apparently the Fates don't mess around when it comes to the mating bond. Even in our other lives, we were drawn to one another."

I scrunched my face. "Were you Jasper, too?"

Alaric barked a laugh that was so hearty, it made my heart feel instantly lighter. "No, Astoria, I wasn't your *dog!*"

Still confused, I asked, "How did you know he was a dog?"

Alaric stopped laughing and tucked a loose strand of my hair behind my ear, love twinkling in his eyes. "Because I was your friend, Maverick, in that life. Your friend, Maverick, who had a very serious infatuation with you and used to bring Jasper little bits of bread and other treats or trinkets in an effort to win your heart."

I smiled up at him. "I – Jessina – was infatuated with Maverick, too," I told my husband. "But she... I... was always waiting for him to ask me out and he never did."

Alaric reached for my hands and intertwined our fingers together. He lifted one set of hands and placed a kiss on my knuckles before doing the same with the other set.

"The bond was always pulling us together, despite Erina's messed up magic," Alaric said, gesturing his head over to the sorceress.

"My magic was not messed up!" Erina shouted in an almost sing-song voice. "It was following the rules of balance set by the Fates!"

Alaric groaned as he leaned into me. "She's never going to shut up about the balance, is she?" he whispered in my ear.

I giggled and Alaric pulled back, smiling down at me.

"We're not too far from Gelu," he informed me. "Want to fly there and rest for the night? It would probably be a good idea to let my family know that we're alive."

I nodded. It had already been an overwhelmingly exhausting and emotional day. I wasn't ready to accept everything the Fates had done, but I was ready to reconnect with the mate that the Fates had chosen for me. We would stop in Gelu, see his family and then spend some time alone together.

Alaric let Erina and the apprentices know of our new plan and we got on our creatures and made our way to Gelu. While I was in dire need of a bath and a good night's rest, I knew that our arrival would be complicated. With Fiah veiled from all of the other kingdoms and Alaric's mysterious disappearance, we didn't know how Alaric's parents would react to the return of their son after almost two centuries.

Alaric suggested that we land just ahead of the castle's gates and that Erina and the apprentices stay behind so as to not create chaos unnecessarily. Snow was falling from the sky as Alaric and I walked up towards the guards, hand in hand. Although he had a smile on his face, I could feel the tension radiating off of him. Besides the fact that this was a sensitive situation, Alaric's relationship with his brother, Elix, had always been challenging. As the first born and heir-apparent, Elix always believed that his brother would try to kill him for the crown. Despite the fact that Alaric didn't have any ambition to be the ruler of Gelu and even after we were married, Elix still felt that he couldn't trust him. Since I didn't have any siblings, I couldn't empathize with Elix, but I did understand that in some kingdoms, fratricide would sometimes occur to obtain power, unfortunately.

"Hello!" Alaric called out to the guards. I had been to Gelu only a handful of times and none of the faces now staring at us looked familiar to me.

"Do you recognize any of them?" Really what I wanted to know is if any of them would recognize *him*.

"Who goes there?" one of the guards asked. But before Alaric could answer, another guard came around from the other side of the wall, his face alight.

"Well, well, well. The Lost Prince returns home!" he exclaimed, walking towards us.

Alaric's pace picked up as he approached the guard. "Renfred! You're a sight for sore eyes!" Alaric let go of my hand and embraced his friend.

"It's so good to see you, Alaric! Where have you been all these years?"

Alaric let go of Renfred and took a step back to look at him. "It is a long story, my friend. And one I look forward to telling you all about! But first, my wife and I must talk to my parents and brother." Renfred's gaze fell on me. "May I present the Princess of Fiah, Astoria?"

I smiled, grateful that Alaric wasn't preemptively calling me Queen.

Renfred dropped down to his knee and bowed his head, the remaining guards looking on. "It is a great honor, Princess Astoria. We all heard of your disappearance. I'm glad to see you looking well. Both of you." He spoke so solemnly and if I had known him better, I'd believe he was getting choked up. He had probably grieved his friend for many years.

"The honor is mine, Renfred," I told him truthfully. "My husband has spoken of you often and in high regard. Please rise. A friend of Alaric's is a friend of mine."

Renfred stood up and immediately put his arm around Alaric, turning towards the castle. The guards continued to watch them, looking dumbfounded. I'm sure it was like seeing a ghost. In fact, it felt like we *were* ghosts. So many years had passed, but the castle looked the same. Maybe a little older and worn, but it was outrageously beautiful. Gelu's castle was known as the Glass Castle, its shining surface resembling ice. And covered in snow, it looked utterly magical. The castle had been built with the kingdom's icy climate in mind. While Gelu experienced short springs and summers, most of the year, it was winter.

Renfred escorted us towards the castle and we told him where the rest of our group was waiting nearby. He assured us that he would personally greet them and that they would be put up in rooms while we met with the king and queen.

When we entered the Glass Castle, the energy immediately changed. The hustle and bustle shifted to hushed tones as the staff realized that their prince had unexpectedly returned home. Most fae smiled and waved enthusiastically, while some looked taken aback and unsure. But despite the few questionable glances, Alaric waved to maids and servants, smiling and shaking hands. He was beloved and I was in awe. Not of my husband, but of the fact that after so much time had passed, he was still cherished. It really was possible to leave an impression on the world and make a true difference.

My joy was short-lived when the realization that Scarlet had been trying to make a difference punched me in the gut. How would her kingdom react when they found out that their princess was taken from them? Murdered in cold blood. She had said that she had been sheltered for most of her life, but there had to be some loved ones left behind that would be impacted by her death.

I redirected my attention back to Alaric as we were brought into the throne room to await the king and queen's arrival. He smiled at me and reached for my hand, squeezing reassuringly. I smiled back at him, my heart picking up speed as my soul recognized its other half. Alaric was the ice to my fire. He completed me.

Growing up, I always believed that the opposite of fire was no fire. My magic was either present or it wasn't. But there was no complement there. Nothing to truly balance it. The opposite of light was no light, but it had a name. In the absence of light, there was darkness. But together, they are an interconnected force... The stars shining brightly in the night sky.

Once I met Alaric, I knew I had met the male that would complement me... balance me. And when the fire inside me is too hot to handle, Alaric cools me down. Warmth was always my comfort, but once that mating bond pulled me towards Alaric, it was ice that I yearned for in my veins.

When Alaric arrived at my mother's Solstice party the night after our bond snapped into place, I felt the deepest peace. I remember I was talking with a courtier that I was friendly with, Arraballe. She was telling me a story about her husband and an incident he had with their cow when my body instantaneously relaxed. My breathing hadn't felt uneasy before, but it somehow felt easier suddenly. And my magic created a tingly sensation throughout my whole body. I looked around the room that was filled with hundreds of my mother's subjects and was immediately drawn to Alaric, his eyes already on me. My magic danced excitedly as the bond tried to pull me towards him. I excused myself and drifted over to Alaric, not once losing eye contact with him. When I approached, he immediately placed his hands on my shoulders and trailed them seductively down my arms, the spots where his fingers lingered creating a pleasant static sensation along my skin.

"Happy Solstice, Princess Astoria."

"Happy Solstice to you, Prince Alaric."

We smiled at each other and remained like that for several moments, just silently staring at one another. My body felt like it was on fire, but Alaric's touch burned like ice. And I wanted to burn with him for all of eternity.

We spent the rest of the evening dancing together, sharing stories of Solstices past and laughing. There was so much laughing. When I was with Alaric, it was as if the rest of the world fell away and there was no one but him.

And now, as we waited for his parents, in my eyes, there was still no one but him.

The doors to the throne room were flung open and Alaric's mother entered hurriedly, followed closely behind by his father. His mother stopped short and gasped when she saw Alaric. She covered her mouth and began to cry before running towards her son.

"I didn't believe it!" she exclaimed as they embraced. "My baby has come home!" She sobbed in Alaric's arms, tears streaming down her face and falling onto Alaric's tunic as he kissed the top of her head. She was a petite woman, barely over five feet tall, so Alaric at almost 6'3" towered over her.

The king approached Alaric and clapped his shoulder as his wife continued to cry. "It's good to see you, son. It seems you have much to tell us."

The queen loosened her grip on Alaric to free him enough to pull his father into their embrace. The three stood frozen momentarily as I watched on, a single tear falling from my eye that I quickly brushed away. I was so happy for my husband and the beauty of this moment, but I would have none of this upon my return home. No mother to cry happy tears with. I was alone.

No! I shook my head, clearing the thought. I was not alone. I had my mate. And I had my kingdom. The kingdom that my mother died to protect. And as long as I kept it safe, my mother would always be with me in my heart.

The queen composed herself and then looked towards me. "Astoria, dear, we're so glad to see you, as well." She walked over to me and gave me a motherly hug. It was so tight, I felt like I could barely breathe, but at the same time, it felt so good. "I was sorry to hear about your mother," she whispered in my ear.

"It's good to see you, too, Your Majesty," I squeaked out. I wasn't entirely sure how she had known about my mother's sacrifice – only myself, Alaric, Erina and her apprentices were informed of her plan before she executed it – , but I didn't have the mental capacity to ponder it at the moment. Or the strength, since Glacia was currently squeezing it out of me.

"Oh, none of that 'Your Majesty' nonsense, dear. You're our daughter! You'll call us Glacia and Renese."

Glacia released me and I tried to discreetly catch my breath before we smiled at one another. "Yes, Glacia."

"Come! Sit!" Renese instructed as he motioned us towards a table. We all sat down and settled in. "Tell us everything! Where have you been all these years?"

Before we could answer, the throne room door was thrown open again and Elix entered, stomping towards us. "Yes, brother, where *have* you been?"

Alaric stood to greet his brother, but Elix halted him with raised hands. Apparently he was not in the mood for pleasantries.

"Elixender, please," Glacia pleaded. "Your brother has been gone for so long. Please let's have a happy reunion with none of this one-sided rivalry."

I looked down towards my lap and smirked, grateful that Glacia saw this opposition for what it was.

Elix sat down and nodded towards his brother, urging him to tell our story.

"Well, there is much we can tell you, but still much we don't know," Alaric began. "To our understanding, the King of Tellus had plans to invade and destroy Fiah. Astoria's mom was given notice of this and took action to protect her kingdom. She went to the sorceress of Fiah and had a spell done to veil the kingdom from Tellus, but also Gelu and Spirare. There needed to be a key created to undo the spell, and that's where Astoria comes in."

Alaric gestured to me to continue. "My mother sacrificed herself to protect Fiah and turn me into the key that will somehow save the kingdom. When Fiah was cloaked, my soul was put into a phoenix, which allowed me to be reincarnated after each of my deaths."

Glacia gasped and looked towards Alaric. "What happened to you?" she asked, barely keeping her composure.

"Apparently because of our mating bond, the Fates tied us together. So while I wasn't the Firebird, my life was connected to Astoria's and I was reborn, as well."

Renese cleared his throat before speaking. "I assume in each of your lives you weren't… yourselves? What I mean is, you didn't know who you were?"

We shook our heads. "No, we didn't," I said. "Otherwise, we would have come back to tell you what was happening. From what I remember, we were living in Tellus in each of our lives. I guess hidden in plain sight? We looked different… What you're seeing now is an illusion, courtesy of Erina."

"They wouldn't have recognized Alaric, anyway. The few times Gelu had anything to do with Tellus, we kept the boys away," Glacia informed us. Her disdain for Tellus and its king was evident by her scowl.

"So how are you back here now?" Renese asked, as Elix continued to remain silent. His narrowed eyes at Alaric and at me said everything Elix didn't say with his mouth.

"We entered the Endless Forest Trials. Are you familiar with this competition?" Alaric asked. Both of his parents nodded their heads. "In the last trial, I solved the riddle and killed one of the other contestants. Almost immediately, Astoria and I remembered who we really were."

"And who was the contestant you killed? What was the connection there?" Renese inquired.

It was my turn again. "The Princess of Tellus."

Glacia nodded solemnly. I was surprised that her reaction wasn't something stronger. Maybe word had already gotten to the other kingdoms that Scarlet had been killed.

"We later found out that she was my cousin. Somehow, her blood was tied to the spell."

Glacia nodded, her lips pursed, as if understanding something that I didn't.

"That's all we really know. We're headed to Fiah with the sorceress to uncloak everyone in the kingdom. From there, we have to figure out how to stop the king."

"Fools," Elix muttered, his silence finally broken with this one-worded insult.

All heads turned to the heir-apparent.

"Elixender..." Renese warned. He was practically growling at his son, making his annoyance abundantly clear.

"What do you think has been happening in the realm since you were so thoughtfully hidden away and protected from harm? Did you think Remis would just stop when Fiah was out of his sights? No!" Elix barked, slamming his fists down on the table. Everyone jumped, but no one said a word. He laughed sardonically. "No! He came after Spirare. He came after *us, damn it*! We have been fighting a war with Tellus for decades upon decades! But it's okay because Princess *Astoria* and Prince *Alaric* were safe and sound!"

"Which we are grateful for," Glacia said, her voice barely above a whisper. "I think your brother is just feeling hurt –"

"I am not *hurt,* Mother! I am angry!" Elix interrupted, his voice echoing throughout the room. "I am angry that so many have suffered and it's all supposed to be okay because the key to everyone's happiness is here, right in front of us! Hooray! Thank you, Astoria, for coming to save us all!" he exclaimed sarcastically. "Please, do tell us, what is your big plan, Your Royal Highness, Heir to the Fiah Crown?"

"Elix," Alaric said sharply, "we did not know that the king was growing madder. We didn't know about the attack on Fiah until just before Astoria's mom told her. She sacrificed herself immediately after and all of the pieces locked into place. It was too late. There was nothing we could do. But we're here now and after less than a day of being able to process all of this, my wife and I are going to eat a hot meal and go to bed so that we can properly answer your question tomorrow. Until then, I beg your pardon, but we're retiring for the evening." Alaric stood up and pulled out my chair, but before I could stand, Glacia put her hand over my forearm to stop me.

"Your mother sent a message," she stated simply, her eyes boring into mine. "Before she died, she sent a message to warn us of Remis' plan. Elix is speaking in anger, but the truth is, your mother did what she had to – what she thought was right – to protect her kingdom and even took what little time she had left to try to help us. We just don't have a sorceress as powerful as Erina. But there's more. I know who informed her of the mad king's plan."

My eyes went wide.

"Yrsula and I were friends before either of us became queen. Which means that I was also familiar with your aunt. Yve married Remis before any of us knew about his addiction to black magic. She didn't agree with it. *She* was the one that informed your mother of the attack."

For a moment, I wasn't sure if I was breathing. My aunt was a traitor to her kingdom? What would Remis do to her if he found out? Then I remembered that one hundred and seventy-four years had passed. He might have already found out...

"My aunt...? Is she..."

Glacia closed her eyes regretfully and I already knew the answer. "She's gone. But she was not killed at Remis' hand. After the spell took effect and you all disappeared, Remis and his spies scoured the area for a sign as to what happened, but to no avail. After a period of time, he set his sights on Spirare and later, Gelu. For all that Remis knew,

Yve was devoted to him. So much so that a few decades ago, she got pregnant with their first child."

"Scarlet," I whispered.

Glacia nodded. "Yes, Princess Scarlet, your cousin. When she was born, Yve immediately knew something wasn't right with her. The child's eyes were bloodshot all of the time and the healers couldn't fix them. She would bleed and her blood would be so dark, it was practically black."

"Yes!" Alaric shouted, startling me. "That was how I knew to kill her during the trials. The riddle said something about piercing the heart of the one with the darkest blood to save the kingdom and when I saw it, something inside of me snapped."

Glacia continued with her story. "Yve wrote to me to ask if I had any knowledge of childhood ailments like the ones Scarlet presented with. Unfortunately, I could offer no assistance. It was shortly after I returned her correspondence that I learned she had killed herself."

I gasped in disbelief. Why would my aunt leave her child alone to be raised by a mad man? "Are you sure Remis didn't have a hand in her death?" I asked.

Glacia shook her head. "My dear, there were witnesses that saw her jump off a cliff."

"Are these witnesses reliable?" Alaric asked, thinly veiled skepticism lacing his voice.

"Yes, son. They were actually the ones who brought Scarlet back to the castle."

"What?" I cried. "She jumped with Scarlet nearby?" I was instantly brought back to my time as Tory and remembered Scarlet's reoccurring dream – the one where a female jumped off a cliff. Scarlet wasn't just dreaming... She was remembering.

"Yes, some of the castle's servants had seen Yve leave with the baby in a basket. They were very fond of your aunt and were concerned that she looked like she had been crying. They watched her from a window and as she approached the cliff, they ran out to stop her, but were too late. They immediately brought the baby to the king and informed him of his wife's death."

Glacia took a deep breath and Renese put his hand on his wife's leg. I was familiar with this gesture, as Alaric often did this to me when I got overwhelmed.

"I don't know what possessed her to do what she did. And I don't know how this is all linked to the trials that you were a part of. But I've carried the weight for so long of not being able to help either of my friends and I'm hoping that what little I can offer to you now might avenge them."

I dropped my head and covered my face with my hands. This was all too much. When I woke up this morning, I was Tory, a female who was about to compete in the final game of the Endless Forest Trials and just wanted to win while also keeping her friends safe. And somehow, I had quickly become Astoria again. An uncrowned Queen with a hidden kingdom that she had to save from a mad, power-hungry king. A female who had lost her mother, aunt and cousin she barely knew for reasons that she still didn't understand, but desperately needed to figure out. And a wife who needed to reconnect with her husband who had been just out of reach for lifetimes.

Alaric looked at me, "I think *now* we will retire to our room."

14

CHAPTER
FOURTEEN

There was a knock at the door and a maid from the kitchen entered with trays of steaming hot beef stew, crusty bread and red wine. She set the trays down on the table and I immediately reached for the bread, scooping a hearty amount of stew onto it and shoveling it into my mouth. I was so hungry. It felt like it had been a lifetime since our last meal at the Phoenix Mansion.

Alaric chuckled softly as he poured us both glasses of wine. He sat down facing me and tucked a loose strand of my hair behind my ear. When was the last time I had bathed?

"What are you thinking about, Astoria?" Alaric asked, his voice low and concerned.

I took a sip of my wine and rolled my eyes with pleasure as its rich taste coasted my tongue and hit the back of my throat. "That I can't remember the last time I had a hot bath, but however long it's been, this wine makes the wait worth it."

Alaric smiled and leaned in to kiss my forehead. He laughed. "Good. Because I was worried that the fate of the realm was weighing on you," he said sarcastically.

I groaned, placing my face into my hands. "What are we going to do?"

Alaric got off of his chair and kneeled between my legs. I opened them further to accommodate his body. He placed his hands around my waist and looked deeply into my eyes.

"Tonight, we are going to simply be Astoria and Alaric. Tomorrow we can be the Queen and King of Fiah," he said.

"Technically, we're not..."

"Buh, buh, buh!" he interrupted me as he placed a finger over my lips. "Tomorrow's problems."

I gently bit down on his finger and watched Alaric's eyes darken with desire, his pupils blowing out so wide that only a thin ring of blue surrounded them. My stomach immediately sank. I was so used to being playful with my husband that I forgot for a moment that it had been one hundred and seventy-four years. One hundred and seventy-four years of living lives apart and with others. Had Alaric been with other females? The idea made me hot with rage. But I had been with other males. I remember that it never felt as intense as when I was with my mate, but it had happened just the same. And neither one of us was to blame, but the thoughts still hurt. What if Alaric's past relationships had been meaningful? What if he had had something deeply intimate with other females? Something deeper than what we had had before?

I was so confused and Alaric clearly saw it on my face because his eyes were now filled with concern.

"What's wrong?" he asked.

I closed my eyes for a small moment and when I opened them, they were filled with tears. "I'm… I'm not sure if I'm ready," I said quietly. I waited for him to say something. Anything. But he just looked at me. Was he mad? Why did I have to be questioning all of these things? One upon a time, I had a beautiful relationship with my mate. We knew each other inside and out. We almost always knew what the other was thinking. Alaric and I used to be constantly in sync. It wasn't always perfect, but it was perfectly us. Sometimes we fought, but we would quickly make up. And the make up was always insanely wonderful.

Alaric wiped a lone tear that was streaming down my face. "That's okay," he gently replied. "We have time to rebuild what we've lost."

"Alaric, it's not that! I don't think that we lost anything!"

"But we did," he stated simply. "We lost time. And during those lost years, we changed. We're not even physically right yet in these bodies. I understand what you're feeling because I'm feeling it, too."

Alaric stood up and placed one arm behind my back and one under my knees, lifting me off of the chair. He kissed my forehead and then gently placed me on the bed. I drew down the covers as he went around to the other side of the bed and climbed in. I nestled up against him. We didn't need any more words. Alaric was my mate and just like my soul found its counterpart once before, it would do it again. I was sure of it and I knew in my heart that Alaric was, too.

* * * * *

My bath the previous night had not gone forgotten, but once Alaric placed me on the bed and I curled up next to him, my breathing evened out and I no longer cared about the dirt and sweat caked all over my body and clothes. I quickly drifted off to sleep, but as the sun teased my eyelids, I was very aware of my stench and the fact that Alaric was no longer in the bed by my side. I rolled over and opened my eyes, quickly scanning the room for him. When I sat up, I heard water being poured in the bathing chamber and got up to investigate. A maid was filling the tub with water as Alaric placed wildflowers in a vase next to a pot of steaming coffee.

"Good morning, my love!" he exclaimed when he saw me enter the room.

I rubbed my eyes and then pulled my hands away, smiling at my husband. "It certainly looks like a good morning."

The maid placed a few drops of lavender essential oil into the tub before stepping out and leaving us. Alaric walked up to me and placed his hand at the hem of my tunic. "May I?" he asked, his eyes almost pleading.

I smiled and lifted my arms over my head. Alaric peeled my tunic off and then tossed it aside. He then placed his hands on the waistband of my pants, hooking a finger in my undergarments, and shimmied them down as he kneeled on the floor. I wove my fingers through his hair and gently massaged his scalp. He looked up at me and then reverently placed a kiss on my stomach before standing and taking my hand to lead me towards the tub.

I brought my magic to the tip of my finger and dipped it into the water to heat it up before Alaric helped me in.

I couldn't help the moan that slipped from me as I submerged myself into the hot, scented water. *This* was magic!

Alaric grinned and reached for a cup, pouring the coffee into it. He added some sugar and a splash of creamy milk. When he handed it to me, I took a moment to savor the beautiful color and then sniffed the rich deliciousness.

More magic, I thought.

It was funny because while we lived in a world of magic that was gifted by the Fates, some of the simplest things in life could be seen as magical if you appreciated them enough.

"Good?" Alaric asked as I took the first sip.

"Soooooooo good!" I exclaimed, settling deeper into the tub and resting my head on the edge. I closed my eyes and took a few deep breaths. "Are you going to join me in here?" I asked.

"No, I showered when I got up," Alaric told me.

"Mm," I replied. I desperately wanted to feel his skin against mine, but I also knew what it would lead to, so I decided not to press him any further. "Thank you for this. It's exactly what I needed."

Alaric sat on the edge of the tub and poured a dollop of hair soap into this palm. Wetting his hands, he began to lather my hair with suds. "Did you sleep well?" he asked.

"Fates, that feels good," I groaned as he massaged my head. "I slept very well. What about you?"

"Lying next to you, I slept better than I have in a long time," he answered and I felt the truth of that in my bones.

I nodded. The mating bond had been humming inside me ever since we became Alaric and Astoria again. The hum was happiness. It was peace. Feelings so conflicting with the war we were about to face.

"Your brother is going to demand answers today," I sighed.

Alaric chuckled. "Let Elix make all of the demands he wants. He is not the king."

I sighed again. "Fine, the *king* is going to want answers today. I know he's your father and he's grateful to have you back, but he is still the king and he's been fighting a losing battle while we were gone. Now we're back and we have to figure out how to stop this."

Alaric gently poured a pitcher of clean water over my head to rinse my hair. He then began massaging out the knots in my neck and shoulders.

I moaned deeply. "Stop distracting me!" I giggled, swatting his hands away. He put them up by his head, raised in defeat.

"Okay, okay! I'll stop!" he laughed.

"Don't you dare!" I exclaimed, turning to try to grab his hands. Instead, he caught both of my wrists in one hand and held them over my head. Alaric's pupils dilated, consuming his whole eyes. His gaze wandered to my wet breasts and my nipples pebbled as my breathing turned into pants. I could feel my cheeks flush under his heated stare.

Alaric cleared his throat and shook his head, releasing my hands and reaching for a towel.

"Here," he rasped as he held it out for me.

Trying to calm my breathing, I reached for the towel with shaking hands and wrapped it around my body. Alaric held onto my elbow and arm as he helped me out of the tub. I reached for him, squeezing his bicep and giving him a soft smile.

Thoughts swam through my head as I dressed. Alaric sat on the bed, staring out the window and I wondered if he was also deep in thought or if he was simply offering me the courtesy of dressing as privately as possible without him leaving my side. It was so quiet in the room, except for the sound of rustling fabric as I put on a tunic and leathers.

Alaric eventually broke the silence. "Scarlet was your cousin." He said it as if it was some kind of epiphany.

"Yes, dear," I replied, my tone teasing. "I'm aware of that."

"No, I mean, there's something there! Your mother's blood was the key to the spell, but Scarlet's blood was the key to ending it. You're the key to ending the king. There's something symbolic about the fact that Scarlet was the last of your shared bloodline and that she was the last of the king's."

I was following his train of thought. "Erina keeps going on and on about the Fates and their demand for balance. What are we missing?" I flopped onto the bed and stared at the ceiling. Alaric laid down as well, but faced me and propped his head up, resting it in this palm.

"I'm sorry," he said softly and earnestly.

Surprised, I lifted my head to look at him. "For what?" I asked.

With his free hand, Alaric brushed my cheek. "For killing Scarlet."

His apology caught me off guard. He didn't need to apologize. He had been just as much of a pawn in this game as Scarlet was.

"Alaric," I began, but he cut me off.

"No, Astoria, I already know what you're going to say and I need you to listen to me. Yes, we didn't choose what happened to us and yes, I did the thing that set us free, but I still took Scarlet's life. And I didn't hesitate. I don't know why I didn't hesitate. I killed your cousin, but before we knew who she was, she was your friend. She was our friend. And I killed her. And I'm sorry." Tears welled in Alaric's eyes. When was the last time I had seen him cry? "How am I any different from the apprentices killing Charlie?"

I sat up in the bed and grabbed his face. He closed his eyes – or maybe he flinched – but he got to say his piece and now I needed to say mine.

"Because you weren't yourself and you weren't acting of your own free will. But Alaric, if there is anything for me to forgive – if you need to hear the words – then I forgive you," I told him.

Alaric opened his eyes and met mine. He placed his hand over one of mine and squeezed it.

"I do not fault you for the actions you took. *Especially* actions you took when you weren't yourself."

His gaze suddenly hardened and his body tensed. He pulled away from me, rolling onto his back and closed his eyes again, rubbing them with the heels of his hands.

"Astoria, there's something I need to tell you," he said resolutely.

I held my breath, for what, I didn't know.

"In my other lives, I... I wasn't... What I'm trying to say is, I wasn't faithful to you, Astoria. To our marriage." Alaric turned back to me and stared into my eyes.

But what was there for me to say? I had been no different. And yet, I just told him that I couldn't fault him for the things he did when he wasn't himself. Could I forgive myself of those same things?

I took a deep breath. "Alaric," I began. I could see he was hanging on my every word and I so desperately wanted to put us both out of our misery. But I just didn't know how. Maybe the only way to move forward was to revisit the past? "In one of my lives, I was a striker in a forge. And there was a handsome blacksmith, Tibias. I would often find myself staring at him while we worked and thought it was nothing more than an infatuation. But the more we talked and got to know one another, the more my feelings for him grew."

Alaric was trying to restrain his face, but I could see his lip starting to curl as his fists tightened on the bedsheets. I knew this was hard for him to hear, but it was important.

"One day, he kissed me and I realized that my feelings were not one-sided. Tibias and I courted and eventually, we were intimate with one another."

Alaric was clenching his jaw so tightly that I was afraid his teeth were going to crack. I needed to get to my point faster.

"Afterwards, I quickly realized that I didn't love Tibias. And Tibias didn't love me. We had a spark, but it never turned into a flame. Tibias said that just like heat was used to shape metals, over time, we could shape our relationship into something different. But there was no denying that the harder we tried, the more obvious it became that love was out of reach for us." I took a steadying breath. "Alaric, I have to believe that the reason these relationships never felt right to me was because of you... My one and only true love. We were both unwillingly unfaithful. It was not something we would have chosen. Just like I know that you wouldn't have chosen to kill Scarlet if you had been yourself."

Alaric swallowed and nodded. "I don't want to live in the past," he stated, his voice raspy. "Astoria, I have only *truly* ever wanted you. I knew I loved you from the moment I saw you. It's as simple as that. The more I got to know you, the more I loved *about* you. My love for you is endless, Astoria. It can't be shaped into something else. It can only continue to grow."

And then Alaric kissed me. His lips met mine and we fit together like two pieces of a puzzle. Fates, I had missed kissing him. I had missed his soft, but firm, full lips. As I melted into the warmth of his mouth, I felt his tongue against the seam of my lips and opened for him. Our tongues danced together, igniting a spark in me that I hadn't felt for so long. I moaned as Alaric leaned into me, laying me back down onto the soft bed, his hard body at my front a stark contrast to the plushness at my back. His weight felt so satisfying on top of me and I ran my fingers through his hair, gently tugging, needing more of him. He broke the kiss and nestled his nose against my neck. Then he trailed a line of kisses from my shoulder to my neck to my jaw and back to my lips. I was about to wrap my legs around his waist when there was a knock at the door.

Reluctantly, Alaric rolled off of me as he answered, "Yes?"

The maid from earlier entered the room. She averted her eyes when she saw us still in bed. "I apologize for the intrusion, but His Majesty has requested your presence in the dining room," she squeaked. "Promptly."

"We'll be down shortly," he replied, trying to mask his annoyance. Once the maid left, Alaric gave me a quick kiss and then winked at me. "Later."

And the promise of later was what I would hold with me as we got through the now.

15

CHAPTER FIFTEEN

When we entered the formal dining room, Renese, Glacia and Elix were already seated, platters of eggs, bacon, herbed potatoes and fruity pastries adorning the table in front of them. Alaric and I greeted everyone and then sat beside each other.

"How did you two sleep?" Glacia asked. She was the epitome of a constantly worrying mother and my heart momentarily squeezed.

"Very well, thank you, mother," Alaric answered, smiling brightly at her as he poured me a glass of juice.

"We're glad to hear it," Renese said and I couldn't help but notice how Elix rolled his eyes at his father's declaration.

Fates help me, I wanted to stab him sometimes. If Elix didn't have to control himself, maybe I didn't need to either.

As if sensing my anger, Alaric squeezed my thigh under the table, sending a jolt of electricity through me. I instantly remembered his promise of what was to come and I settled back down. The least I could do was enjoy this decadent breakfast laid out for us. A servant approached me and spooned some eggs onto my plate as another filled my cup with more coffee.

"Well, we wanted to talk with you two some more of what has transpired in the past few years and get an idea of how you're planning to deal with Remis. Obviously, you have our army at your disposal, but you need to strategize." Renese stabbed a couple of potatoes onto his fork. I didn't know how bad things had been since we left, but if the forked potato was any indication... they hadn't been good.

Renese chewed his food before continuing. "Remis has been somewhat out of control for centuries. It started when he began dabbling in black magic. To our understanding, the dark arts have always been forbidden because the magic is *created* instead of using what already exists – a gift from the Fates. We were always of the belief that they would punish him for using this terrible form of magic, but as he got stronger and more powerful, we worried that the Fates were leaving this in our hands. You know how the Fates are... always seeking balance. We did research on black magic, but there is so little information on the subject. It was never meant to be used, let alone harnessed. But then we learned that since it is a form of magic not granted by the Fates, they could not control Remis. So we began growing our army. We knew the day would come when he would come for us and so we prepared as best as we could. We believe that it was around this time that Remis decided to conquer Fiah and Yve contacted Yrsula. And, of course, you know the results of that..."

It bothered me that my mother didn't do more to help the other kingdoms. Why couldn't she have cloaked the others, as well? Or why didn't she let them in on her plan so that they could follow suit with their own magic? I now knew that she had warned them while she could, but it didn't feel like enough and I hated that I felt that way.

Glacia interjected. "After you disappeared, rumors started to circulate that Fiah had been defeated by Remis. A prophecy started being told about a Firebird destined to save the missing kingdom. But as is the nature with rumors and prophecies, they start to change over time. Stories are passed down, fae and humans die and details are eradicated, the stories becoming altered as the next generation records and tells them. The particulars were so unclear, we had no idea that the Firebird prophecy had anything to do with you, Astoria."

Renese took a sip of water and cleared his throat. "Tellus has changed. I don't know how much you saw or knew while you were there."

Alaric nodded. "There's a lot of civil unrest amongst both the fae and humans. The humans are incredibly poor and are often punished for it. Meanwhile, the fae have to participate in Yielding Day every year and give up some of their magic to Remis. They grow weaker while he grows more powerful."

"Correct," Renese replied. "He has more power than he ever should have had. He's unstoppable and indestructible and has been trying to take over each kingdom to have access to even more magic. It's what further fuels the dark magic. Which is why Spirare began taking matters into their own hands over the past few decades."

"What does that mean?" I asked.

Renese looked over at Glacia who nodded at her husband. "Are you familiar with the macarong?" he asked, his voice noticeably lower than it had been.

With furrowed brows, Alaric and I shook our heads. Whatever a macarong was, it was clearly meant to be a secret as evidenced by Renese's hushed tone.

"We don't know their origins, but they are creatures that can be... made – fae that face death and are given a second chance at life," Glacia explained, her voice barely above a whisper, as well.

"I don't understand," I admitted. "How is that possible? All souls are supposed to go to the After Realm with the Fates after they die."

"Each macarong has something called an immortal ember. From what we understand, it's a part of their soul. When a fae dies, if done quickly, the macarong can give their immortal ember to the fae and gift them life. Many believe that this is an act of violence against the Fates, but what many don't know is that the macarong are stronger than the average fae. In fact, they're more closely related to the mythical vampires. Spirare has gathered thousands of them... And built an army with them," Renese told us.

I still didn't understand. "Can a macarong defeat Remis if he's using black magic?" I asked.

Elix finally spoke. "Likely not. But an army of macarong can defeat an army of fae."

Alaric's eyes widened. "Brother, what are you saying?"

Elix smirked and it unsettled me in so many ways. "I'm saying, *brother,* that we joined forces with Spirare and created our own army of macarong to ensure Gelu's survival."

The room started to spin and I felt like I was going to vomit. Elix's choice of words didn't go unnoticed. He didn't say that they built an army... he said that they created one.

Alaric gasped as he realized what I had. "Father, no! Please tell me this isn't true!"

Renese paused and I noticed the dining room begin to darken.

A storm brewing? I wondered.

Renese looked Alaric directly in the eyes. "It is true," he confirmed. "But each one of them chose this for themselves and for the good of the kingdom. No member of this army became a new creature against their will."

I placed a hand on my stomach and took a sip of water, desperately trying to keep my breakfast down.

Tellus had black magic.

Gelu and Spirare had an army of vampire-like creatures.

Fiah was still safe. Not in an ideal condition, but safe. Fiah was a peaceful kingdom with a small army of fae. How long before we weren't safe anymore? How long before one of these armies turned on us? If we went back to unveil Fiah, what fate would we be opening our subjects up to?

Without warning, a flash of lightning lit up the dining room followed by an extraordinarily loud clap of thunder that seemingly made the walls of the castle shake.

Elix rolled his eyes. "Your doing?" he asked in a bored tone while looking over at Alaric.

My head snapped to my husband. I had had so much on my mind that I completely forgot about Alaric's storm-wielding magic. He was incredibly powerful at manipulating the weather and his heightened emotions normally brought the nastiest of storms. I suddenly recalled the one time he used his true magic during the trials. While Ricky had conjuration magic and easily brought the rain to put out Scarlet's fire, it was really Alaric's storm magic that had come through. Just like the times fire had simmered at the surface of my skin during our time at the Phoenix Mansion. It wanted to be let out, but as Tory, I didn't really understand what the feeling was. And if I had, I probably wouldn't have been able to wield it.

Alaric was staring intently at his brother. I placed my hand on his cheek and turned his face towards me. "Hey. Let's go take a walk."

He nodded and I looked to his family. "If you'll excuse us," I began, although there was no option of *not* excusing us. "We'll be back... when we're back."

I stood up and took Alaric's hand in mine, his vacant stare alarming me more than I wanted to let on.

"Take your time," Glacia said. She knew her son well and she understood. "We'll see you at dinner. We're having a feast in your honor this evening."

I bowed my head and led Alaric out of the dining room, worrying my lip as we made our way through the glass halls. Rain was coming down in sheets and I knew the grounds would flood soon enough if I didn't rein Alaric in. The cold temperature would allow the rain to turn to slush first, but the flooding would be inevitable.

Practically running towards the entrance of the castle, I dragged Alaric behind me, sparing a glance at him. He was still lost to his emotions. I threw the doors open with such force, the guards jumped. But I didn't have time to concern myself with them.

"Alaric, my love, I need you to breathe," I told him as I led him out into the storm. Rain poured down our faces and our clothes clung to us, the sight immediately returning me to a moment many years ago... our first kiss.

Alaric returned to Fiah a fortnight after our Solstice celebration to declare his intentions to formally court me. With every trip to my kingdom, Alaric and I were brought closer. The bond always purred whenever we were in each other's presence, but we wanted to have a mental and emotional connection to one another that was as strong as the physical one that was demanding we join together.

Spring was always my favorite season. There was something so beautiful about the rebirth of nature. Colorful flowers, lush greens and rolling rivers came alive and I was always in awe of this other kind of magic. So when Alaric came for a visit and insisted we have a picnic lunch, my heart was filled with so much joy.

He ensured that we had the most delicious spread of food: Roasted vegetable sandwiches, a platter of cheeses, a salad with a bright lemon dressing, fruit and custard tartlets, buttery chocolate croissants, divine milk and dark chocolates and a bottle of sparkling wine. He even made sure that bunches of pink and magenta peonies, my favorite flower, adorned our picnic blanket. Alaric carried a chess board with him and all of the pieces. He had learned how to play chess from the humans in his kingdom and after teaching me a few visits prior, I fell in love with the game of strategy.

It was an absolutely perfect afternoon.

But spring isn't known just for its beauty, but also its unexpected showers. And one came in so quickly that we were soon drenched, ruining what was left of our respite and ending our game just as my queen was about to checkmate his king. Despite the fact that my wet hair was clinging to my head and face in a most unattractive way or that the kohl around my eyes was staining my cheeks, I couldn't help but smile at the way Alaric looked at me.

"What?" I asked him, grinning from ear to ear.

He drew his hand from one side of his body over his head to the other side of his body and the rain immediately stopped. A rainbow appeared over us like a multi-colored archway standing out against the now cerulean sky.

My eyes filled with wonder at this incredible magic that my mate possessed. I could feel Alaric's stare, so I glanced over at him. There was a moment where I believe we were both holding our breaths and then Alaric leaned in, his lips meeting mine.

The kiss was incredibly gentle. Alaric's hand brushed my face and then made its way to the back of my head where he laced his fingers through my hair. I melted into this kiss. This new beginning. The bond felt like a warm static radiating from my heart out to my limbs and through my fingers and toes.

When Alaric pulled back and smiled at me, I knew that he could feel it, too.

"You're mine, Astoria. I promise you that as long as I live, there will always be a rainbow for you after the storm."

In the present, desperate to pull my husband out of the anger that was causing chaos around us, I asked, "Alaric, do you remember the first time we kissed?"

He blinked. It wasn't much, but it was something.

I ran my hands up his arms and interlocked my fingers behind his neck. "You cleared the skies of a storm that rained down on our picnic and created a beautiful rainbow. I knew then that even if we weren't already destined for each other, that I would love you forever. You are my rainbow after a storm. You are my everything."

Alaric's eyes softened. I pulled him down to me and kissed him as tentatively as he had kissed me the first time. It didn't take long for him to kiss me back. I felt his tongue slip against the seam of my mouth and I opened for him. Desperate in a different way than I had been moments before.

The cold raindrops hitting my face were such a stark contrast to Alaric's warm lips. He pulled me against him and I wrapped my legs around his waist. He broke the kiss and chuckled into the crook of my neck.

Suddenly, the rain came down at a much slower pace and the clouds started to clear from the sky. Once I felt the heat of the sun on my face, I tossed my head back and looked up, knowing exactly what I would find.

A rainbow.

I kissed Alaric again. "We're going to fix this," I told him.

With his eyes closed, he nodded. "I know."

I put my hands on his face and looked him in the eyes. "But I need you here with me."

Alaric nodded again. "Until the end of time. There will always be a rainbow for you after the storm."

* * * * *

Alaric and I spent the remainder of the day in our chambers. We decided it was best that we didn't make our presence known to everyone. It would lead to too many questions about where we had been, how we got back and how we planned to stop the king and we weren't prepared to answer those questions. So, instead, Alaric located a chess set and we played while racking our brains for any clues to how to defeat Remis.

"I had a strange vision before I came back to myself," I admitted to Alaric. I still didn't understand what I had seen and hadn't been ready to talk about it just yet, especially since it didn't necessarily mean anything.

Alaric moved his pawn, careful to not over-emote. "Oh, yeah? What did you see?"

Fates, I loved him. He was trying so hard to be casual, but I could tell that he was anxious to hear what I had to say. I very infrequently had visions, if you could even call them that, but when I did, they often came to fruition.

"It started off as if it were a glimpse into the past. I saw the apprentices cast the spell that turned me into the Firebird. And then I *was* the Firebird and I was flying over the forest. I eventually flew to a city, I'm not sure where exactly, but it looked like it could have been Tellus. Everything was up in flames… and Scarlet was standing in the middle of the chaos." I scrunched my face up at the last part. It still hurt to think about her.

Alaric nodded his head slowly, thinking. "What do you think it means?" he asked.

I shook my head as I moved my bishop across the board. "I don't know. Everything happened so quickly once we were… back… to ourselves that I didn't have too much time to think about it. But the more I do, the more it's been bothering me. It could simply be my brain thinking about the trials, especially with everything up in flames and Scarlet's… death." I paused when I saw Alaric flinch. It had been murder, but it wasn't his fault and I would die on that hill. Regardless, I didn't think I'd ever be able to assure him that I didn't blame him.

"So what makes you think that it was a vision instead of just a nightmare?"

I took a deep breath. "It all just felt too real. I can't explain it. And in my vision, Scarlet was holding a sword." I narrowed my eyes at him. "She wasn't killed with a sword. She didn't even *have* a sword! Why would my brain put a sword in her hands?"

Alaric put his rook down and placed his elbow on the table, his chin resting on his fist. He looked at me thoughtfully. "Do you remember any other details? Like what the sword looked like?"

"Not really... I was too far away. But when she pointed it at me – "

Alaric cut me off. "I'm sorry, what do you mean 'when she pointed it at me'? Pointed it at the you in your vision or the bird you?"

I wanted to laugh at how ridiculous that sounded, but this was serious. "The bird me," I replied with a straight face. "When she pointed the sword up at me, I remember seeing the flames dance off of a black stone in the hilt."

"Like, an onyx?"

I nodded and Alaric furrowed his brow.

"What's wrong?" I asked.

Alaric stood up and walked over to a bookcase. He ran his finger along the spines, obviously looking for a particular title. "I'm not sure. I mean, maybe nothing. But in some ancient cultures, onyx was used in amulets and talismans for protection." He removed a book and opened it up. I approached him as he flipped through the pages. He landed on one and I leaned over to see what it said.

"The black onyx stone is said to act as a shield," I read aloud. "But..."

Alaric already knew what I was about to say. "Not a shield for Scarlet... Remis!"

My eyes went wide. "You think that I saw Remis' sword? That it's how he's wielding the black magic?"

"What if his sword is imbued with black magic?"

The realization hit me. "Then we can kill him with his sword."

16

CHAPTER SIXTEEN

It was a stretch. But it was all we had. We decided it would be best to not discuss it with Alaric's family until we had the opportunity to talk to Erina and see if our theory was plausible. Could a sword imbued with black magic kill someone who was unkillable? Would there be consequences to using black magic indirectly? And if so, would those consequences be worth it?

The more I thought about it, the more it seemed possible that Remis' sword could be the answer to all of our problems. Especially since my vision linked Scarlet to the sword. We already knew that our shared blood connected us. It only made sense that there would be a connection to Scarlet and her father.

Alaric and I dressed for dinner and it was the first time in a long time that I actually felt like the royalty that I was. Glacia had ensured this by sending up several dresses, as well as a diamond necklace and tiara. The tiara was nothing compared to my crown, but the gesture made my heart swell. The gesture was that of a mother taking care of her daughter. I couldn't have my mother with me, but I was grateful for the next best thing: a compassionate mother-in-law.

I decided on the emerald green gown that was made of silk and practically backless. It hugged my body and made me feel beautiful. I wasn't the only one who felt that way. When Alaric saw me in the dress, his eyes darkened with desire. I did a quick, but somewhat dramatic, spin to give him the full view.

With a face-splitting grin, he said, "Soon-To-Be-Queen Astoria, you look stunning. I'm in awe of you every time I look at you, but tonight you look exceptionally gorgeous. Would you do me the immense honor of allowing me to escort you down to the ballroom?"

I smiled back as I took his arm.

We made our way to the ballroom, music floating through the halls. I squeezed Alaric's arm with joy. It had been so long since we had been together in a setting like this.

When we entered, the room was filled with more fae than I had anticipated. Everyone was conversing, drinks in hand, as servants walked the room with platters of hors d'oeuvres. My mouth watered as I saw a plate of beef tartare drift by. Swallowing hard, Alaric and I made our way over to Glacia and Renese.

"You both look so regal," Glacia said, a smile pulling at her lips and pride filling her eyes.

"Thank you so much for the gowns and accessories, Glacia. I really appreciate it," I told her, taking her hands in mine. I gently squeezed them, hoping to truly show her how much the gesture meant to me.

Alaric looked around the room. "I thought this would be a small gathering, father. We had discussed keeping our presence to just those on a need-to-know basis."

"There isn't just nobility here tonight, son," Renese replied. "Take a closer look. These are some of our mac-arong soldiers."

A storm began brewing in Alaric's eyes, but before his anger could get too far, Renese placed a hand on his son's shoulder. "Those who fight for us should know who they're fighting for... just as you should know who chooses to fight for you... for us."

As if on cue, we were approached by a small group. The king greeted them. "Ah, yes! Astoria, Queen of Fiah. Alaric, Second Prince of Gelu and King Consort of Fiah. Allow me to introduce the general of our army, Pyta Grinroff, and two of our sergeants, Sergeant Brinker and Sergeant Mineer."

The three service members bowed to us. "It's an honor to meet you both. We are so grateful for your return," General Grinroff said.

"Thank you, General, but the honor is ours. Thank you for your service and sacrifice," Alaric replied. I could see a mix of emotions on his face. He had so many questions, but he was genuinely grateful for those who would give their lives to protect our families and kingdoms.

"We understand that you have some... concerns about how we began this journey and we'd like to give you the opportunity to ask anything that's on your mind," Grinroff went on.

Alaric took my hand and squeezed it. "Thank you. We really appreciate that. We didn't learn about the macarong until our return to Gelu, so you can imagine, we were taken by surprise in hearing of your existence and how you come to be. My wife and I would never expect anyone to embark on this journey unwillingly and we just want to make sure that your presence here is of your own free will."

General Grinroff and his two sergeants nodded their heads along as Alaric spoke. Brinker was the first to speak. "As you know, macarong are made creatures. Historically, a fae that has died can be given an immortal ember within the first few moments of death to be brought back to life as a macarong. Many of us here have made the choice to become this creature because we believe in what we're fighting for. We want to use our new and heightened abilities to give the kingdoms a better chance at defeating the Dark King."

"Forgive me for asking," I began, "but how does it work? You agreed to allow someone to kill you? And then turn you?"

"No apologies necessarily, Your Majesty," Mineer said, a genuine smile on his face. "Yes, that's correct. We believe in this cause and if we're willing to die to save our kingdom, dying the first time knowing that we'll be brought back hardly seems like a sacrifice."

I took a deep breath. The subjects of Gelu had already given up so much for a cause that shouldn't be their battle to fight. Meanwhile, my subjects were just suspended in time. Sure, their lives would be changed in different ways, but... it was all so much and why? Because Remis was a crazy tyrant who was stealing magic to become more powerful? He needed to be put down. No one should have the power to ruin so many lives.

Brinker spoke up. "If it's any relief, Your Majesty, our deaths were painless. The kingdom's alchemists gave us a potion that slowed our heart rates. In the moment that they stopped beating, a macarong was standing by, ready to transfer their ember."

I nodded my understanding. That alleviated some of my pain for these creatures, but not much. It was still a choice I didn't want them to have to make.

"Thank you, to all of you," Alaric said. "And thank you for speaking with us this evening. We appreciate everything you've done and continue to do for us. Sincerely."

All three macarong soldiers bowed and took their leave. I watched as they gathered towards a group of other soldiers, all of whom seemed jovial, laughing as they indulged.

"Son, I'd like you to walk with me. It's good for everyone to see their lost prince. Come," Renese said, taking Alaric by the arm and leading him away from Glacia and me.

"Good," Glacia said. "I've been wanting to talk to you. Alone."

Her whispering of the last word caused a chill to run up my spine. Glacia led me to a corner of the ballroom, grabbing two glasses of sparkling wine on the way. She handed me a glass and faced me, smiling as if I had just said something amusing. We looked like we were having a casual conversation and that made me uneasy.

"There's something that I need you to know that I've not told to either my husband or son," she began and I understood she was referring to Elix. Glacia took a deep breath. "What you all know is that your mother sent word to us that our kingdoms were in trouble and to prepare. What you don't know is that she sent me another message."

I sucked in a breath. What was Glacia about to tell me? Would it break my heart?

"Go on," I urged her.

She closed her eyes for the briefest of moments before continuing with her story. "Your mother was very concerned for her sister's safety. As I mentioned, we were all friends, so they both trusted me... As I had trusted them centuries ago when I told them my secret." She paused and I felt like I was about to stop breathing. What realms-shattering revelation was she about to share with me? "In addition to my ability to manipulate elements, I have a second power... I can speak to animals."

My eyes widened in shock. I had never heard of the ability to speak to animals. Our magic usually centered around the elements, objects or things within us, like Tory's memory magic. It was something our brain was able to do and didn't use outside forces. But our magic never used something with a soul.

Glacia could obviously see that I was processing the information she gave me and allowed me a few moments to gather myself. She smiled softly.

"Something special about Gelu is that we have a large population of snow foxes. And there were two that I had an exceptional relationship with. They agreed to travel to Tellus to watch and protect Yve. If the king showed any ill intent towards her, they were supposed to report back to me so that I could take action. But Remis never raised a hand to her. He didn't necessarily cherish your aunt, but he held her in high regard. So when my snow foxes returned and informed me that Yve killed herself, it came as an immense surprise. That's when I learned the truth."

I waited with bated breath.

"After your cousin was born, she started to show odd signs. Yve had brought her to different healers, but they said that her behavior and strange physical traits were not something that could be healed. Yve set out to find Erina, to no avail. Your mother's sorceress is revered throughout all of the kingdoms for her extraordinary talents, but since Yve couldn't locate her, she had to find another sorceress and did so in Spirare. It was there that Yve learned that death and blood can create protection spells and deduced that that's what her sister must have done. Spirare's sorceress had heard the prophecies and believed that the spell Erina used was tied to Remis' blood. *His* blood spilling would bring an end to the spell. What no one foresaw was Scarlet's birth. It created a magical loophole because she carried Remis' blood and somehow made her... wrong."

I couldn't stop myself from cringing, but quickly plastered my conversation face back on as Glacia continued.

"Because the Fates always demand balance, Yve believed that her sacrifice would protect and save her daughter, so after the sorceress created her own spell, Yve killed herself. I sent my foxes back to Tellus to watch over Scarlet, but you know how that ended.

When you arrived here with Erina, I took the opportunity to speak with her about all of this and why Scarlet still died. Erina told me that Yve's death had nothing to do with the original spell and no other magic would negate it. She, unfortunately, died for nothing, leaving Scarlet essentially alone and misunderstood. And her death was still inevitable if Remis wasn't killed first."

My knees gave out and I grabbed onto a wall sconce to stabilize myself. "Where's... Erina..." I breathed through gritted teeth.

"Astoria, I didn't tell you this so that you'd take action against Erina. I needed you to know the full story. We don't know what small detail might be the one that saves us all." Glacia looked pleadingly into my eyes.

"There is no punishment to mete out," I stated, though I wasn't quite sure that was true. "I just want to speak with her."

Glacia nodded her head in understanding. "We put her and the apprentices in the guest chambers on the second floor of the west wing. She should be there now. But from one queen to another, tread carefully, Astoria."

I bowed my head in thanks and gathered the bottom of my dress in my hand as I marched towards the morally grey sorceress and her minions. They were always playing games and were protected under the guise of the Fates' balance. But I was tired of it. If we were going to save the kingdoms, Erina needed to come clean once and for all.

Alaric made eye contact with me from across the ballroom and took a step forward, but I put my hand up to halt him. I could fight this battle alone.

He said something to the macarong he was speaking to and then quickly chased after me. We approached the doors together and burst through them.

"Where are you going?" he asked me, trying to keep up, which was funny because I was in heels and he was not. My fae abilities were being heightened by my anger, propelling me forward.

"I'm going to see that bitch, Erina!"

"Whoa! Whoa!" Alaric grabbed my arm to stop me. "What's going on?"

"Alaric, let go of me! I just want to talk to her!" I yelled, trying to pull out of the embrace he had on my arm. "I love you, but I can do this without you."

He released my arm, looking crestfallen. "The whole point of our bond, Astoria, is that you never have to. Tell me what's wrong and let me help you make it right," he pleaded with me.

I closed my eyes and took a deep breath to steady the energy surging through my veins. I wasn't mad at Alaric, so I needed to stop yelling at him. He was just trying to support me.

"Erina keeps withholding information and I'm tired of it. My aunt killed herself because of it and Scarlet's death occurred because of a magical loophole that she could have avoided," I explained. There was more that wasn't my story to tell, so I omitted the parts about the secret letter and Glacia's unique abilities.

Alaric nodded his head. "Got it. Let's go," he said, gesturing towards the stairs.

I scrunched up my face. "That's it? You have no other questions."

Alaric took my face in his hands, firmly, but still gently. "You are my mate and I love you. I trust you. I didn't need you to tell me what was going on to get me on board with this attack, I just wanted to know so I knew how to support you."

I kissed him and then headed towards the second floor, my husband behind me. Once we arrived at the guest suites, I banged on each chamber door until all three of the apprentices and Erina opened theirs.

"I want to talk to you, Erina." It was a demand and not a request.

Erina opened her door wider. She was welcoming us in, but I could feel her hesitancy. "What can I do for you, Your Majesty?"

I pointed at her apprentices. "You three! I want you in here, too." I was frustrated and trying to keep my composure, but I could quickly feel that diplomacy was about to fly out the window.

"Why did you link the spell to Remis' blood and not him specifically?" I asked, venom dripping from my voice.

Marcus, Francois and Gebert looked at each other before Erina answered. "I'm not sure I understand your question, Your Majesty."

"My aunt killed herself trying to save her daughter from becoming a sacrifice." I glared at her.

"Ah... you spoke to the Queen of Gelu." Erina sighed. "There was an unavoidable error... Yve got pregnant with Scarlet. The spell was supposed to break when Remis died, but then Scarlet was born, so her blood became the blood that triggered the end of the spell, leaving Remis still alive and very powerful."

"So let me make sure I understand this," Alaric said. "You never considered that Remis would reproduce?"

"In a word, no," Erina replied. "Remis and Yve hadn't produced an heir in centuries. We had no reason to consider it, let alone know that the Fates would choose blood to mean bloodline and not his *actual* blood. We thought that when Remis was finally killed, Fiah would be safe to be un-cloaked."

I sat down on the bed and buried my face in my hands. The Fates. They really made a mess of things. But why? Why did they commit the atrocity of allowing Remis to have black magic that can destroy the kingdoms, but also gift me with a mating bond? A bond so strong that it tied our souls together even when mine was supposed to be somewhere else? Were we all just pawns in the Fates' game of chess?

I wouldn't get any answers tonight, but there was something that I desperately wanted to do.

"Erina, we'd like to speak with you tomorrow regarding Remis and his black magic. Please join us in the conservatory tomorrow at sunrise." I turned to Alaric. "Come with me."

17

CHAPTER
SEVENTEEN

I led Alaric back to our bed chambers and once the door was closed behind us, I threw my arms around him and kissed him deeply. I felt him smile against me as he lifted me off of my feet and backed me up towards the bed. Before I could hit it, he broke the kiss to scoop me up in his arms and gently lay me down.

I couldn't fix my kingdom's problems tonight, but I could be with my mate and husband. My protector. My biggest supporter. Alaric was my everything and always would be.

"I don't know if I'm still the woman you fell in love with," I said, my voice trembling. "I know that parts of her are still inside me. I know that every day of my lives, something always felt like it was missing and I know now that that something was you. You are what completes me. I don't know if I can be the woman that completes you, but I want that more than anything."

Alaric furrowed his brow and looked at me like he didn't understand before saying, "You are my *everything*, Astoria. I would burn the world down if it would take away every moment that made you think that you were anything less than my heart and my soul."

He kissed me then. Softly. So soft and almost painfully slow, as if he were pouring every ounce of love into this one kiss.

"Most beings… humans… fae… go their entire lives without ever feeling what you and I feel for each other."

I looked at him, not knowing what to say, but knowing that I wanted him. Needed him in a primal way. It was as simple as needing air to breathe.

"I know we're not wholly us yet… our real bodies are still in Fiah, but I need you, Alaric. I need to feel our souls unite." I lifted my head off of the bed to close the distance between our lips. This kiss wasn't tentative. This kiss was the end and the beginning. The end of what was lost and the beginning of what was found. We were together again and all that mattered in this moment was rediscovering each other.

Alaric broke the kiss with a mischievous gleam in his eyes and then peeled off my dress. He kissed my jaw and then my neck, languidly making his way down my chest and stomach. He then placed a kiss on my inner thigh before lifting it over his shoulder and licking my throbbing core. His tongue swirled through my slick heat before flicking the bundle of nerves at my apex. I bowed off the bed, Alaric's name on my lips as I moaned. The sound must have snapped the tight leash that he was keeping himself on and he became like a famished man, feasting on me like his favorite meal.

"I need you." My plea. My prayer.

Alaric looked up at me before saying, "You already have me."

"No, I need you inside me," I told him, writhing on the bed.

"As you wish, my queen," he said before pressing a thick finger inside me. The delicious feel of his tongue and finger pumping in and out of me were quickly becoming my undoing. It wasn't what I had meant when I told him that I wanted him inside of me, but then he curled that finger and I saw stars. I wove my fingers through his hair and pulled his head closer to me before he chuckled against where I was most sensitive. I was already so close that the vibration was all it took to have me tighten against him and then shatter.

As I came down from my ecstasy, Alaric lifted his tunic over his head and then took off his pants, his cock hard and thick. He stroked himself seductively before placing his tip at my entrance. Bracing his arms on either side of me, he slowly glided himself in, stretching and filling me.

The feeling was euphoric and the bond hummed with satisfaction as the two of us became one again. Alaric waited for me to adjust to the size of him before sheathing himself entirely. He thrust in and out, slowly at first and as the pleasure built in both of us, he increased the pace. I wrapped my legs around his waist, allowing him to go deeper, our moans filling the room.

"Fates, Astoria, you feel so good," Alaric said through gritted teeth. "You *make me* feel so good."

His thrusting soon became erratic and I could feel my release building.

"I love you, Astoria," Alaric told me.

His words were my undoing. I came hard, screaming and not caring who heard. Alaric followed after me and then collapsed on top of me, panting hard while pressing kisses to my neck.

"I love you," he repeated. "I have and always will love you, Astoria."

I brushed a lock of his hair off of his forehead and then ran my palm along his cheek, pausing at his chin. "I love you, too."

Alaric rolled off of me and pulled me into his side. I put my arm around his abdomen and rested my head on his chest. Hearing the beats of his heart in tandem with mine made me feel incredibly at peace. He wrapped his arms around me tight, drawing circles on my shoulder with his thumb. No matter what was happening around us, in Alaric's arms, I would always be home. He was my sanctuary.

"I want us to have a grand coronation," Alaric declared. "The biggest one that Fiah has ever seen."

I lifted my head to look at him. "I think a large celebration is the last thing we should be thinking about."

Alaric shook his head. "I disagree. I think that all of the kingdom should bear witness to how much their new king loves their queen. And I think that once the dust settles from the fall out of being cloaked, before we go to war, Fiah deserves to celebrate what we all have… each other."

I smiled at my incredible husband. Of course he would be thinking like this. He was going to be the most considerate king the realm had ever seen.

"I think that sounds wonderful." I relaxed back into the warmth of his body.

We didn't speak for a while, content in our comfortable silence. Eventually, Alaric spoke up.

"Can I ask you something? What you said to Erina… How she said that you spoke to my mother… What did my mother tell you? How did she know about your aunt and Scarlet?"

I smiled into his chest, knowing he would eventually ask me this. "I love you so much and don't want to keep anything from you, but it's not my story to tell. You'll have to talk to her yourself."

Alaric didn't question me any further. I soon heard his breathing become deeper and knew he had fallen asleep. I followed him into the darkness, as I always would.

* * * * *

The next morning, we headed down to the conservatory at sunrise to meet with Erina. While it was probably the most beautiful room in Gelu's castle, it was also the best for having private conversations. With the walls being made entirely of glass, it was impossible for someone to make their way in unseen.

When Erina entered, she bowed to me and then to Alaric before joining us at the table that was kept in the conservatory with these confidential meetings in mind. I gestured for her to take a seat.

"We wanted to talk to you about Remis and his magic. We have a theory on how to kill him, but as our expert in all things magic, we wanted to consult with you first before putting any plans into action," Alaric explained to the sorceress. He then looked to me.

"When I... came back to myself, I had a vision," I began tentatively.

Erina looked surprised. She knew that they were a rare occurrence, so I'm sure the admission ensnared her attention even further.

"I saw a city being destroyed by fire. Chaos everywhere. And then I saw Scarlet. She pointed a sword with an onyx stone embedded into it towards me. Alaric and I discussed what these things could mean. Obviously Scarlet is dead, but since she is Remis' daughter, his blood, we think that maybe she represented him. And we know that onyx has protective properties. Could it be possible that the onyx is storing his magic? That it's imbued into it?"

Erina considered this for a moment. Before she could answer, Alaric interjected.

"It's imperative that you don't keep anything from us, Erina. The whole truth and nothing but the truth. Please." It saddened me to hear the slight sound of desperation in his voice. The sorceress had been less than forthcoming on so many occasions, but in order for her to truly help us win this war, we needed her absolute honesty and nothing less.

"It is all possible," she began, choosing her words carefully. "I can not say for certain if it's the case, but it all sounds very plausible. Scarlet was the key to releasing you because she carried Remis' blood. She represents the bloodline. And you're correct, onyx is used to shield from danger, which is why Remis has been using the black magic for all along. It would make sense that he would carry it with him for protection or to call on it when needed. Historically, stones are used as amulets, but a sword would suffice. More than suffice since it's a weapon he could still defend himself with."

Alaric and I looked at each other, silently agreeing to our next question.

"If we were able to use the sword against Remis, could we kill him?" I asked. I held my breath waiting for the answer and could feel the tension in Alaric as he did the same.

"We can't enchant objects for only one user. If something carries magic, it does so for whomever the bearer is. It's a similar idea to the vessel that carried your soul. Although our intention was to take just yours, my queen, your mate's went with yours."

Alaric loosed a breath. "So you're saying there's a chance?"

"I believe so, Your Majesty."

Alaric reached over and grabbed my hand, squeezing it with excitement. We could do this! We could kill Remis and end his reign. We could get vengeance for my mother and aunt and Scarlet.

"But…" Erina cut off my thoughts and I immediately felt a chill run down my spine. "There could be a cost. Whoever wields the sword would be wielding the dark magic. There's no telling what consequences there could be to that."

We had all lost so much because of Remis. It wasn't fair that we finally had a way to put an end to this evil, but at an unknown cost. I would die for my kingdom. I knew Alaric would do the same. We had an army of macarong who had already died for our cause. But when would the cost we paid be enough? How many more had to die to stop one corrupt king?

Alaric and I looked at one another. Each answer led to another question.

"We'll figure it out," he assured me. "We'll go back to Fiah and figure it out." He nodded as he spoke, as if trying to convince himself of his own words.

"We'll figure it out," I echoed back, my voice barely above a whisper.

We didn't have any other choice.

18

CHAPTER
EIGHTEEN

After our meeting with Erina, we headed to the training field to watch the macarong. They were definitely a force to be reckoned with, utilizing their enhanced strength with their magical abilities, the ones that were standard to all fae, as well as the ones gifted by the Fates.

Which led to a question: If the macarong were considered an abomination because they, in theory, took souls from the Fates, why would the Fates allow them to keep their magical gifts? It was almost as if they approved of these new creatures. All was definitely not as it seemed.

The macarong had learned to use their skills in tandem with one another, barely breaking into a sweat at they executed different skills meant to attack and defend.

"You see those soldiers over there?" General Grinroff asked as he pointed to two macarong who looked identical to each other. They were engaged in a sword fight that looked more like a partner dance, each moving as a perfect complement to the other. Both smiling, their fangs were on full display. "That's the Pearsem twins. They're both telepaths and can speak into each other's minds. It's an excellent form of communication on the battlefield, as they can coordinate with one another during an attack."

It was really fascinating to watch them work so efficiently. It reminded me of how Alaric and I were often as in sync as the telepath twins. It made me wish that we could speak into each other's minds. Not necessarily as a war strategy, but just to feel even closer to him.

I looked at Alaric, mischief gleaming in my eyes. "Do you want to train with me for a little while?" I asked him before turning to Grinroff. "Would that be okay, General?"

He nodded. "It would be more than okay. In fact, I would encourage it. I think it would be great for morale for the soldiers to feel like you're one of them."

Alaric grabbed my hand, a smile stretching across his face. "Let's go!" He pulled me along as we headed to an area of the field that wasn't occupied. We were close enough to feel like we were joining the macarong, but far enough away to keep them out of immediate danger.

It had been so long since I had used my fire magic to its full extent. Sure, I had been using it to keep me warm in the cold weather and I had been doing small things like heating up water for baths or tea, but my magic was capable of so much more. And right now, it was begging to come out and play.

Alaric backed away from me, grinning from ear to ear. "Are you ready, my queen?"

I giggled as I brought my magic to my fingertips and shot a teasing spark at his foot. His mouth dropped open in feigned surprise and I could hear some of the macarong chuckle behind me.

"The question is, are *you* ready, my king?"

He blew me a kiss as dark grey storm clouds began to fill the previously cerulean sky. Large drops of rain began to fall and I watched as the surrounding macarong looked around, already in awe of what they were seeing.

I raised my hands to my husband and winked before flames shot out of my palms. But before they could harm Alaric, he motioned in the sky and a gust of wind and heavy rain redirected my shot away from him. He winked back at me and waved his hand again as the rain quickly began to hail, pelting down on my head.

"Ow!" I exclaimed, face scrunched up as I rubbed my head. With my other hand, I sent multiple balls of fire at him.

Alaric used the hail to build a wall of ice to block my shots. The flaming balls began to cut through the ice, but they died out before they could break the wall. I sent more fire out in tiny streams to cut precisely through Alaric's ice wall, but when it finally crumpled, Alaric was no longer there. In his place was a snowman with a face that looked just like Alaric's, but with an expression that was clearly added to mock me. When I looked past the snowman, I saw my husband in the distance, already building a friend. I smiled before throwing my head back in pure laughter. He wasn't building his snowman a friend… he was building him a mate. A snow-woman that looked so much like me that I couldn't help but cease fire and race towards Alaric, jumping into his arms and planting a kiss on his cheek.

"Stalemate?" he asked, a grin splitting his face from ear to ear.

I nodded. "Only for you."

"Only for me," Alaric repeated before kissing me. Around us, I could hear the macarong soldiers cheering. I pried my lips off of Alaric's and looked around, both of us laughing. A rainbow appeared overhead and Alaric winked at me.

"Okay, okay!" General Grinroff exclaimed, clapping his hands. "Everyone back to your sparring." Alaric put me down and we both faced the general. "That was a stunning display. Your talents will definitely be useful during battle. Thank you for giving us a demonstration of what you're capable of."

"No thanks necessary, General," Alaric began. "We'll be leaving Gelu this evening for Fiah. We know we're leaving the kingdom in excellent hands and couldn't be more grateful."

General Grinroff bowed to us and then turned back to his soldiers.

"Ready, my queen?" Alaric asked, offering me his upturned hand.

I gave him an affirmative nod of my head and placed my hand in his. As we made our way back inside the castle to gather a few items, most importantly, the vessel needed to uncloak our kingdom, I noticed Renfred leaving his post and jogging over to join us. Alaric had been able to steal a few moments with his old friend during our stay in Gelu, but I wished they had had more time together. They were close when Alaric was still living in the castle, before he met me, and I wanted Alaric to have more people he could trust around him. Around us.

"My friend!" Alaric exclaimed. "It seems that this is good-bye for now!" He let go of my hand to shake Renfred's but Renfred did not take it.

"Not necessarily, old boy," Renfred said, jabbing him in the shoulder "With King Renese's permission, I have been granted leave."

I narrowed my eyes at the guard. "What do you mean?" When I looked at Alaric, he was grinning. "What's going on?"

As if knowing the answer already, Alaric asked, "Where will you go?"

Renfred grinned back. "With you, of course! To Fiah. If you'll have me."

Well, look at that! Wishes sometimes do come true!

I smiled up at my husband who looked to me for confirmation that he didn't need.

"We'd be honored, Renfred," I replied, but before the words were even fully out of my mouth, Alaric had Renfred in a headlock and the two were grappling with one another. I rolled my eyes. Fae males and their antics...

I cleared my throat, but a smile dusted my lips. They straightened up and both bowed to me, causing me to shake my head and roll my eyes again.

When we finally reached the castle doors, Erina and the apprentices were already waiting for us. Prissy was nearby, flapping her wings when she saw me. I walked up to her to stroke her muzzle and give her little tickles which made her snort with amusement.

"We're ready when you are, Your Majesties," Erina announced.

While our traveling companions waited outside, Alaric and I went to say our farewells to his parents and brother. Glacia was the first to embrace me as Renese shook his son's hand. We then switched parents and while hugging Renese, I noticed a look of peace on Alaric's face over his mother's shoulder. He had decided not to talk to her about what she divulged to me. He felt that if she wanted him to know, she would have already told him. And if the time ever came that she was ready to open up to him about her secret, he would welcome it and accept whatever she had to say.

I thought that Elix wasn't going to grace us with his presence, but just as we were each pulling away from Glacia and Renese, he entered the room. There was no love in his eyes, so definitely no love lost.

"Safe travels," he said with a tone that made it clear he didn't really care if we made it back to Fiah or not. He leaned against a column in the center of the room, folding his arms over his chest. Elix had the emotional intelligence of a wet mop. Why couldn't he just hug his damn brother? Bastard.

And with that, we were finally on our way home.

* * * * *

The journey to Fiah – and the needed stops along the way to relieve ourselves and eat – took a little over two days. It was a fairly easy flight, which was appreciated more than the Fates could know. The last thing we needed was *another* problem to deal with.

We landed on a hilltop – if you could even call it that – in what appeared to be a remote area, but I knew exactly where we were. It looked nothing like the kingdom that I loved. There wasn't a single tree or patch of green grass in sight. In fact, it looked like the area had been plagued with a drought. It was desolate and uninhabitable. Even though I knew better, my eyes filled with tears. I couldn't help it.

Alaric and I dismounted off of Prissy, who also looked less than thrilled at the appearance of our home.

"It's okay, girl," I assured her, disappointingly digging my foot in the ground and kicking up sandy dirt. "We're going to fix this."

Erina and the apprentices joined us. She reverently handed me the vessel. "Please take this, Your Majesty."

When I held it in both of my hands, I could have sworn it was vibrating. Or humming? I couldn't explain it, but there was a sense of rightness that caused me to shiver. Almost like the hum of the mating bond. The vessel was sensing something about me being on my land.

"Is the vessel sentient, Erina?" I asked, surprised.

She shook her head. "No, Your Majesty. But it 'knows.'"

Erina and her layered words. What the heck did that mean? I decided I didn't want to know. I just wanted to be home. "What do we do now?" I asked her. I noticed the apprentices were chanting something, but I couldn't make the words out. Slowly, they joined hands and spread themselves in a circle. Erina guided me towards them, Alaric keeping in stride, not letting me out of a distance greater than arms length. He didn't trust Erina. He never would. And I loved him all the more for it!

Marcus and Gebert let go of their joined hands momentarily and Erina nudged me towards them. Taking slow, deliberate steps, I stood in the center of the three apprentices as they closed the circle again and continued chanting in hushed tones.

The vessel continued to hum, but the humming started to feel different. Like it was speaking to me in a silent language. I felt a pull at my magic and the very strong need to pour fire into the vessel. I did as I desired – as the unspeaking voice demanded. Neither one of us was the other's commander. We were working in unison, feeding into each other in some hidden way.

Hidden like the kingdom in front of me no longer was.

My eyes widened and I gasped at the sight. It was like watching the impossible come true. After almost two hundred years, Fiah was part of the realm again. No longer veiled, it was a spectacular sight to behold!

"You did it!" Alaric exclaimed, in awe of what he was seeing, as well. He looked at me, his eyes even wider than mine, as he took in our surroundings.

No longer were we standing on a giant mound of dirt, but rather, a lush hilltop covered in the greenest grass imaginable and dotted with stunning Cherry Blossoms that were in full bloom. Standing under the ancient stone archway that greeted visitors to our kingdom or welcomed Fiahans home, I couldn't help but smile, remembering this archway had appeared in the third trial. Erina really had put all the clues right in front of Tory. A laugh bubbled up and escaped my lips.

Birds flew overhead as if they had already been en route to somewhere. It made me wonder if they had been frozen in mid-air. Three butterflies fluttered around me, one landing on my nose before the little family took off again. I smiled and then looked to the group. For the first time since Selection Day at the trials, the apprentices were smiling. Renfred looked like he was just thrilled to not still be in Gelu's frosty weather, a pleasant color tinging his cheeks. And Erina was... well, she was Erina.

"We should hurry down," the sorceress suggested. "Everyone will be waking up and the longer you wait to address everyone, the greater possibility of confusion."

She was right. As much as she drove me crazy, Erina did exactly what she had promised my mother: she froze the kingdom, kept it safe and brought me home to save it once and for all.

Alaric quickly brushed his lips against mine before Erina teleported the three of us inside the castle. Now that we were back in Fiah, Erina's powers were much stronger, thank goodness!

As I looked around, I realized we weren't just inside the castle… We were inside Alaric's and my bed chambers. I looked around the room and saw the doors leading out to our balcony that overlooked the courtyard. I saw the fireplace and mantle where I displayed some of our most cherished gifts. And I saw the four-poster bed and soft, white blankets where our bodies were still laying on top as if perfectly preserved in time. I looked at our sleeping faces, still in awe at how similar they were to the ones we were wearing.

Erina was chanting and waving her hands before I even realized what was happening. I was so grateful for this sense of urgency.

"Do you feel strange?" Alaric asked, taking his eyes off our bodies and turning towards me. When I turned to look back at him, his current body began dematerializing. I immediately realized by the look on his face that my body must have been doing the same. Before I could reply, I was suddenly on my back, staring up at the coffered ceiling.

I was in my real body again!

I quickly sat up and saw that my former one was gone in a plume of smoke, as was Alaric's. I turned to my husband, immense joy spread across my face. There wasn't a chance for a single word to leave my lips before Alaric's were on mine and I could feel every ounce of his happiness.

We were us again.

We were whole.

With no time to savor this moment, we raced out of the castle and hopped back on Prissy to make our way into town. Flying would have been the fastest way to get there, but concerned that we'd frighten everyone further, we decided against it. My beautiful pegasus understood the assignment and raced as fast as her legs would take us towards the town.

All around us, fae and humans were waking up. Erina had explained to us that everyone would feel slightly disoriented – the side effect of being held in the same state for so long while time kept moving. Some looked dumbfounded while others waved in greeting with groggy smiles on their faces. But everything looked to be intact. The stone facades of the buildings were as charming as ever. Flowers of all different colors bloomed inside window boxes, making Fiah look like what I imagined the inside of a rainbow resembled.

"Follow us!" Alaric called down to them. We wanted to lead them into the town square so that we could give a formal declaration.

Once we got to our destination, we halted in front of the town wishing well. This had always been one of my favorite places to observe the town in its peaceful glory. The town was where food would be purchased for family meals, dresses were altered before a ball and children would play while their parents hoped for them to exert all of their energy. I loved watching it all! It was life and it was beautiful.

And it was time to take it all back.

"Subjects of Fiah!" I yelled from atop Prissy as everyone began to gather and the chatter died down. "We know that you may be confused right now and we have much to share with you!" I took a deep breath. "My mother received word that the King of Tellus was going to be attacking our kingdom."

Gasps resounded through the crowd. I could see the immediate panic and knew I had to assuage it quickly.

"Please stay calm! In an effort to protect you all, the queen took measures to keep the kingdom safe. She had the sorceress spell Fiah and all of you to keep you hidden from the mad king."

The crowd started to calm, but I could still see the looks of confusion and concern. This was going to be the hardest part.

I took another steadying breath. "You've all been frozen in time for almost two hundred years."

I waited for chaos to erupt, but instead, I was met with stoned silence. Wide eyes met mine, waiting for me to continue.

"The queen sacrificed herself to keep you all safe. I know you all will have a lot of questions. There's still much we're trying to figure out, as well. But rest assured, we have a plan to defeat Remis! We will need all of your help, though! Please trust that we intend to keep Fiah a safe and peaceful kingdom. It was my mother's dying wish that I will uphold until my last breath."

I was met with stunned silence for the briefest of moments before someone in the crowd yelled, "Long live Queen Astoria! Long live King Alaric."

I wish I could have been stoic. More queen-like. Instead my eyes filled with tears. Alaric scooped me up into his arms so that I could gather myself and not allow the tears to turn into a full sob.

These were my subjects. They were scared and confused, but they trusted me. And I would do everything in my power to never lose that trust.

19

CHAPTER NINETEEN

The next few days flew by in a whirlwind. Alaric and I settled back into the castle, taking up our old room. I wasn't ready for us to move into my mother's former suite yet. I knew that we'd have to do it eventually, but with everything we had been through already, having the stability of our old chambers was a comfort at the end of each day that I didn't want to give up.

Our days were mostly filled with meetings. Meeting after meeting after meeting. Under normal circumstances, I would think so many meetings tiresome, but there was just *so much* that needed to be discussed.

We met with the fae to ensure their magical abilities were still intact. Where the subjects of Tellus were often afraid to display their gifts, the fae of Fiah were encouraged to do so. We always believed in the beauty of our inherent magic and the gifts of the Fates and how they made us strong, both as individuals and as a kingdom.

We met with the humans to help them with their grief. While they had been frozen in time for nearly two centuries, it seemed that their lives had been extended and were just picking back up where they left off. But their loved ones in other kingdoms had not experienced the same and while it felt strange to grieve deaths that occurred so long ago, to these humans, it was like it had just happened yesterday.

We met with our very small military to discuss the upcoming war and to tell them all we knew about the macarong, their history and their powers. If we were going to be successful and defeat Remis, we needed to work in tandem with Gelu's forces. Which was a huge reason why Renfred joined our army and filled the role of Lieutenant General.

Just as we were finishing up our last meeting of the day, a female voice called out, "Hullo! Hullo!" as two heads popped their way into the doorframe.

I nearly shrieked when I saw their faces. Practically knocking over my chair, I raced to the female and locked her in my embrace as Alaric joined me at my side to greet the male.

"Malisande!" I exclaimed, hugging her small frame as tightly as I could and stroking her long, blonde hair. "Oh, my dear friend, I've missed you so much!"

"It's good to see you, too, Astoria," she squeaked out. "But I can barely breathe well enough to express it."

I quickly let go and took a step back. Malisande's green eyes shimmered with happiness.

"Brick, I'm so glad to see you well!" I said as Alaric switched places with me so that I could embrace the male while he embraced Malisande. Brick was a sturdy fellow that I could barely wrap my arms around. He laughed heartily as he lifted me off of the ground.

Malisande was my lady in waiting and Brick was her husband who became the castle's cook after they married. While they were part of the royal staff, they were so much more than that. They were our best friends and confidantes.

"Where have you been?" I asked, wishing they had come to find us as soon as we arrived back in Fiah.

"We were anxious to see you, but wanted to give you a few days to settle in. While *you* haven't seen us in a very long time, we feel like we just saw you yesterday."

I couldn't help but chuckle. She was right, of course.

"Are you all right, though? With everything?" I asked. Regardless of how smooth this transition was going, everyone would be adjusting at their own pace.

"We're fine! We're fine!" she exclaimed, brushing me off before looking at me with a serious expression. "But we are very sorry to hear about the queen. The former queen. Your mum. Sorry, I'm not good with condolences. They make me nervous." She threw up her hands, waving them in front of her face and hanging her head.

I gave her a hug. There was nothing more to say.

"Awl'right! Awl'right! Enough of that!" Brick drawled. "Whaterya eatin'? What kind of mush 'ave they been servin' ya in Telly that I can wipe clean from yer palates?"

Brick's way with words... or sounds... could be deceiving. While he didn't have the privilege of a proper education as a child, he could cook better than anyone I had ever met. After he married Malisande, I put a good word in with my mother, who quickly snatched him up from the tavern he was wasting his talents at.

Alaric laughed. "Believe it or not, I don't recall the food being half bad there."

Brick narrowed his eyes at Alaric who immediately threw his hands up in surrender.

"*Nothing* was as delicious as anything you've ever made, Brick, I assure you," I interjected before the cook killed my husband.

"Aye! Att'll be for sure! Hows about I whip ye up a roast duck wit cherry sauce and mashed po-ta-toes?"

Alaric looked like he was salivating and I couldn't imagine anything tasting better. I could practically taste the butter in the mouth. We both nodded emphatically which made both Malisande and Brick erupt into laughter.

"What's so funny?" Alaric asked, looking at me to see if I was in on the joke. I shrugged, just as confused as he was.

Malisande was laughing so hard, she could barely catch her breath. "Oh, we're sorry! It's just that... well... it's actually the last meal we had before everything happened. So technically, we just ate roast duck with cherry sauce and mashed potatoes a few nights ago."

I eyed my friend. *This* was what was so humorous? Then again, I suppose with the absurdity of the whole situation, we really did need to laugh at these types of things. I hugged her again. I just couldn't stop hugging her.

"Oomph!" she gasped as I knocked the wind out of her, her arms flapping helplessly at her sides. "Well, enough of that," she said, pushing me away. "We have a lot of catching up to do. I'll see you tomorrow afternoon for tea?"

I smiled. Before the spell, Malisande and I enjoyed tea together every afternoon. The tea was wonderful, but it was the court gossip that I most looked forward to. It was never anything too scandalous, but I always found the stories so interesting. As a princess, I didn't get to experience these things first hand, so tea time with Malisande allowed me to live vicariously through the court.

"Yes, tea tomorrow." I took her hands in mine and squeezed them affectionately.

"Aye! And I'll be servin' ye pie holes later dis evenin. An' don't rush me if ye want perfection! I won't 'ave it!"

Alaric clapped Brick on the shoulder and his eyes softened. "Thank you. Thank you both."

"For what?" Malisande asked.

"For being our friends," Alaric replied with a sweet smile. I could tell he was as happy to see Malisande and Brick as I was. It was just a bit more normalcy in our new lives.

* * * * *

"You really didn't remember?" Malisande asked me. We were sipping tea in the solarium and I was telling her about the spell, my past lives and everything at the Phoenix Mansion that led to Alaric and me finally being able to come home.

"Not a thing," I replied, taking another sip of tea. It was an herbal blend that I had loved in the old days. The old days... I guess that's what I was calling my pre-spell life now.

"But you remember each of the lives you had during the spell?" She was leaning in so closely to me, clearly absorbed by my tale.

I nodded. "I didn't remember them while we were under the spell. Each life at the time was the only one that existed to me. But once the spell was broken, they all came back to me in pieces."

"And Alaric was with you in each life?"

Reminded of my mate and our unique bond, a smile tugged at my lips. "He was. I obviously didn't know it at the time. We weren't always 'together,' but he was always there."

Malisande sighed dramatically. "That's so romantic! I mean, truly! The fact that your mating bond kept your souls connected like that? What could be more beautiful?"

I shrugged with a coy grin on my face.

Malisande placed her tea down on the table. "Okay, let's talk about your coronation!" She clapped her hands in excitement.

"Well, we want to do it as soon as possible. Alaric is adamant about wanting it to be a giant celebration. We have a long journey still ahead of us, but he wants everyone to come together and have this moment. To feel the love we're all fighting desperately to preserve."

"You know, I can hardly believe it's finally here," Malisande said, her voice brimming with anticipation. "When we were young, I used to dream of this for you. I had obviously hoped for it to be under different circumstances, but it's something that you've been preparing for your whole life."

Malisande's reminder of our childhoods together instantly brought me back to all of the times we would play coronation in the courtyard. She took so much joy in playing priestess and placing my small tiara on my head each time, declaring me the Queen of Fiah and insisting any servants nearby clap and cheer for me.

It was a simpler time, but a happy one.

"It still doesn't feel real," I replied, my voice coming out in a rasp. So many emotions were bubbling at the surface. "But it feels right. Alaric was always meant to be a king, despite his birth order."

"And *you* were always meant to be a queen." Malisande paused. "You and Alaric have built something truly special. This coronation is a celebration of your love."

I smiled, a twinkle in my eye. "I must admit, I was hesitant to have such a big celebration at a time like this, but I'm looking forward to what's being planned! The grand feast, the music, the dancing... And the procession? The streets will be lined with flowers! It will be a beautiful day!"

"A beautiful day for a beautiful queen."

My eyes met Malisande's.

"It will be a spectacular day," I whispered into my tea.

"You and Alaric have been through so much. You deserve it."

"I often can't believe my good fortune to have been gifted this mating bond by the Fates. I truly could not have asked for a more perfect partner."

Malisande nodded, her eyes full of affection. "The love between you two is something special. And everyone will feel it. The way you support each other – it will fill the whole castle – the whole kingdom – with understanding that this war with Remis needs to take place. And that there's no one better than you and Alaric to protect us."

I smiled and nodded my head once for emphasis. "Tomorrow, we'll celebrate. We'll dance, we'll laugh, we'll make memories."

Malisande reached over and squeezed my hand. There was so much love in her eyes for me, but she couldn't possibly know that I loved her even more. I would do anything to protect her and her future with Brick.

The coronation wasn't just about crowns or oaths – it was about the love that bound *all* of us together. And wasn't that the most beautiful thing of all? Tomorrow we would celebrate. And then we would show Remis that love conquers all.

20

CHAPTER TWENTY

I woke up in the morning with a smile on my face and Alaric's arm wrapped around my waist as I felt his chest rise and fall with his breaths against my back. I arched my back the smallest bit and was rewarded by Alaric's sleepy moan. I turned in his embrace and kissed his jawline.

"Good morning, my handsome prince!" I whispered cheerily. "Today's the last day I'll be able to call you that."

Alaric smiled, his eyes still closed. "Astoria, you can call me whatever you want as long as I draw breath. And even then, the After Realm won't be able to stop me from answering to your call."

He rolled me onto my back and leaned in to kiss me, but we were interrupted by a knock at the door. Alaric groaned with frustration. "How does this keep happening?"

I giggled. "Come in," I answered as I sat up in bed, stretching my arms over my head while I attempted to stifle a yawn.

My maid, Leeza, walked in, carrying a large, white box. "Good morning, Your Highnesses. I apologize for the interruption, but we're on a tight schedule today."

I leaned over and kissed Alaric's forehead. "Out," I told him as I swatted his hip.

"Ugh, what?" he replied as he propped up on his elbows.

"I have to get ready and I want you to be surprised when you see me." I kept grinning, knowing how miserable this was making Alaric.

"Astoria, love of my life, this isn't our wedding. I can see you in your dress," Alaric tried to reason, rolling over towards me and burying his face into his pillow.

I bounced out of the bed, his arms shooting out as he tried to reach for me, to no avail. "Alaric," I pretended to whine. "Humor me, please? I promise it will be worth it."

He shifted so that his head was still resting on his pillow, but his face was no longer smushed into it. He smiled back at me. "Mm... I'm sure it will be." There was a twinkle in his eye and I knew exactly where his mind had gone.

"Shoo!" I exclaimed, swatting at him again. When I looked back up, I saw Leeza, still standing in the doorway, trying not to openly laugh. Alaric and I had to be the strangest royals in all of the realm.

It took some coaxing, but eventually Alaric left for the bed chamber he would stay in when we were courting. Left alone with Leeza, I was ready to start the day as a princess and end it as a queen.

She prepared my bath and I took it upon myself to open the box that contained my coronation gown. I pulled the dress out, placing it up against my body, when I saw an envelope fall to the ground. When it hit the floor, I saw the wax seal and immediately recognized it.

My mother's seal.

I tossed the gown onto the bed and picked up the letter with shaking hands. What was this? And how did it get in my dress box?

I broke the seal and slowly pulled the letter out. It was definitely from my mother, written in her perfect penmanship.

My Dearest Daughter,

If you're reading this, all has gone to plan and you'll be getting crowned today. I've asked the modiste to hold onto this letter until your coronation. I want you to know how proud I am of you and Alaric. I knew you would get here.

The first time I met Alaric, I saw your father in him. And although he passed before you were born, I can assure you that the two share many qualities that make a great king and husband. Be each other's rock and there will be no storm you can't withstand.

Know that I am in the After Realm today, smiling down at you. The road ahead will not be an easy one, but I will always be by your side because I am always in your heart.

All of my love,
Your Mother

Hot tears were spilling down my face, blurring my vision. I wiped them away, but more fell in their place. I missed her so much. I would never stop missing her. But I would always make her proud. And I trusted Alaric to do the same.

Leeza stepped out of the bathing chamber and let out a small gasp when she saw me crying on the floor. "Your Highness, are you all right?" she asked as she tentatively stepped to my side.

I wiped away a fresh batch of tears.

"Yes, Leeza, I'm fine, thank you."

She gave me her hand to help me off of the floor. "Your bath is ready."

I nodded and made my way into the bathing chamber. I placed my hand into the tub to heat the water before removing my nightgown and then submerged myself fully. Holding my breath, I let the water that filled my ears warp the sounds around me. I stayed beneath the surface, allowing the increasing burning sensation in my lungs to ground me. The pain was a tingling sensation compared to the overwhelming pain I felt at the loss of my mother. She had been gone for almost two hundred years, but to me, it was a recent loss. I understood how the humans felt to grieve their loved ones because I felt the same way.

Once the pain became too much to bear and I felt lightheaded, I reemerged, gasping for air. I saw poor Leeza jump, but being the professional she was, she reined her feelings in and started lathering my hair with soap.

I focused on the feel of Leeza's fingers massaging my scalp. The hot, lavender-scented water. The bittersweet taste of the coffee my maid had brewed for me while I was insanely holding my breath under water. Today I would be

Queen. And my mother was so sure that this day would come. It didn't seem fair that she couldn't share the day with me. But I knew in my heart that her words were true. She was always with me.

Once I was cleaned and dried, Leeza braided my auburn hair into an elaborate coronet before lining my eyes with a dark kohl and dabbing tinted beeswax onto my lips. I slipped out of my silk robe and into my gown. Mother and I had designed it when I was younger. A crimson velvet adorned with gold embellishments and a train to match. Leeza buttoned me up from behind and then finished the look off by placing two teardrop shaped diamond earrings in a gold setting into my ears and a necklace to match around my neck.

"You look… breathtaking…" Leeza stated and I could tell from the way she said it that she truly meant it. She gently took my hands and squeezed them. I knew what she wanted to say, but was afraid to for fear of making me cry again. But there were no words necessary. My mother had already said them in a letter written long ago: she was proud of me.

Leeza escorted me towards the stairs where Alaric was waiting with Renfred. They were deep in conversation until Alaric spotted me out of the corner of his eye and like a magnet, his gaze was drawn to mine.

"Astoria," he loosed a breath as we walked towards each other. I swear, he looked more in love with me than he had on our wedding day. But he looked equally good, his velvet robes matching my dress. "You look like a dream." He took my hand and placed a kiss atop it as he bowed to me.

A smile pulled at my lips as I curtsied to him, bowing my head in reverence.

"What are you doing?" he asked. His brows furrowed in confusion, but he had a grin on his face.

I stood to face him and clasped his hands in mine. "We are equals in every way and I have the same respect and admiration for you as you do me. Soon, everyone in the kingdom will know that."

I didn't know it was possible, but even more love poured from his eyes. The prince who wasn't meant to be the king because of his birth order, but was always meant to be *a* king. My mother was right. Alaric was going to rule Fiah alongside of me and was going to show the kingdom and those that surrounded it just what it meant to be a kind and gracious leader. We would never be like Remis, using fear to rule and taking from our subjects.

"Shall we?" Alaric asked as he offered me his hand and walked with me down the staircase to our future.

A carriage was waiting for us just outside the castle doors and took us into the town. Fae and humans lined the streets, cheering, waving flags and throwing flowers at us as we rode by. I couldn't help but to laugh and wave in return.

Once we reached the center of the town, we were brought to the raised dais that was built specifically for the coronation. There were two wooden thrones that were intricately designed with golden filigree and flowers carved into them. Despite only being used for today's ceremony, someone had put a lot of effort into these works of art. Already standing atop the dias was the high priestess with our crowns gleaming beside her in the sunlight.

We joined the high priestess and she began chanting her blessings. Then Alaric and I took our solemn vows. She raised my crown, and the air seemed to still, as if the entire realm held its breath in reverence. I lowered my head, my expression unwavering as I thought of my mother and imagined her standing beside me. With a solemn gesture, the high priestess placed the crown on top of my coronet. It fit perfectly, as it was supposed to, but the feel of it still surprised me. The town square erupted in a chorus of deep, resonant cheers and I smiled back at them.

Then, Alaric stepped forward and with eyes shining with quiet resolve, lowered his head. The square held its breath once more. Alaric raised his head, his new crown resting with ease atop his silvery-white hair. The cheers that followed were just as thunderous, though there was something more tender in them. My people recognized Alaric's grace, his wisdom, and the heart that would lead them all and they accepted him wholeheartedly.

"I love you," he whispered to me.

"I love you, too," I replied, my heart bursting with happiness.

Together, we stood, the king and queen, united not only in our own destiny, but in our kingdom's. The golden crowns above our heads glinted as symbols of our power and our promise. Alaric's hand reached for mine, our fingers interlocking in a perfect bond as we turned to face our people. The silence that followed was filled with the weight of history, the sacredness of the vow we had just taken, and the unspoken understanding that this moment would echo through the annals of time, forever etched in the memory of our kingdom.

A cheer rose, louder this time, and the Kingdom of Fiah had its rulers again. Our reign, heralded by crowns, was now officially upon us.

* * * * *

The feast back at the castle that evening was beyond anything I could have imagined. Brick and the rest of the kitchen staff had really outdone themselves. There were roasts of chicken, duck, pork and beef with a gravy for each. Mounds of mashed potatoes and roasted root vegetables adorned the serving tables. Savory and sweet pies, fluffy breads and rolls and desserts made with the most beautifully colored frostings were laid out as far as the eye could see! And wine! Lots and lots of wine!

It was truly an incredible sight.

Music echoed throughout the ballroom as everyone danced. It was impossible to not be part of the merriment. Even the most stodgy of courtiers could be found in the center of the room, shifting their weight from side to side.

I smiled down at everyone. This was exactly what Alaric and I had wanted. A true celebration. In this moment, everything was perfect.

Alaric looked over at me and took my hand in his. I looked down at our hands and then back up at him.

"May I have this dance, Queen Astoria?" He winked at me. Fates, I loved that wink!

I bowed my head ever so slightly. "You may, King Alaric."

We stood from our seats and Alaric led me to the center of the ballroom as partygoers cleared the way and made space for us. Alaric wrapped his arm around me and pulled me towards him as we swayed in time with the music.

"I love you," he whispered in my ear. "I have always loved you and I always will love you."

My heart picked up pace in my chest and I sighed against him. "I love you, too, Alaric." I paused before continuing. "I truly don't have the words to express how I feel about you and how you make me feel."

Alaric nodded, understanding.

"So what do we do now?" I asked, resting my head on his chest.

Alaric chuckled and the sound reverberated through me. I looked up at him curiously.

"Now we go back to our room and I show you how damn sexy I think you look in that crown."

21

CHAPTER
TWENTY-ONE

Alaric wasn't kidding. As soon as the song finished, he scooped me up in his arms and carried me out of the ballroom. The sound of drunken cheers and whoops followed us out as we made our way down the hall and towards the stairs up to our suite.

Still cradling me, Alaric used some of his fae magic to open the door to our chambers and I gasped softly. The entire room was illuminated by the soft, golden glow of candlelight. Red rose petals created a trail from the doorway to the bed and there were at least a dozen vases of peonies scattered throughout the space. It was breathtakingly beautiful.

I turned my head up at Alaric and he was smiling a toothy grin.

"You?" I asked.

"Who else?" he shrugged his shoulders, which lifted me slightly up and then down along his body. I kissed his cheek as he walked slowly towards the bed and placed me down gently beside it. Slowly and incredibly methodically, Alaric began to undress me, undoing each button with immense attention to the task. Finally, the gown fell to the floor and I carefully stepped out of it. Before I even fully turned to Alaric, his lips were on mine, hot and greedy.

I pulled away and brought my hands to my head to take the crown off, but Alaric stopped me.

"Leave it on," he instructed with a grin.

"As you wish, Your Majesty," I acquiesced with a curtsy.

I crawled along the bed towards the center as Alaric pulled off his tunic and pants with a speed so contrary to how slowly he had undressed me, I couldn't help but stifle a laugh. He reached for his crown, but I tutted him.

"Absolutely not. That's an order."

Alaric cocked his head to the side with a smirk on his face as he joined me on the bed. He pulled me into his lap so that I was straddling him.

"Is that your first official order, Your Majesty?"

I nodded affirmatively. "It is. And if you don't obey my command, I'll be forced to chain you up in the dungeons."

"Is that a promise?" he asked, his icy blue eyes staring deeply into mine.

Instead of answering him with words, I answered him with my lips. It was the only answer he really ever needed.

I sat back a bit and looked at Alaric, taking his face in my hands.

"Hi," he said.

I smiled. "Hi," I replied.

"What are you thinking?" he asked me as he tucked loose strands of hair behind my ear.

I huffed a laugh. "That you're the luckiest male in all the realms." My smile was so wide that I was sure Alaric could count each and every one of my teeth.

He shook his head in disbelief. "You don't think that I know that? That I don't think about that every time I look at you?"

Then he kissed me again and this kiss was a different kind of promise. The mating bond responded in kind, vibrating through my soul. Alaric tipped my head back and I opened for him, letting out a deeply satisfied moan.

Alaric was already hard beneath me, so I seized the opportunity to chase my release by rolling my hips along the length of him, eliciting a guttural moan from him. Fates, I needed more. So much more.

I dragged my fingers down his chest and over his abs, relishing the feel of all of his hard parts against my softer ones.

Alaric grabbed his erection and I lifted up slightly onto my knees. He brought the tip to my entrance and a breathy moan slipped through my lips as it slid through my wetness. Alaric gave me a devilish grin which I reciprocated as I slid down onto him. Our moans filled the room as I slowly continued riding Alaric, his hands on my hips guiding me. Needing to feel closer to him, I leaned over, my hardened nipples grazing his chest, and kissed him again.

Alaric moved a hand to my back and gasped, "Stay with me here."

I nodded and felt my core throb as I picked up the pace, Alaric using the motion to thrust into me. My eyes rolled to the back of my head. Fates, I was so close.

Before I could register what was happening, Alaric wrapped his arms around my waist and in one swift motion, rolled me onto my back so that he was hovering over me, my legs now wrapped around him.

He slammed back into me to the hilt and my moan turned into a scream of his name. Hearing his name on my lips made him increase his pace. I was panting as he slid in and out of me over and over again. His thrusts soon became erratic and I knew we were both close.

"Are you going to come for me, my queen?" he said through gritted teeth.

I raked my nails down his back and nodded my head.

"Say it," he demanded as he placed a hand between us and pressed his thumb into the bundle of nerves at the apex of my thighs.

"Yes!" I shouted.

Alaric plunged into me harder and deeper as his thumb circled my center at just the right pressure and pace. Suddenly, stars shot through my field of vision as I clamped down on him, my core spasming and inevitably bringing him to his release, wringing out the last of my orgasm.

He panted into my neck, his warm breath tickling my sensitive skin. I took several deep, steadying breaths and wove my fingers through Alaric's hair to massage his scalp.

Alaric's head suddenly snapped up, confusion on his face as he realized something. "Does Fiah even have a dungeon?"

Completely satiated, I tossed my head further back on my pillow and laughed. "Of course not!" I exclaimed. "We have a few holding cells, though, so don't get any ideas or I *will* make good on my promise."

Alaric kissed my forehead and rolled off of me so that he could sit up in bed. "Come here," he said, gesturing to the space between his legs.

My eyes went wide. "Already?" I asked in surprise.

He chuckled. "Not yet. Just come here," he repeated, curling his pointer finger at me and then gesturing in front of him. I made my way over to him and he turned me around so that my back was just inches from his chest. He slid his hands from my arms, the contact making me shiver, and then used them to carefully remove my crown and put it on the nightstand beside him. He then took his off and went back to my head, gently undoing my coronet. His fingers ran through my hair, detangling it and fluffing it out so that it was a mass of waves cascading down my back.

"Perfect," he whispered before pulling my hair to one side and then placing a kiss on my shoulder. I turned back around to him and he tipped my chin up so that I met his gaze. "I'm so proud of you," he told me. He tucked a loose strand of hair behind my ear.

Tears welled up in my eyes again. Fates, would I ever get through a day without being so emotional?

"I am so honored to be your mate, husband and now king, Astoria. Knowing and loving you has been my greatest honor."

I grabbed Alaric's face and kissed him again. I didn't have the words to truly tell him how I felt, so I showed him instead.

* * * * *

Late the following morning, Malisande and I sat on the balcony of my suite, drinking coffee while watching Alaric and Renfred sword fight in the courtyard, the rest of our army about three hundred yards away. After keeping me up all night, I didn't know how Alaric managed to get up and train. I was content to sip my hot beverage with my dearest friend. Watching my husband get all sweaty again was an added bonus.

"You look… happy," Malisande ventured.

I gave her a soft smile. "I am, Mal. I am."

"No, I mean, you look *really* happy," she laughed. "I'm guessing the rest of the night was… eventful… after you left the party?"

I choked on my coffee, trying hard to swallow it before it came back up. "Malisande!" I exclaimed, feigning shock. "You're a lady!"

She giggled. "And you're the Queen of Fiah, but you still got some last night, am I right?"

I tossed my head back and laughed so hard, Alaric and Renfred ceased their fighting to look up at me. Alaric grinned and then winked at me before going back to training. It had been so long since he'd wielded a sword, that I was glad that he was finding the time to strengthen his abilities.

I looked back at Malisande. "Yes, we were… very busy last night." I considered my next words. "And this morning."

Now it was Malisande's turn to laugh heartily. "Good for you, Astoria."

In the distance, I could hear a knock at the door. "Come in!" I shouted as I turned in my chair. I saw Leeza step in, holding a letter. She walked onto the balcony and handed it to me.

"This came for you today, Your Majesty."

I turned the envelope over in my hand to inspect the seal. It wasn't one that I had seen before. Curious, I broke it and opened the letter, also not recognizing the handwriting. It was who the letter was addressed to inside that took me by surprise.

Tory and Ricky,

My stomach dropped. There was only one person who would call us that. I just couldn't believe he was writing to us.

You can imagine my surprise to discover your true identities after the trials… came to an unfortunate end. There is a lot that is still unclear to me, but just know, I will keep your secret. This favor will come at a price, though. One I will collect at a later date. Once I have finished grieving, I hope that I will be received at your kingdom so that we can discuss our experiences in greater detail.

There were no pleasantries to end the letter, just his signature - *Beaumont.*

He would keep our secret. Or so he thought. However he discovered our identities, they were no longer a secret. But my guilt over Alaric killing Scarlet would be the thing that granted him the favor he sought. Within reason, if it helped right the wrongs that were committed against Scarlet, I would give him what he asked for.

I looked up and saw Malisande staring at me. I could feel that my whole demeanor had just changed and she was probably giving me the space I needed to come to terms with whatever I was reading.

"It's okay," I assured her, waving off her concerned look. "The human from the trials that Alaric and I had befriended – "

"The one who was romantically involved with Scarlet?" Malisande questioned. She gave me her best scandalized look that would always cross her face when she was giving me the court gossip, wiggling her eyebrows up and down.

I nodded. "He wrote to us. He thinks that he's carrying some great secret of our hidden identities. He obviously doesn't know the full extent of everything we've been through. He wants to join us at court in the future." I decided against sharing the part about the favor. I didn't want to paint Beau in a bad light and something about the demand wasn't sitting right with me. I needed to know more before discussing it any further with anyone other than Alaric.

I didn't have much time to process Beau's letter before I noticed an odd black circle just behind Alaric. I blinked a few times, trying to clear my vision, but instead, the circle kept getting larger and looked like it was spiraling.

"Alaric!" I screamed. "Behind you!"

Instinctively, both Alaric and Renfred turned to see what I was pointing at, but retreated back a few steps. We were too far away for his voice to sound like anything more than a murmur, but I saw Alaric's mouth form the shape of "What is that?" to Renfred. The black hole was now larger than both of them and the realization of what was happening came to me as a male body stepped out of the void.

"It's a portal!" I yelled as I pushed Malisande back inside my suite to safety and King Remis of Tellus stepped through.

Remis was now standing in Fiah.

My Fiah.

Remis acknowledged Alaric and then immediately looked up and made eye contact with me. A chill ran down my spine. I brought my fire magic to the surface and I could feel it simmering at my fingertips, awaiting my command.

"I hear congratulations are in order," he stated and although he wasn't yelling, I could somehow hear him as if he were standing right next to me. "A restored kingdom and a coronation. How lovely for you!"

Alaric said something in return, but his voice wasn't being amplified like Remis' was. I leaned forward, trying to use my magic to hear better. Whatever Alaric said, it didn't please the mad king. He snarled and said something back, but I could no longer make out any of what was being said. He waved Alaric off and said something that made Alaric blink in confusion. Renfred turned to me – the same odd look spread across his face – and before I knew what was happening, at a speed that was almost unfathomable, Remis unsheathed his sword and sent it towards Alaric. Alaric was quick and raised his to deflect the blow, the clash of steel meeting steel making me cringe with fear. Immediately, the soldiers in the distance were racing towards Alaric.

Renfred swung his sword and in one swift motion, Remis pushed Alaric back and turned his attention towards the attacker. Alaric was already on the offense, but Remis fought like he had nothing to lose. Or rather, that he *couldn't* lose. Even two against one. Even with an army of soldiers closing in to defend their king.

Sparks flew as their blades clashed again and again. They were too close together for me to use my fire magic and not risk hitting Alaric or Renfred. Remis swung again and Alaric ducked and then, faster than my eye could track, Remis thrust his sword forward.

Into Alaric.

Alaric fell back and crumbled to the ground, his eyes vacant.

I felt the mating bond snap and I screamed a blood-curdling scream, but I couldn't hear it. Everything fell away in slow motion. I couldn't hear anything but the high-pitched ringing in my ears. All I could feel was an unbearable agony as I shot a blaze of fire towards Remis. Of course, his magic protected him.

"I'll be seeing you, Little Queen," he said as he looked up at me, smiled and waved. Remis stepped back through the portal and it closed around him just as the army burst forward a moment too late.

Renfred ran to Alaric as I turned and raced out of my chambers and down the stairs at a speed I didn't know was possible. Everyone I passed was nothing more than a blur of colors. I tried to tug on the mating bond, but it was barely there. It was just a thread.

But it was a thread. It was something.

I yelled maniacally for a healer. Over and over, I kept screaming for a healer as I threw every bit of my magic into my legs and finally fell to Alaric's side, taking his hand in mine. His lips tugged ever so slightly to one side, but his eyes were glazed over and there was blood everywhere. So much blood. Remis' sword protruded from Alaric's stomach.

But it wasn't Remis' sword. Not the onyx sword.

Why would Remis run Alaric through with a sword that wasn't imbued with black magic?

There was no time to question it. I looked at Renfred and suddenly realized that we were surrounded by the entire army. They were circled all around us with looks of shock and fear spread across their faces. Had I pushed past them when I was running towards Alaric? I couldn't remember, but knew that I must have.

I looked back at Renfred and tried to keep my voice steady as I said, "I need you to pull out the sword on my count."

He nodded, but Alaric squeezed my hand. I looked down at him, tears falling in streams down my face.

"I have loved you irrevocably," he said, his voice a raspy whisper. "Death changes nothing. I will wait for you in the After Realm, my love."

The tears wouldn't stop flowing. Was this what the Fates had in store for us all along? If so, then they were just as evil as Remis and I would stop at nothing to destroy them all.

"Absolutely not," I cried. "Don't you dare die on me, Alaric. You *can not* die! I won't allow it! Do you hear me?" I was screaming. Daring the Fates to stop me. If they took Alaric from me, I would burn the realm to ashes.

"Astoria," he sighed, his breathing becoming more labored.

"No." It was a command.

An order.

A plea.

I looked at Renfred and nodded at him before he placed his trembling hands on the pommel and then pulled the sword out of Alaric in one swift motion. Alaric bowed off the ground, but I immediately placed my hands on the wound to cauterize it. Alaric winced in pain, but pain was good. Pain meant he wasn't feeling the numbness of death.

Three of the castle's healers dropped to their knees. I removed my hands and allowed them to place theirs on Alaric's body. A white light emanated around his abdomen and I desperately prayed to whoever would listen to me to save my mate.

He was good. He was everything kind and wonderful that belonged in this realm. I needed him by my side. I couldn't do this without him. I wouldn't.

"We've done all that we could," one of the healers, Rhodiola, told me, her eyes not meeting mine.

"What – what does that mean?" I stuttered. I looked down at Alaric with wide eyes. This couldn't be the end. It just couldn't.

"The rest is in the hands of the Fates," the healer, Rosea, stated. "He needs rest, Your Majesty."

I nodded, barely processing what she said. I tried to say 'thank you,' but my throat was so dry that no words came out. They bowed their heads solemnly to me and then slowly walked back towards the castle. Everything started to spin as I looked back at Alaric. The last thing I saw was several of the soldiers carefully lifting him onto a make-shift gurney before everything went black.

22

CHAPTER
TWENTY-TWO

I woke up in my bed in the middle of the night.

Alone.

I was alone.

"You're not alone," a female voice said next to me and, startled, I jumped. "Sorry, I didn't mean to scare you. I was telling you that you weren't alone to avoid frightening you."

Malisande. She was sitting in a chair that she had moved from the corner of the room to the side of my bed, a book in one hand and a candle in the other. Fates bless this female.

"Where's Alaric?" I asked and I could hear the terror in my raspy voice.

"He's resting in a guest room. The healers thought it best."

I was already climbing out of my bed. "The healers were wrong," I mumbled.

Malisande stood up and squeezed my arm. "Astoria, please. Stop."

I growled at my friend and immediately felt awful. This wasn't her fault, but she was keeping me from my mate and right now, I needed Alaric more than I needed air.

Malisande let go of my arm, but didn't back away. "Astoria. Renfred is outside your room. He needs to talk to you and then you can go join Alaric. But, please, talk to him first."

I looked at her face and considered what she said for a moment before leaning back and sitting on my bed. I nodded to her and she left the room to get Renfred who literally was right outside the door. I didn't know how long I had been out, so I had no idea how long he had been waiting there.

Renfred looked me over as he approached the bed. "How are you feeling?" he asked.

I took a deep breath. "Not great, Renfred. But better than Alaric, I'm sure," I grumbled and then dropped my head in defeat. "Thank you for helping me. For helping him." I lifted my gaze to Renfred.

He bowed his head. "Always," he said. "But I need to talk to you about something that Remis said before he... you know..."

"What is it?" I asked anxiously, wringing my hands in my lap.

"Remis said that he always knew that his daughter would get in his way. He just didn't know that bribing some fae named Beau to kill her would set all of this in motion."

My lips formed a straight line as my brow furrowed. "That doesn't make any sense." I replied.

"That's what Alaric said."

I scratched my head. "That doesn't make sense at all. For one, Beau is human. He's not fae. And he didn't kill Scarlet. Alaric did." Something wasn't adding up and I couldn't figure out what it was. Beau's letter and then Remis' arrival? What was I missing?

Renfred shrugged and shook his head. "I don't know why he said it. Maybe he was intentionally trying to throw us off to catch Alaric off guard." He cringed on the last word. Guard. He was supposed to be guarding Alaric and he failed.

"Renfred, it wasn't your fault," I tried to assure him. "This was all Remis. And he will pay dearly for what he did to Alaric." I was growling again. Like an animal. This is what Remis had reduced me to. Not a queen, but a beast.

But if the beast was what he wanted, the beast was what he was going to get.

Suddenly, I felt a tug in my chest. It was so slight that it felt more like a palpitation, but it was there. A second thread!

"I have to go!" I exclaimed, jumping off the bed and running for the door. No one was going to stop me from seeing my husband again. I didn't know what room they had put Alaric in, so I followed the pull inside of me. Down the hall, just a few doors down from my own, I knew Alaric would be there.

I cracked open the door, hoping it wouldn't creak and wake Alaric from the sleep he desperately needed to heal.

I knew he needed his rest; I just wanted to watch him do it. He was lying on the bed, shirtless, his bandages exposed. They looked free of blood, so there was that to be grateful for. The cauterization worked.

I looked through the items sitting on the nightstand beside him. A tonic for pain and a tonic for infections. There were also some herbs – chamomile, rosemary and turmeric – that I remembered from my studies would reduce any swelling Alaric was experiencing.

"Astoria," Alaric croaked. Without thinking, I grabbed the pitcher of water by his bedside and poured him a glass. I was planning to cradle his head and pour the water into his mouth, but he surprised me by taking the glass from my hands. He lifted his head off of his pillow ever so slightly and tipped the water slowly into his mouth.

"Hello, my love." I was doing everything in my power not to cry again as I placed a hand behind his head to cradle and support it. He handed me the glass and placed his head back down, panting hard. I brushed the hair out of his face.

"That feels good," he murmured, his eyes closed.

There was a chair beside him that I pulled closer. "Then I'll keep doing it," I replied softly, gently brushing his locks with my fingertips almost rhythmically. "How do you feel?"

"Like I was stabbed." He started to laugh, but it became a series of coughs. "Ow. Don't make me laugh."

"I'm pretty sure you just did that to yourself." Instead of appreciating the sound of Alaric's laughter, my mind wandered back to where it shouldn't have and I couldn't stop the tears from falling down my cheeks again. "You almost left me."

Alaric took a deep breath that sounded more like a wheeze. "I've been trying really hard not to."

I nodded, although I knew he couldn't see me.

"Will you lie down with me?" he asked.

I didn't answer, but pushed the chair back and climbed onto the bed slower than I ever have in my life. I didn't want to hurt him, but, selfishly, I needed this as much as he did. He put his arm out to the side and I placed my body alongside his, careful not to touch his wound as I wrapped my arm gently around him. I rested my head on his chest and then he wrapped his arm around my shoulder, letting out a big sigh.

"I don't know what's worse," he began, still speaking slowly and with his eyes closed. "Getting fileted by a sword or the bond severing."

I could only speak into one of those things. "The bond didn't sever, Alaric. Not entirely. Can't you feel it?" As if hearing my words and wanting to prove them to my mate, what little was left of the bond hummed. He smiled and a tear slid free from his eye, falling down his cheek and onto his pillow.

"I feel it."

I released a breath that I didn't realize I was holding. "I'm going to kill him," I said aloud. Maybe to Alaric, but more for my own benefit. How dare Remis try to take what is mine? And how dare he make my mate cry? "I'm going to kill him," I repeated, my teeth gritted to the point of pain.

"Astoria, I would really rather you didn't talk about other males when you're in bed with me. It's not good for my ego."

I wanted to playfully hit him, but decided against it.

"You almost left me," I told him again.

"I promise I'll try to not do it again."

"Good," I replied.

Alaric grunted and I looked up at him, worry etched on my face. "What's wrong?"

"I wanted," he grunted again. "My body isn't cooperating."

"What are you talking about?" I demanded. I untangled myself from Alaric to give him room for whatever he was trying to do. "What do you want?"

"Maybe if you sit on my face. My mouth seems to work just fine."

My eyes went wide, my brows shooting to the top of my forehead. "Are you out of your damn mind?" I shouted in utter shock.

He chuckled. "My very beautiful and queenly mate is lying in bed with me after a near-death experience. It's the least I can do to thank the Fates for my good fortune. It was worth a shot, anyway."

Alaric reached for me and I settled back against him. I wanted to point out the very *bad* fortune of getting stabbed in the first place, but it didn't feel like the time. Moreso, I quickly realized that his breathing was becoming more even. Soon it got heavier and I knew that he was asleep. I thought about going back to my room, but knew I wouldn't be able to sleep without him. So I closed my eyes and breathed in Alaric's scent as a third thread wove together with the other two.

"Thank you," I whispered to the Fates. And then, exhausted, but satisfied, I fell asleep, too.

* * * * *

I woke up before the sun rose, the sound of Alaric's even breathing almost coaxing me back to sleep. After I disentangled myself from his arms, I tiptoed out of the room, careful to not creak any of the wooden floorboards. I had someone that I needed to see, but first, I made my way down to the kitchen.

Despite the early hour, the kitchen staff were already buzzing around, preparing the day's meals. The scents permeating through the room were intoxicating and my empty stomach growled in anticipation. When was the last time I ate? I immediately spotted Brick and made my way towards him.

"Good mornin', Yer Majesty!" he exclaimed cheerfully. "Hows ower king doin'?"

"He's doing much better," I replied. "I was hoping you can put something special together for him for breakfast. He probably won't eat much of it, but we need to get his strength up. Lots of meat and lots of vegetables. And fruit juice! He hates it, but I'll make him drink it."

I noticed an odd look on Brick's face. "Yer Majesty, it's already bein' taken care of. Whaddya think I am, eh? Some louse that dodn't love ower king? Ye offend me!"

I was about to apologize. I mean, he was right. I was just being overprotective. But before I could speak a word, Brick was pushing me out of the kitchen.

"Out witcha!" He laughed as he tossed me out into the hall. I turned around, feigning irritation, but was met with a plate of eggs and potatoes. Before I could open my mouth to say 'thank you,' the door closed behind me. I tried to furrow my brow, but my face refused to obey and was stuck in something that looked remarkably like happiness.

Alaric was alive and healing. Our mating bond was quickly restoring itself. And now I had even more of a reason to destroy Remis. He would never touch the ground of my kingdom again.

"Erina!" I shouted as I knocked on her door. "I need you! Now!" I popped a potato in my mouth and moaned at how good the butter and salt that coated my tongue tasted.

I heard a thump and then the rustling of clothes before Erina finally came to the door looking flushed. I couldn't help but notice the tail of a brown robe entering the bathing chamber.

Interesting, I thought. *I wonder which one it is... Probably Marcus...*

I shook my head to knock the image out of my head.

"How can I help you, Your Majesty?" Erina asked, glancing me over. "Is the king okay?"

I found it very entertaining that she wasn't inviting me in. "He's doing well, thank you. I wanted to talk to you about Remis' unannounced visit. We have wards surrounding the castle. How did he break them?"

Her eyes widened. "Do you think I – ?"

"No!" I exclaimed before she could finish her sentence. No, I didn't think that she was working with Remis. That would be ridiculous. She orchestrated the whole damn spell to protect Fiah. The last thing I would suspect was her involvement with the mad king.

Erina let out a small breath. "I imagine that the wards can't withstand black magic. I can't say for sure, since it's never been tested, but it's the only explanation."

"Is there a way to create stronger wards? We can't risk any more unanticipated attacks. And we need weapons. What is the magical equivalent to the onyx that holds Remis' black magic?"

"Your Majesty, please. Take a breath."

I didn't have time for a breath. I needed to protect my kingdom and everyone that I loved in it.

All of a sudden, I staggered backwards with wide eyes until I hit the wall, my plate of breakfast hitting the floor with a loud crash. I grabbed my chest with one hand and tried to steady myself as my knees buckled beneath me. I could barely breathe. Something was wrong. Something was very, very wrong and it felt all too familiar.

Without a second thought, I started to run towards Alaric's room. I could hear Erina's muffled voice, asking me what was wrong and then heard her footsteps behind me. I was running as fast as my legs could go, but felt like it was happening in slow motion.

Not again. This could not be happening again.

I threw the door open to Alaric's chambers and found him doubled over on the floor, gasping in pain.

"Alaric, what's wrong?" I asked, panicked. I dropped to his side and looked him over. His skin was practically colorless and his eyes… were wholly black. When Erina saw him, she immediately called for the healers who were suddenly by my side.

"Poison," I heard one of them say.

"What – what do you mean?" I stammered. "He was fine just a little while ago!"

"Delayed release, Your Majesty," another replied almost at the same moment that a different healer ran out of the room.

The sword. The sword that wasn't Remis' onyx one. He didn't need black magic to kill my husband. He just needed poison.

The healers adjusted Alaric's body so that he was spread out on the floor. His breathing was incredibly shallow. Too shallow.

"No," I cried earnestly. "Absolutely not! *You promised me!*" I was screaming. Again. It was happening all over again. Except this time, Alaric was now unconscious.

The healer that had previously left the room came back holding the vessel that once held my soul in one hand and a bottle that contained a liquid that was as orange as fire in the other. She handed both to Erina who knelt beside me.

"What is that?" I asked, wiping tears from my cheek and looking back at Alaric. Fates, he looked like death. This couldn't be happening…

Erina grabbed my arm, the act bringing my attention back to her. "Your Majesty, this is very important. I need you to listen to me."

I looked at her, but I could feel the glazed look in my eyes. My head felt heavy and the room was beginning to spin. I was so tired of it all. So sad and so tired.

"When I put your soul into the Firebird, only you were supposed to be reincarnated. But the Fates had other plans. They tied Alaric's soul to yours."

"He's *dying*, Erina! He's fucking *dying*!"

"He's not dying, Your Majesty. He's not dying." She seemed so sure of something that I could feel wasn't true.

"Since we returned to Fiah, I've been studying old texts and discovered that once in recorded history has there been a bond like yours and the king's. When their threads were severed completely, they both died, one shortly after the other. I couldn't risk all that we've worked for... All that your mother did. I loved her, Your Majesty. She was the most selfless creature to ever exist and I promised to protect you. I couldn't risk losing you if you lost the king. So I found a way to save you both."

Tears continued to stream down my face. I felt like I was gasping for air. It was then that I suddenly became very aware of the pain surging through my body. The sharp sting in my abdomen... The clenching sensation in my chest.

That's when I understood what Erina was saying: Alaric wasn't dying.

We both were.

"Your Majesty, I need you to trust me. Do you trust me?"

I did. Erina wasn't perfect, but I always believed that she loved my mother. And if she promised to protect me, I believed that she would. I nodded my head, having trouble catching my breath.

Erina closed her eyes, looking relieved. "Good. I need you to drink this."

She handed me the bottle of orange liquid that I took with trembling hands. I quickly eyed it before I tossed my head back and took a large gulp. Erina grabbed the empty bottle back from me.

"I'm going to put your soul back into the Firebird. The king's will go with yours and be safe until we can get the poison out of his body. As soon as he's in the clear, I'll bring you back."

I choked on a sob. "We won't be put in other bodies? Until someone dies?"

Erina shook her head. "Not this time. I promise. Marcus has been busy making a potion that will circumvent that. No prophecies to fulfill this time. As soon as the poison is out of the king, I'll bring you back."

I took a deep breath. What choice did I have, but to go along with this? If Alaric died, I would, too. Which I was grateful for. But what would come of the kingdom? I needed to do this and I needed it to work.

"Do it," I demanded.

Immediately, Erina began chanting and just as quickly, the pain started to subside, replaced by an incredible heat. My magic was being summoned by Erina's spell. It was consuming me. I grabbed Alaric's hand and tucked myself into his side before the world as I knew it disappeared.

23

CHAPTER
TWENTY-THREE

I was soaring high above Fiah. Higher into the clouds. I flew so high, I felt like I would wind up in another realm soon enough.

Which, apparently, I did because I was suddenly standing in front of the gates of the After Realm. I don't know how I knew that's where I was. I just did. I looked down and saw my legs. My fae legs. I was no longer the Firebird, but rather, I was myself. To prove it further, I brought my hands in front of me.

Definitely fae and not a bird.

The silver gates were glowing with an ethereal light and they emitted a warmth that I wanted to walk towards. It was like a pull that felt oddly similar to the mating bond. Was Alaric beyond the gates? Did Erina's spell not work? Fates, was I dead?

I felt the beginnings of a panic attack wanting to take hold of me when a figure emitting the same white glow as the gates approached and my heart felt a tug. But it wasn't my mate that was now standing in front of me.

It was my mother.

"Mother?" I cried, my shock overwhelming me. I ran to the figure and when I was sure that it was her, I threw my arms around her shoulders and squeezed as hard as I could.

"Hello, honey," she replied, rubbing my back in the calming way she always used to do.

I pulled back to get a good look at her. "Am I in the After Realm? Am I dead?"

My mother smiled softly. "Yes, you're in the After Realm, but no, you are not dead, my dear."

I cocked my head in confusion. "But you're dead and you're here?"

She offered me her hand. "We don't have much time. Walk with me."

Without hesitation, I laced my fingers with hers as she led me inside the gates of the After Realm. It was truly a stunning sight. Everything surrounding us had a soft glow. The gold trees with teal-colored leaves. The shimmering pink lake. The puffy pale yellow clouds. They all glowed with this beautiful light that made me feel warm. Safe. I felt so much peace walking in this place known for being where the souls of the dead are held.

"I'm very proud of you, Astoria," my mother told me. "The female you've become is nothing short of incredible."

We approached a bench and she gestured for me to sit down. I looked around and it was abundantly clear that we were the only ones around. "Mother, I need to get back to Alaric. He's dying. I can't lose him like I lost you."

My mother looked as if she was considering this, almost lost in thought. Finally she spoke, her voice so soft and melodious. It was as if music was playing whenever she opened her mouth.

"You won't lose him, honey. You can't. I made sure of that."

I knew that I should feel alarmed by her last statement, but I didn't. I felt... I just felt. Like my body was absorbing all of the serenity and love in this place.

"Where is everyone?" I asked. I mean, where were all of the dead souls? Why was no one else here?

"Hmm? Oh, that. Astoria, there's something that you need to know and I need you to listen to everything I say very carefully. Can you do that, sweetheart?"

I nodded my head. It felt fuzzy – like it was full of cotton and butterflies – but I nodded it just the same.

"Astoria, when I offered myself to set the spell, the Fates deemed my sacrifice to be so selfless that they granted me a higher power."

Incredulously, I looked at my mother. "A higher power?" What did that mean?

She nodded with a smile on her face. "I transcended as one of the Fates, dear."

I jumped off the bench. That couldn't be. They were the Fates. They just 'were.' Fae didn't become them... But that couldn't be true because here was my mother, someone I trusted with everything I had, telling me that she was one of the highest beings in creation. And something inside me just knew – just accepted – this as the absolute truth.

The Fates really did work in mysterious ways. My mother had not been gifted with any Fates-given magic, but the Fates gave her their ultimate gift: The honor of becoming one of them.

Suddenly, things started to click into place. Alaric's soul following mine when the spell was cast. Us being tied together until death. My mother saying that she made sure that I wouldn't lose Alaric.

She must have known exactly what I was thinking because she looked at me and bobbed her head, urging me to confirm my understanding.

"Erina said that there was only one other couple in history to have a bond as strong as mine and Alaric's. She said that if one of us passes on, the other's soul will join."

"It's true," my mother stated simply. "I learned of that couple many years before my death. Their love knew no bounds."

"Mother, I don't understand what's going on. I feel like I know this is all true, but it defies reason."

She smiled at that. A wide grin that made my heart leap. "Love defies reason, Astoria. The love between mates. The love between a mother and a daughter. The love that is the After Realm. You see, my darling, it's the Fates' responsibility to maintain the balance in all things. While remaining neutral parties. In my life, I made sure Fiah remained a peaceful kingdom, but that doesn't mean that those who live there don't face their own struggles. After life, the After Realm is where their souls come to experience true peace for all of eternity. It's the balance. It's the love the Fates have for all of those they serve. Astoria, do you know why the dark arts are forbidden?"

I shook my head from side to side. A wordless answer, but an answer nonetheless. The *why* never really mattered to me. I just accepted it for what it was.

"Black magic is sourced from the souls that have not yet made their way to the After Realm. When someone uses the dark arts, they are stealing the souls from their eternal serenity. It is the purest form of evil to deny a soul the love of the Fates."

"So why don't you stop Remis? Rid the realm of black magic entirely?"

My mother sighed, but a smile remained on her face. "Neutrality, my dear." She paused, looking deeply into my eyes. "I can't tell you what's to come. All I can tell you is that the Fates do not approve of Remis' ways. Long ago, they tied your soul to Alaric's. I just strengthened the bond."

"But I thought you must remain neutral," I pointed out.

"Why would making love stronger be considered biased?" She cocked her head at me, but a laugh escaped her. It was such a beautiful sound and one that I had greatly missed.

I opened my mouth to reply, but a blinding white light suddenly appeared behind my mother. As it grew in size, it reminded me of Remis' portal. Except I felt a strong pull towards this one. It was urging me to walk towards it.

Taking my hand in hers, my mother led me towards the white light. Was it calling to her, too?

"It's time, my dear," she said, taking me into her arms.

I wasn't ready to go, but yet, I wanted to. I wanted to go home, but I didn't want to leave my mother behind. I missed her so much. "I feel so weak," I sobbed against her shoulder.

She rubbed my back and then pulled away from me. "You are stronger than you know Astoria." She brought her hand to my chest and placed it on my heart. "You have a heart of gold, my love. Your power is in your heart." She gently guided me towards the portal. "Time works differently here," she informed me. "You've been gone long enough. You need to return to Fiah. To Alaric."

"I love you, mother!" I exclaimed as the light overwhelmed me.

"I'm always with you."

And then I woke up.

* * * * *

"Welcome back, Your Majesty."

I was in my bed, staring at the ceiling when I heard Erina's voice.

"Why does it smell like burnt toast?" I asked, sitting up slowly and rubbing the back of my head.

"You were on fire," Erina said in a matter-of-fact tone.

"Ah," I replied, as if that fully answered my question. "I feel like shit."

"You were on fire."

I shot Erina a glare. Fates, she could be a pain in my – Wait. "Where's Alaric? Is he okay? Did it work?" I was scrambling to get off the bed, but Erina jumped out of the chair she was sitting on and halted my attempt.

She smiled at me. Erina rarely smiled. It felt odd and unsettling. But also, *Erina was smiling*!

"Did I not tell you that I would bring you back when he was healthy again?"

My eyes went wide with elation. "He's really okay? Like, *really* okay and not okay like the last time?" I tugged on the mating bond and felt a strong tug back.

"The poison is completely out of his system. It has been for a few days now. He's not fully back to his old self, but he will be in the next day or two."

Did she say that the poison had been out of his system for a few days? "Erina, how long have I been out for?"

"It's been a week, Your Majesty."

A week? How was that possible? I was just talking to my mo – My mother. She had said that time worked differently. Was that real? Had I really been to the After Realm? It all felt real. I was used to having the occasional vision, but this felt different. It felt like an actual memory.

I wasn't ready to talk about it. I needed to let everything my mother said settle in me. And I needed to see my mate!

"Erina, thank you. For everything."

Erina smiled again. Fates, I was never going to get used to that. "It's my pleasure, Your Majesty." She dipped her head and I raced out of the room and towards Alaric's chambers. I threw the door open and realizing he could be sleeping, quickly reached for it before it slammed against the wall.

Gritting my teeth at the close call, I looked up and saw the love of my life smiling at me.

"Hi," he croaked, his throat obviously dry from lack of use.

"Hi," I squeaked as I walked tentatively towards him. I wanted to jump into his arms. To kiss every inch of his body. But I didn't know how he was feeling and was afraid to break him.

"You won't break me," he said.

I scrunched up my face in confusion. "How did you – "

"It was written all over your face," he replied with a grin. "Come here." He stretched his arms out towards me and I climbed onto the bed so that he could envelop me in his love. "I almost left you again. Even though I promised not to."

"It wasn't your fault," I told him as I nuzzled my face in the crook of his neck. "How could you possibly know that you were poisoned?"

I felt him shrug. "Still..."

I sat up and grabbed his face. "No. Not 'still.' You didn't do anything wrong. Remis is just... he's pure evil."

The memory of what my mother said slammed into me. Remis preventing souls from finding their peace was truly the epitome of evil.

"I need to tell you something. I'm still processing it my-self, so bear with me."

Alaric's face showed no emotion as he waited to hear what I had to say.

"I saw my mother."

Alaric's eyes widened in shock and somehow I knew it was the shock of the fact that I saw my mother and not the shock of the crazy statement I just made.

"Go on," he instructed me, rubbing my forearm affectionately with his thumb.

"It wasn't a vision. I don't think it was. It felt... different. I was in the After Realm and my mother... she... she was one of the Fates." I cringed and quickly began to regret not taking more time to think this through. It sounded absurd.

"Okay," Alaric started. "How is that possible?"

Encouraged that he wasn't flat out telling me that I was insane, I went on. "She said that her sacrifice was deemed so selfless that they granted her higher power. They made her a Fate. It's why we're so strongly tied together. The Fates gifted us the mating bond, but she strengthened it. Something about love defying reason."

Alaric nodded along as I spoke. "Erina mentioned something about our souls being tethered to one another's. That if I had died, you would have died, too. I guess we have your mother to thank for that."

"You believe me? You believe that I saw her?"

"Of course I do. Why wouldn't I?"

I worried my lip before settling back down into Alaric's heat. Not the heat of a fever, thank goodness. Just his natural, wondrous body heat. "I don't know. I guess because it sounds fantastical. My mother's one of the Fates and ensured that we'll never be without one another."

"It's a blessing, Astoria. We'll never have to live a day without the other. And while I would rather wait in the After Realm for you for hundreds of years to ensure you lived a long, happy life, I know that we're stronger together. We always have been. This gift from your mother just enhances that."

I told Alaric about the dark arts and why they're forbidden and shared everything I could remember from my conversation with my mother and my time in the After Realm. When I was done filling Alaric in, I asked, "So what do we do now?"

"Whatchyer gon do now is eat and put some meat on yer bones. Ye both look too thin an' too pale. When was the last time ye saw the sunlight?"

I burst out laughing. So focused on Alaric when I entered his room, I forgot to close the door and Brick had just barged in. But his intrusion was welcomed because he was carrying two trays of what looked like pastries and my eyes immediately focused on the chocolate croissants.

Brick's tone changed as he approached us and placed the trays down, one on Alaric's bedside table and one at the foot of the bed. "In all seriousness, howarya feelin,' the both of yous?"

Alaric reached out a hand to shake Brick's. "We're good, ol' boy. Thank you."

I nudged the platter on the bed with my foot. "I know that I'd be better if I had one of your famous chocolate croissants in my mouth." I looked up at Brick and gave him my most charming smile.

He grabbed two croissants and handed one to each of us. "Eer! Stick that in yer gullets! I'm off. Just wanted to bring ye both somethin' to snack on before dinner."

"Thank you!" Alaric and I shouted in unison as Brick left us alone and closed the door behind him.

"These really are delicious," I told Alaric, flicking a bit of pastry off of his mouth. We were getting buttery flakes all over the bed, but I didn't care. "But seriously, what do we do now? We need to kill Remis. And we need to do it fast."

"We need to give the armies more time," Alaric replied. "And while we do, you and I are going to rest. We're no good to anyone, let alone entire kingdoms, if we're not at full strength."

He was right, of course. But the longer we waited, the more anxious I was becoming. I wanted to end this once and for all. Two hundred years was a long time to wait for a peaceful existence. And I didn't just want an existence. I wanted a beautiful life with my husband, ruling over our kingdom.

"Fine. We'll wait," I acquiesced. "But while we wait, there are two things we need to figure out: how we're going to get Remis' sword and a Plan B in case we're wrong about it being the solution."

Alaric kissed the top of my head and lazily brushed back the hair that was curtaining my face. "Yes, my queen."

We spent the next few days within our chambers. Alaric moved back into our suite and we laid low and rested as much as we could. Soon, Alaric was back to his normal self and looking healthier than ever. Brick said it was because of him constantly plying us with food and I was hard pressed to disagree. It also helped that our friends were visiting us regularly to check in on us. Malisande stopped by every afternoon for tea and despite tea not being Alaric's preferred choice of beverage, some days he joined us, while other days he used that time to bathe. Renfred also popped in with updates on how the soldiers were faring with their training. Things were moving along and they were preparing the best course of action to proceed with this war. An attack on Tellus would be coming, but it had to be executed properly.

I was starting to believe that things were finally getting better when Leeza entered our chambers one afternoon, a letter in one hand and a sorrowful expression on her face.

"Leeza, what is it?" I asked, grabbing the letter from her. I turned it over and when I saw the seal from Alaric's parents, I prepared myself for the worst.

"It's the King of Gelu, Your Majesties. I'm so sorry, but the king is dead."

24

CHAPTER
TWENTY-FOUR

No, that couldn't be right. I must have misheard Leeza. I turned to Alaric and saw his crestfallen face. No, I hadn't misheard her. I broke open the seal as Leeza told us that the town is already mourning his death. They somehow found out about the king's passing just before the letter arrived.

When it rains, it really does pour, I thought absentmindedly. It felt like we were just getting dealt blow after blow.

"The letter is from your mother," I uselessly told Alaric as he stood over my shoulder reading. "She says that his heart stopped working." I looked up at Alaric. "Can fae's hearts just stop working? I thought that was only a human malady."

"I thought so, too," Alaric said, suspicion lacing his voice. He took the letter from me and continued reading. "I have to go to Gelu," he stated.

"*We* have to go to Gelu," I corrected him. I couldn't imagine letting him out of my sight. Not so soon after our near-death experience.

Alaric shook his head. "No, Astoria. You need to stay here. The queen can't take leave as a war is brewing. You need to stay here to show your determination and to give your subjects hope."

Frustrated, my mouth pressed into a hard line and my brow furrowed. "But I thought we were stronger together."

Alaric took my hands in his and held them to his heart. "We are. And we'll continue to be. I won't be gone long. Just long enough to pay my respects and conduct a small investigation. If this was Remis' doing, we'll make him pay. But if my father died at someone else' s hands – if it was an inside job – we need to know who did it. We need to know who our enemies are, Astoria."

He was right, of course. My sensible husband. But a certain word struck me while he spoke. In the midst of me thinking I was losing him, albeit differently, again, I had forgotten that this was Alaric's *father* we were talking about. His flesh and blood.

I reached up and wrapped my arms around his neck. "Are you okay?" I asked, weaving my fingers through his hair.

"I will be," he replied with a sigh, his eyes closed. "He was a king and all kings' lives are at risk."

I flinched. My father and Alaric's father's lives were both ended too quickly. And in recent weeks, my own king had been targeted. I knew that this was the trade off; that being royalty came with both rewards and risks. But I hated it, regardless.

"I need to go be with my family and take time to grieve his death while I'm gone. But I will be back. I *promise* that I will return to you."

"You promised not to almost die again and look how that turned out," I mumbled under my breath. It was meant to be a sarcastic comment, but I instantly realized that my timing was off and regretted it.

Alaric didn't seem to mind, though. He drew me into his arms so that I was flush against his body. "I have an idea."

I was definitely curious. "I'm listening..." I drawled with a smile on my face.

He kissed me quickly on the lips. "It's a surprise. Stay here." He ran out of the room and left me wondering. I sat down on the bed and stared out the window. I was going to worry about Alaric the entire time he was gone, so I knew that I needed something to distract me. Something like... Plan B. I would work with Erina in Alaric's absence to find another magical way of killing Remis, but I would also spend some time with Renfred to brush up on my defensive skills. The last time I had to fight in any capacity was during the trials.

The trials... they felt like a lifetime ago. Technically, they were a lifetime ago... Tory's lifetime, at least.

Alaric raced back into the room holding a plain, white box. He looked giddy, which was surprising since he just learned that his father had died. Or been murdered.

"What's in the box?" I asked. I kneeled on the bed as Alaric sat down, his weight making the edge of the mattress creak.

"When we were in Gelu, General Grinroff told me about this enchanted stationary that some of the soldiers use to communicate with their loved ones while they're away visiting other kingdoms or engaged in battle. It's very expensive, so not widely used or known about, but Grinroff was able to give me some leads on where to get some."

Puzzled, I looked at the stack of paper. "How does enchanted stationary work?" It looked like ordinary paper, but when I gently touched a piece with my fingertip, I could feel the soft buzz of magic.

"I can write you a message on it and when I fold the paper, you will find it somewhere nearby. I'm told within arm's reach. When it's opened, you'll be able to hear my voice reading you the message."

My eyes went wide with excitement. "So, if we keep writing messages back and forth, it will be like we're talking to one another? I won't be able to see you, but I'll be able to hear you?"

He chuckled. "It will be as if we're in different parts of our suite. You in our bed and me in our bath."

I leaned over and pressed a kiss to Alaric's mouth. "I love this. I love you. What a thoughtful gift!"

"I figured it would come in handy one day. I had hoped under better circumstances, but here we are, just the same." He smiled as he said it, but it didn't reach his eyes.

I brushed a lock of silvery hair from his face. "Go to Gelu, Alaric. But come home soon."

Alaric pulled me towards him so that I was pressed against his body once again. He kissed me deeply and I kissed him back with just as much ferocity. This wasn't goodbye. It couldn't be.

* * * * *

The next day, I headed down to the courtyard where Renfred was already waiting for me. The sun was barely up, orange and pink streaking the cloudless sky. I could already feel the humidity permeating the air and knew it was going to be a hot day.

"Good morning, Your Majesty!" Renfred exclaimed as he met me and handed me a sword.

I reached out to take it from him. "Good morning, Renfred. Please, call me Astoria," I told him.

He looked at me hesitantly and then opened his mouth, an objection clear in his eyes.

I put a hand out to stop him. "I insist. At least while we're out here, please. I'm not your queen, I'm your mentee."

"My mentee," he repeated slowly as if seeing how the words tasted in his mouth.

I gave my head a good nod. "Yes, I'm your mentee and you are my mentor and unless you want me to start calling you sir, I expect you to call me Astoria. Plain and simple Astoria." I smiled a toothless grin.

Renfred took a breath that looked like it pained him. "Fine," he replied. "Astoria," he bit out.

My grin widened, almost all of my teeth now showing. "See? That wasn't so hard, was it?"

Renfred rolled his eyes. "First things first, let me see your stance."

I brought my sword in front of me and spread my legs apart, bending my knees slightly. Fates, it had been so long since I wielded a sword. It felt strange, but good. It made me feel stronger than I had in a while.

"Good," Renfred stated, stepping behind me. "Is it alright if I make some adjustments?" I looked behind me and saw that he was holding out his hands, asking for permission to touch me.

"Yes, Renfred, of course."

"Bring your legs a bit closer together," he instructed as he placed his hands on my outer thighs. "Good." Then he moved to my hips to square them. "Now loosen your grip on the pommel. Your knuckles are turning white."

My gaze drifted down and, Fates, he was right! I immediately opened my hands and wiggled my fingers before gripping the sword again.

"Excellent! Now let's work on some basic maneuvers. Just to get you used to the feeling again." Renfred stepped in front of me and drew his sword.

We began to move. Slowly at first, increasing our speed and getting into a rhythm as we went. Ever so often, Renfred would shout directions at me.

"Watch my shoulders!"

Clang!

"Move with your sword!"

Clang!

Soon, I was sweating and panting... And it felt incredible. I had forgotten how empowering it felt to train like this. I sat down in the grass and Renfred dropped a waterskin at my side. I grabbed it and quickly removed the top before I gulped down its contents.

"Tomorrow, let's work on combining your sword skills with your magic so that they're working in tandem with one another," Renfred suggested.

I took another large gulp, the sound making me choke out a laugh. "Okay. Thank you, Renfred. This was so helpful."

"It's my pleasure, Your – Astoria." He smiled sheepishly and then his gaze changed. It was as if he suddenly went somewhere in his mind.

"Are you okay, Renfred?" I dropped the waterskin at my side and stood up to face him.

He blinked a few times, clearing his head, and directed his eyes back to mine. "Can I... talk to you about something?" he asked hesitantly.

"Of course you can! You're one of Alaric's oldest friends and most trusted confidants. You can talk to me about anything."

Renfred took a deep breath. "I'm worried that he's too strong."

I already knew the answer, but I asked anyway. "Who's too strong? Remis?"

Renfred nodded. "Astoria, I felt his power that day. Not just his strength or his Fates-given abilities. I felt the ripples of black magic coming off of him and it terrified me. It still does."

And just like that, all of my new-found strength and empowerment flew out the metaphorical window. It wasn't Renfred's fault, but this was the first time someone other than Alaric was speaking my fears out loud. Since we returned to Fiah, the kingdom had blindly backed us up and supported all of our decisions without a negative word in our direction.

Maybe that wasn't fair to think. They weren't doing so blindly. They believed in me and Alaric. But were their beliefs in us unfounded? What had we done to deserve their faith?

We'd returned. We'd broken the spell and come back to save them. And save them we would.

I placed my hands on Renfred's shoulders and looked him in the eyes. "Renfred," I began. "Your concerns are just. And I want you to know that I'm scared, too. So much so that it sometimes feels debilitating. But I have to believe that good will conquer evil. Renfred, it just *has* to. I won't accept any other outcome and in case you haven't noticed, I'm pretty stubborn when it comes to getting my way. Ask Alaric." I winked at him.

My session with Renfred was the beginning of one plan being set into motion: I needed to be able to get ahold of Remis' sword and use it to kill him. If I had to face consequences for using its black magic, then the consequences would be damned, Fates help me! First thing tomorrow, I was going to go to Erina to work on Plan B. I wasn't going to let Renfred down. I wasn't going to let *anyone* down.

25

CHAPTER
TWENTY-FIVE

After a hearty meal of fall-off-the-bone meat stew and vegetables with a side of creamy mashed potatoes, courtesy of Brick, and a nice, hot bath, I was tucked comfortably in my bed that night when a letter suddenly appeared next to me on Alaric's pillow. I almost couldn't contain my excitement. I snatched it and tore it open.

"My darling, I made it safely to Gelu a little while ago." The words were written on the paper, but I could hear Alaric's voice as if he were right beside me. Quickly, I reached over to open the drawer of my nightstand and pulled out a piece of stationary and a quill with some ink.

Hello, my love! I am so relieved to hear it. How are your mother and Elix? I wrote before folding up the paper neatly. Instantly, it disappeared from my hands as if it had never been there at all.

I grabbed the hairbrush that was also in the nightstand drawer and began brushing my hair as I waited for his reply. I felt so much lighter once I heard from Alaric. It was as if I had been holding my breath since he left and was waiting to exhale, the pressure in my chest instantly alleviating.

I heard a small sound and looked back towards Alaric's side of the bed where a new letter was now sitting. I tossed the brush aside and grabbed it, somehow ripping it open faster than I had the first. I needed another hit of Alaric's voice.

"My mother is taking it hard. They had been together for almost four hundred years, so the pain is pretty intense. Elix is... Elix. He's been a bit more reserved with me than usual, but I've already heard talk around the castle that he's planning his coronation."

I rolled my eyes and sighed. That sounded just like Elix. My heart broke for Glacia, though. I couldn't imagine – didn't *want* to imagine – what she was going through.

An awful thought came to my mind. One I desperately wished hadn't. I licked my finger and used it to separate another piece of stationary from the stack.

Do you think E had anything to do with it? Also, can we agree to burn these after each conversation?

Fates, I truly hoped that Elix didn't have a hand in Renese's demise. I didn't really think he had it in him. His ill-tempered behavior tended to be directed at his brother. And from what I had seen during our last stay in Gelu, Elix and his father shared most beliefs on how the kingdom was to run. Unless he was desperate to take the crown faster, I didn't see any reason why he would want his father out of the picture.

A new note appeared and my heart skipped a beat out of nervousness.

"I don't think so, but I haven't ruled it out. And yes, burn, baby, burn!"

The last few words ended in Alaric's laughter, which made me laugh. It was good to hear that deep, booming sound. I could feel it in my soul.

Well, give your mother a hug for me and get some rest. I'm going to meet with Erina tomorrow about some things. I'll write to you after.

"Things I should be concerned about?"

Quickly, I scribbled on the page, *Just working on Plan B. I'll keep you posted!*

Alaric must have been writing just as quickly because I barely took a breath before another note appeared. "Wait! How did your training go with Renfred today?"

I smiled thinking back on my training session and the weight of the sword on my hand.

It was good, I wrote. *It felt really good to use my body like that.*

"I wish I was using your body right now."

I burst out laughing. Fates, this mate of mine!

Before I had an opportunity to respond, another note followed his last.

"Maybe you should touch yourself and tell me about it." Alaric's voice was suddenly low and laced with seduction.

Heat pooled at my core as I considered his suggestion. Writing while trying to be sexy felt a little... challenging.

Alaric, this stationary was expensive! I don't want it to run out before you get back. Just come home soon and you can touch me all that you want. Or I'll touch myself and you can watch. Whatever you want. Anything you want.

I tossed my head onto my pillow. I really would give this male anything he wanted without hesitation. The thought of denying him of anything felt no different than denying myself of air.

"Deal. Be home soon! Burn, baby, burn!" he replied and I immediately felt hopeful.

I gathered our used paper in my hands and made my way towards the bathing chamber. The water from my bath had already been removed from the steel tub, so I placed the notes inside and brought a spark to my fingertip. I touched a piece of the paper and watched it go up in flames. The fire quickly spread to the other pieces until they were all ash. I grabbed a jug of water from my nightstand and dumped it into the tub, extinguishing the remaining flames and leaving nothing but a puff of smoke.

I was still smiling, thinking about Alaric, as I got back into bed, covered myself with my blanket and curled into a ball.

* * * * *

The next morning, feeling a little mischievous, I grabbed a piece of stationary from the nightstand and scribbled a quick note to Alaric.

Touched myself while thinking of you. Now off to see Erina! Have a great day!

I chuckled to myself as I folded the note and it disappeared into the thin air. Jumping out of my bed, I headed into the bathing chamber to freshen up. There was still a light smoky smell wafting through the air from the night before.

As I was walking back into my room to get dressed, there was a knock at the door.

"Come in!" I hollered. I opened the door to the balcony, hoping that a good breeze would freshen the air within the suite. When I turned back around, Malisande was standing in the doorway, holding a tray of food that smelled divine.

"First of all, good morning," I said to Malisande as I walked towards her, taking the tray from her hands. "Secondly, where is Leeza?"

"I decided she needed a break," Malisande informed me with a pleased smile. "Honestly, I just wanted to come and say hi. I haven't seen much of you lately." She jutted her bottom lip out to make a pouty face.

Balancing the tray on one hand and wrapping my other arm around Malisande's shoulders, I gave her a squeeze. "I'm sorry, my friend. Join me for breakfast, please."

"Oh, no apologies necessary. I completely understand all of your queenly duties." We headed out to the balcony and I placed the tray down. "And yes to breakfast, I think Brick may have outdone himself on this one."

I took a good whiff of what looked like some sort of eggy pie dotted with greenery. It smelled heavenly. "What is it?" I asked.

"Brick says it's called a quiche. Humans love it. It's usually eggs in a crust, but Brick added some smoked trout and herbs. I'm salivating just thinking about it!"

Malisande and I giggled as I cut into the quiche and served her a slice before placing one on a plate for myself. We took our first bites simultaneously and sighed with delight.

"I had an ulterior motive for coming up here this morning," Malisande admitted as she stared out over the courtyard. My head whipped to my friend and I saw the worry etched on her face. What kind of ulterior motive did she have?

"Go on," I urged her tentatively.

Malisande took a deep breath and I tensed. Whatever it was, it was bad.

"I know that you have so much going on right now. So much to deal with. And I don't want to pile onto that, but I think you need to know..." she trailed off.

My heart was pounding so hard, it was quickly making me lose my appetite. "Know what, Mal?" I asked, trying hard not to grit my teeth in anticipation.

"There has been talk... in the town... of rebel groups."

I pulled back, appalled. "Rebel groups? What do you mean?" How did we have rebel groups in Fiah? What were they rebelling against? A war with the devil? As alarmed as

I was, I was grateful to be hearing this from Malisande. If anyone could get to the bottom of this, it was her.

"They're just rumors, as far as I can tell. I can't seem to find a source. But I'm hearing that Remis has made promises to some humans in exchange for their allegiance to him."

I tried to process what I was hearing, but I just couldn't wrap my head around it. Who would trust a mad king? And why humans? "Promising them what?" I asked, genuinely curious.

"Magic," Malisande replied, finally meeting my gaze. She stared deep into my eyes, waiting for my understanding to set it. And when it did, it hit me like a ton of bricks.

"Remis is using the dark arts to gift humans with magical abilities of their own?" I breathed out in disbelief. That would be insane! But then again...

Malisande's mouth tightened into a firm line as she slowly nodded her head. This was catastrophic. Not only could we have a war amongst our own kind, but the consequences of humans having magic would be devastating. It disrupted the balance that the Fates were always toting to maintain and protect.

"I'm sorry to be the one to have to tell you, but I thought you needed to know. Even if the rumors are unfounded, the fact that they're being said at all is concern enough. At least, that's what I thought – why I came to you."

I stood up and embraced my friend. Fates, I loved her so much. She would never know how much her counsel meant to me. Before I could give her empty words of assurance, there was another knock on my chamber door.

"Come in!" I instructed with a shout.

Leeza entered, head bowed, and said, "There is a man in the drawing room looking to speak with you, Your Majesty."

"What do you mean 'a man'? A human man is here to see me?" I looked towards Malisande whose eyes were wide with fear.

"Yes, Your Majesty. When he was told that the queen would not entertain unexpected guests, he said to tell you that his name is Beau and that he's here for his favor."

Fuck.

This was the last thing I needed right now. To deal with Beau and his feelings. Fates, I still felt bad for what happened to Scarlet, but Beau's timing was horrible amidst the chaos that was currently my life.

I suddenly remember what Renfred had told me after Alaric was stabbed. In the midst of everything that had been going on, I completely forgot!

"Remis said that he always knew that his daughter would get in his way. He just didn't know that bribing some fae named Beau to kill her would set all of this in motion."

I tunneled my fingers aggressively through my hair, wishing that Alaric was here with me so that we could deal with Beau together. That's when I realized that he had responded to my earlier message and that it was waiting for me on my bed.

"Leeza, please tell Master Beaumont that I will join him shortly. Bring him some tea and cakes while he waits. Thank you."

Leeza curtsied and left the room as I first went to my bed to hide the potentially dirty letter under my pillow and then reached into my nightstand for more stationary.

"What are you doing?" Malisande asked. She didn't know about the enchanted stationary yet and I didn't have time to thoroughly explain the concept to her.

"I need to send Alaric a message. This paper has magical properties that will ensure the letter gets to him instantly."

Malisande's mouth dropped open in surprise. "That's incredible!" she exclaimed.

A,
Change of plans.
Beau is here.
Meeting with him now.
Send messages through Malisande.
I love you,
A

I folded the note up and watched it disappear before quickly getting dressed in something more appropriate for receiving guests and then headed towards my door to exit.

"You're in charge of my correspondence until I return!" I called out to Malisande. Behind me, I heard her clap a piece of paper between her hands and then the rustling sound of her opening it.

"*Absolutely not!*" Alaric's voice roared as I left the room and made my way towards the unknown.

26

CHAPTER TWENTY-SIX

"Beau! It's so good to see you!" I crooned as I entered the drawing room. Beau was about to take a sip of tea when he saw me and carefully placed his cup down on his saucer before standing up to greet the female formerly known as Tory.

He bowed to me and I was able to quickly give him the once over. He looked well. Surprisingly so.

"Queen Astoria. Thank you for meeting with me." His tone and demeanor were so formal. It was as if he wasn't the same human that had once fought beside me. Something about that was unnerving. But what was more unnerving was thinking that he had been a hired assassin.

"Beau, of course!" I exclaimed. I wondered if he could hear the falseness to my sugary-sweet tone. "And please, just Astoria. You knew me as Tory so at least it's close." I shrugged and then gestured for him to take his seat again as I settled into the cushioned chair across from him, not taking my eyes off of his. Leeza joined me at my side and poured a cup of tea for me. She looked on edge and I couldn't blame her. She likely could feel the tension radiating off of me. "We didn't get to speak after... everything happened... so I never got a chance to offer my condolences."

I searched his face for any indication that he was potentially a lying bastard, but was met with a cold glare.

"'Everything that happened'..." he trailed off. In that moment, he truly did seem distraught and I realized that I needed to give him the benefit of the doubt. I mean, I would trust him over Remis if I had to choose which to enter a dark room with. I doubted I would trust him, though, if I was unarmed in said room. What did I ever really know about him other than the fact that Scarlet had quickly developed feelings for him?

"Beau, Alaric and I are so sorry about what happened to Scarlet," I said sincerely. I tried to reach across to take his hand, but he jumped up out of his seat abruptly and began to pace.

"'Everything that happened!' 'What happened!' Call it what it was, *Astoria! Murder!* Your husband murdered my girlfriend!"

Okay, this was definitely real, *raw* emotion.

I got to my feet, preparing for whatever was to come next. I desperately needed to talk him down. To make him understand. "Beau, there is so much that I want to tell you.

So much that I can share with you that will make you understand what happened that day."

His head snapped towards me. The previously cold glare had now turned to pure hatred. "And will that bring her back?" he asked. "Will your story bring. Her. *BACK?*" His punctuation made me flinch and instantly regret believing Remis' words for even a second.

Beau could never know how much his question pained me. If I had the ability to raise the dead... I don't know... Would I do it for Scarlet? Hel, why didn't her father who wielded black magic raise her from the dead? He could do it, I bet!

I took a deep breath and let the words flow out of me as quickly as possible. I didn't know if this opportunity would be presented again and he needed to know the truth. "Beau, Scarlet was my cousin. I didn't know it at the time. Alaric and I were under a spell. And the only way to break the spell was to spill the King of Tellus' blood. *That* was the prophecy of the Firebird that you tried to tell us about back at the Phoenix Mansion when we all first met. Tellus was the Dark Kingdom and Fiah the Light. Alaric and I were supposed to return to ourselves and to our kingdom after the King of Tellus was killed. When the spell was created, Scarlet hadn't been born yet. They didn't know that her birth would create a magical loophole." I dropped my hands to my side in defeat. It didn't matter. Beau had been falling in love with Scarlet and these were just words falling on his human ears.

Human ears...

"Beau, are you recruiting humans to join Remis? Are you here in my kingdom, under my roof, as my friend or my enemy?" I brought my magic to the surface. I didn't want to use it on Beau, but I would if I had to.

Without answering, Beau sat back down again, dropping his head and placing it in his hands. He looked like a broken man and I extinguished my magic, no longer in fear of an attack. Regardless, I remained standing a few feet away from him, prepared to defend myself if he chose to leap from that chair and attack.

"Why would I be working with Remis?" he asked, his voice muffled by his hands rubbing over his face.

"I don't know. You're upset with me and Alaric. Maybe you think it will avenge Scarlet's death. Maybe you think having magic will somehow help."

Beau looked up at me. "Tory – Astoria, I mean." He shook his head and then looked at me with more seriousness than I'd ever seen from him. "There's something that I need to show you." He stood up and then dramatically waved a hand over from his head down to his neck. It reminded me of how Erina had waved her hands over Alaric and me before glamouring us. I gasped as he revealed his pointed ears.

"You're... fae?" I exclaimed, shock rippling through my body. Remis had apparently gotten that part right. "But how? Why were you pretending to be human?"

"I have the ability to glamour myself. Remis found out about my abilities and hired me to kill Scarlet during the trials, so I masqueraded as a human to keep her guard down."

So many shocking revelations had been made since we entered the Endless Forest Trials and somehow *this* felt like the most shocking of all! If I were reading this in a novel, this would be the point where I gasped at the plot twist. The plot twist that was right in front of me the whole time.

Remis was telling the truth.

I collapsed in my chair, trying to understand this new reality. "I'm so confused," I admitted, not caring in the slightest how unqueen-like this admission was. "So you didn't actually have feelings for Scarlet? You were an assassin? Why do you even care that Alaric killed her, then? He did your job for you!"

Beau flinched and then quickly exclaimed, "Of course I had feelings for her! I never had any intentions of killing her. At least not once I realized that the king was wrong about her. He believed that she was some great evil that would destroy Tellus. I thought that she was the prophesied Firebird that would *save* Tellus! And even though I was wrong, it didn't change the fact that Scarlet was *good.* There wasn't an evil bone in her body. She wanted to make this realm a better place. Scarlet had been sheltered her whole life from what was going on just outside the palace walls and as soon as she saw the injustices, she knew she had to do something about them. And that was despite the fact that it was her father creating the injustices. Scarlet had no idea how evil Remis truly is. He *sent* her to the trials to die because he knew she'd be the one to get in his way!"

I didn't need convincing that Scarlet was good. If I had it my way, she'd be the ruler of Tellus. She had been kind and selfless and those were some of the greatest qualities a leader could have. I remembered watching her buy bread for a little boy when we went to the tavern in Tellus. I think she thought no one noticed, but I did.

Something suddenly occurred to me. "Beau, what kingdom are you from? You never mentioned it while we were at the mansion."

A smile spread across Beau's face and my blood ran cold. "Ah, well, that will bring me to my favor, then."

I braced myself for whatever was to come. What could he possibly want that I could give him? Certainly not Scarlet.

"I'm from Spirare, Astoria. I don't know if you know this since you were under a spell at the time, but decades ago, Remis attacked Spirare. He decimated much of our infrastructure. And while we rebuilt, we grew our army. It's an army of... creatures."

"The macarong, I know," I interrupted. "Alaric's family filled us in." I was wondering where this was going.

"I want you to fight with us when we're ready to attack. And we'll be attacking soon."

I was overjoyed to hear this. "Done!"

"Done?" he asked, narrowing his gaze at me as if he didn't trust what I had just said.

"I'll even throw in Gelu's army, how does that sound?" I was practically giddy.

"It sounds... Astoria, do you know how to defeat Remis?"

"We have a solid idea," I replied, still not believing my sudden good fortune. "Just get me Remis' sword and I'll handle the rest."

"So you'll take the killing blow?" he asked skeptically.

"Absolutely!"

"And you know it will kill you, too?"

And just like that, my good fortune was speared with a sword.

* * * * *

"What do you mean it will kill me, too?" I asked. "What do you know?"

Beau sighed and rolled his eyes as he sat down and replied, "Apparently more than you, Queeny." For a brief moment, I got a glimpse of the old Beau.

"I knew there would be consequences to wielding black magic, but why would killing Remis kill me? I mean, *he's* using black magic and he's alive."

"Is he?" Beau countered as he gave me a pointed look.

"What are you saying?"

"Legend has it that the realms were created by the Fates who are supposed to be these neutral, all-knowing entities that are always maintaining balance. But after millennia had passed, one of the Fates grew restless and started using his infinite knowledge to manipulate circumstances. To tip the scales towards evil to see how things would play out. He was literally toying with lives out of boredom."

I sucked in a breath. I had never heard of a rogue Fate, but then again, up until recently, I didn't know that new Fates could be chosen like my mother had been.

Beau continued his tale. "The Fates punished him by creating Hel and banishing him there where he couldn't do any further damage. But banishing him didn't eliminate evil. It couldn't. So the wicked Fate found a way to continue his immoral ways. I've consulted many ancient texts over the years and to my knowledge, in order to even have access to black magic, the user needs to sell their soul to Hel. It's the first soul that's used to generate their dark magic."

"Wait, so you're telling me that Remis doesn't have a soul?"

Beau shook his head. "I think that Remis is still walking this realm because the evil Fate is controlling him through his soul. And I think that being the one to cut off Hel's control of the soul will cause their death."

"And you pieced this together from reading ancient tomes in Spirare?"

"Spirare has an incredible library."

A memory surfaced from the trials when Beau was missing from breakfast and Scarlet was worried about him. Alaric had assured her that Beau was probably just off reading somewhere – that he was often pouring over a book. I smiled as I realized that Beau was full of surprises. Not only was he fae, but furthermore, he was a scholar.

"Beau," I whispered. There was something bothering me that I needed to ask. "Where is Scarlet's body?"

He looked at me and blinked a few times as if considering whether or not to tell the truth. "It's in Spirare," he stated simply.

Silently, I nodded. At least now I had a better idea as to where my cousin's final resting place was. "So Remis thinks that you killed Scarlet." It was a statement rather than a question, but Beau still answered.

"Yes. Our deal was, if I killed Scarlet, I would be granted a position within his army... Lieutenant General, to be exact."

"Wait." What was I hearing? "You're the Lieutenant General of Tellus' army?"

Beau's grin stretched from ear to pointed ear. "I'm a double agent, Astoria. I've infiltrated Tellus' military and I feed intelligence to Spirare's army."

Holy. Shit.

Beau really *was* full of surprises!

I scrubbed at my head with my fingers. "So let me make sure I understand all of this: You are undercover as a Lieutenant General in Tellus' army, working with Spirare's army that's composed of thousands of macarong? Spirare, Fiah and Gelu are going to join forces to take down Remis and I'm expected to take the killing blow that will also kill me." And kill Alaric, but I didn't feel that it was necessary for Beau to have that piece of information. "What if I don't want to die? Why can't another fae take the final shot and get turned into a macarong? From what I understand, there are a lot of fae willing to make that sacrifice." I hated the words as soon as they left my mouth, but if there was one thing I learned when I was Tory, it was that information was power. As much as I was willing to die for my kingdom, I knew that staying alive was still the better option. Especially when there were alternative plans.

"Because you're the light," Beau stated matter-of-factly.

My chest suddenly felt tight. "What do you mean?"

"You said that if I got you Remis' sword, that you'd be able to kill him. It's because of the onyx, right? You think that the stone is imbuing the dark magic into his sword?"

Wordlessly, I nodded, not understanding where this was going again.

"The only way that dark magic can kill a dark magic user is if it's wielded by light magic. The ultimate sacrifice."

"But I don't have light magic. I have fire magic. And yes, I understand that fire is a form of light, but I don't really think that's what you're referring to." I looked deep into his eyes, trying to figure out what I was missing.

Beau blinked rapidly again. I was beginning to realize that that was his tell when he was caught off guard. His mouth set into a firm line and he bobbed his head, trying to cover his obvious disappointment. "Ah, I must have made a mistake then." He stood up and bowed to me before looking around the room, seemingly disoriented. "I must be on my way. I'll have a message sent when we're ready to attack. It seems I still have some work to do."

For the life of me, I couldn't understand what was happening. "Beau…" I began, but he was already walking out the door. He stopped in the hallway and paused for a moment before he slowly turned back towards me.

"It was good to see you, Astoria. I hope you find what you're looking for before it's too late."

What did he mean by that? Was he referring to a fae with light magic who would be willing to die for our cause?

"Beau!" I yelled out to him. "Beau!"

But he was gone and a cold chill wrapped around my spine.

27

CHAPTER
TWENTY-SEVEN

After my unsettling meeting with Beau, I needed some time alone with my thoughts. Well, not quite alone. I headed to the stables where we kept not just the horses, but housed Priscilla. She was the only one who could give me what I needed right then.

"Hi, my Prissy girl," I greeted her as I entered the stables. Her particular stall had no door to give her the freedom to fly whenever and wherever her heart desired. And right now, I needed to feel that freedom. "Want to go for a fly, my little love?"

She nudged me and whinnied softly.

I gently climbed on her back and after trotting out into the open field, Priscilla began to gallop until she gained enough speed to set to the skies. Flapping her feathery wings, we soared high above the treetops and over the clouds. Once at a satisfactory altitude, I leaned in and wrapped my arms around Priscilla's neck and rested my head on her mane.

I needed to clear my head, but I also needed a good cry.

I couldn't wrap my mind around the fact that we had three armies at our disposal, ready to wage a war against Remis, and yet it still felt like we weren't any closer to killing him than when we first started out. What was the answer to the riddle? How would Tory solve this puzzle?

Flying through the sky was such a magical experience. Back before the spell changed everything, flying with Priscilla had been one of my favorite things to do on any given day. There was something so incredible about being so high in the sky, making everything – including your problems – seem so small. But now, my problems just felt like they were getting bigger and bigger with no solutions in sight.

After some time in the air, Priscilla eventually brought me back down to the stables. I gave her a big hug around her neck before hopping off and grabbing a brush. As I stroked through her mane, a letter appeared before me, slowly floating down so that I could catch it.

"Are you okay?" Alaric asked. "Malisande said that you took off after Beau left. What happened?"

I didn't have any stationary or a quill, so I promised Priscilla some better grooming tomorrow and ran back to the castle. Malisande was waiting for me at the entrance, a somewhat large and ridiculous stack of papers in her hands.

"These are for you," she said as she handed them over to me. "He's concerned. You should probably talk... er, write... to him soon."

I flipped through the letters quickly and realized that Alaric's most recent one at the stable had been the most reserved. I needed to write back to him fast. He was already dealing with so much back in Gelu and he was probably ripping his hair out waiting for me to respond.

I thanked Malisande and raced up to my room.

I'm okay. I'm so sorry to make you worry. Beau had some interesting things to say that I would rather discuss with you in person. Nothing emergent. It can wait until you're back home.

I folded the note up and watched it disappear into nothing, relieved to finally be able to ease Alaric's mind. I flopped onto the bed and covered my eyes with my hands, taking a deep breath. It wasn't long before Alaric's reply appeared beside me.

"Nothing emergent, but serious enough to not want to put it into writing? I'm concerned, Astoria."

I could hear his concern. I could also hear his silent plea to tell him what was going on. But I couldn't risk this information getting into anyone else's hands. I was treading on extremely thin ice that felt like it would quickly break if I took a step in the wrong direction.

I promise that we will work this out together. Until then, please trust me.

"I do trust you, Astoria. With everything that I am. But I remembered something from before my... accident. Something Remis said."

I already know. Renfred had told me afterwards and the truth came out during my meeting with Beau. I'll explain everything soon.

"Fates, I want to come home to you."

How much longer do you think you'll be staying in Gelu?

"Elix will be crowned in four days' time. My mother has insisted that I return to Fiah immediately following his coronation."

That was the best news I had heard all day.

And your investigation? I wrote.

"I haven't made much progress. Or rather, I haven't found any evidence to the contrary that my father's heart simply failed him."

That seemed strange. After meeting with Beau, I started thinking that maybe it would be a good idea to look through some old books and ancient texts to do some more research on black magic, but now I was thinking that maybe looking into past instances of a fae's heart giving out would also be part of my studies. Admittedly, while I was a good student that my tutors often praised, there were quite a few years before the spell was cast that I wasn't staying knowledgeable on current events. And then, of course, I was gone for so long. Maybe this disease of the heart was now a common occurrence amongst our kind and I just didn't know it yet.

I realized that brushing up on political affairs would probably be in our best interest, as well. Alaric and I sent a few more notes back and forth to each other before I headed off to the small library within the castle. Ours was nothing like Spirare's, but it was nothing to scoff at, either. Hundreds of rows of books wove throughout the space and then there were the books that crawled up the walls, two stories high. The library smelled musty, but in a way that made me feel reminiscent. There was something about the scent of an old book that brought me back to my childhood. Tucked away in a corner somewhere, I would read about imaginary places and pretend that I was there. The main character was always someone I aspired to be and I often found myself imagining that I was the protagonist in the story. It didn't matter if the main character was blonde or human... She was me and I was her. Kind of like how I felt about my life as Tory and my life now. One couldn't exist without the other and when I thought back to those experiences, it was myself that I pictured in my head. Not the different versions of me that had been reincarnated over and over.

I wondered if Alaric struggled with that. I could never blame him for the actions he took while he was Ricky, or any other being. But I knew it weighed on him that Ricky struck without a second thought. Which made me further wonder if Alaric pictured himself killing Scarlet. Was that an image that played on repeat in his head? Fates, I hoped not.

I found a few books that looked like they might be able to help – *Fae's Anatomy, Epidemics of the Realms and their Impacts on the Future, Politics and Peace: A Guide for Royals, The Magic Box* and a book called *The Fates Are Black and White: Magic, Power and the Struggle for Balance.*

I brought the books to a table and spread them out before grabbing *The Fates Are Black and White.* If this war we were fighting wasn't about magic, power and the struggle for balance, then I didn't know *what* we were doing! I flipped through the pages, mainly looking at the chapter titles, but also skimming for key words like "The Fates," "black magic," "dark arts," and "madness." One particular chapter caught my eye. The author talked about how black magic users were quickly drawn to madness, the power they held overwhelming the inherent magic coursing through their bodies. Black magic attacked the brain first, which usually led to the user increasing their magic usage. Then it would attack their heart, deteriorating it until it was nothing but dust. The only thing that allowed the body to continue functioning and give the illusion of life was a sacrifice of more magic... like Tellus' tithe.

I put the book down and paused at the mention of the heart. There was no way Renese was using black magic. I was sure of it. As sure as I was that my husband was my mate. Besides, Renese wasn't crazy. If the black magic attacked the brain first, it further proved that my father-in-law had not touched the dark arts.

It was interesting, nonetheless, and I used a slip of paper to mark the page to go back to later. I continued reading until I stumbled upon something that really piqued my interest.

Fae hearts differ from humans' in that they are not all the same. It is a little known fact that abnormalities exist in some fae, giving them abilities that exceed their Fates-given gifts. When tapped into, their powers are amplified. It is believed that this deviation is passed down through bloodlines and if that is true, one must consider that this ability is prevalent in royal bloodlines especially.

"Your Majesty?"

Startled, I yelped and tossed the book up in the air, catching it before it clobbered me in the head. I swallowed hard. "Hi, Erina. What can I do for you?" Where had she come from? I was so engrossed in my book that I hadn't even heard her footsteps as she approached.

The sorceress stepped towards me tentatively as I marked my place in the book and put it down on the table, but not out of reach.

"I understand Beau was here earlier," she stated as she sat down. "I imagine you have some questions."

I placed my elbow on top of the book and rested my head in my hand. "I feel like I always have questions. Thank you for coming to find me." I don't know when it happened, but at some point after the trials, Erina began to grow on me. Maybe it was because I was just now realizing how close she was to my mother or maybe it was because she wasn't being so cryptic all the time, but either way, when I looked at Erina, I felt a fondness within me for her.

"Beau said that Remis doesn't have a soul. Or, at least, he doesn't think he does. And that the onyx sword isn't enough; that the only way to kill a soulless, black magic wielder is by using 'the light.' Or that they have to have light magic. I forget exactly how he worded it. But he said that the fae with light magic would die if they wielded the sword to kill Remis. That it's the ultimate sacrifice." I suddenly realized that I hadn't actually asked a question, so I decided to start at the beginning. "Does Remis have a soul?" I narrowed my eyes at Erina in question.

She smiled softly at me. "Can I tell you a story, Your Majesty?"

I nodded. I had no idea where this was going, but I knew that if Erina was going to tell me a story, it would be epic.

"Once upon a time, there were seven magical beings known as the Fates that created the realms and everything within them. Brothers and sisters known as Alphaba, Betadon, Deltafy, Gammal, Sigmarae, Epsilonlie and Upsilonly. These beings were all-knowing and vowed to one another to remain neutral in all things. They were the Creators, but also the balance. Back then, there wasn't good and evil, but simply good and bad. And all things needed a balance of both in order for us creatures to live happy lives."

I cocked my head. "But why do we need the bad? Wouldn't just good lead to a happy life?"

"If you only ever had good in life, would you know it was good or would it just simply be?"

I looked at Erina, my face contorted in confusion.

She understood my silence and continued. "Good only exists because there's bad. It's a scale. If you never feel the bad, how do you know if something is good?"

She made sense. Being healthy was a good thing, but only because we knew what it felt like to be sick. We had to experience the bad to appreciate the good otherwise it wouldn't mean as much.

"But Upsilonly was different from his siblings. He was inherently bad. And after millennia upon millennia of maintaining the balance, Upsilonly grew bored and began manipulating situations for his own twisted pleasure. Tipping the scale in his favor. The Fates had created the After Realm as a place where souls could exist in peace after a balanced life, but once Upsilonly created evil, they banded together and created Hel where they banished Upsilonly to keep evil out of the After Realm."

Erina's story sounded an awful lot like the one Beau had told me. Although it seemed fantastical, the fact that their stories aligned said something to me.

Erina continued. "Now that evil existed, Hel was where the truly evil souls went after death. And Upsilonly ruled Hel. Humans now call him the devil... but I call him daddy."

"D-daddy?" I stuttered. "Upsilonly, the King of Hel, is your *father?*"

Erina nodded, a smirk on her face. "Upsilonly eventually married one of the evil souls that resided in Hel and birthed evil witches to combat the good that the Fates did. Upsilonly's own little army against his siblings. Many now know them as The Six, but they – we – were once known as The Seven."

My eyes went wide as I processed what Erina was saying. I had heard of The Six. Similar to how Erina was a member of Fiah's court, The Six were part of Remis'. And they were a force to be reckoned with. Which also meant that Erina wasn't really a sorceress... She was a witch. It now made so much sense that she was considered the most powerful sorceress in all the realm. She was a witch born of the devil himself.

"Witches are able to travel between realms due to their powers and I came to this one to wreak havoc in the name of my father. But even before I came to this realm, I knew that there was something different about me. My sisters, they live for chaos and pain. They are fueled by power. But for me, those things never made me feel complete. I always felt like there was something missing. Then I met your mother... and I was drawn to her like a magnet. She was everything pure and good that made life worth living and I suddenly felt that sense of rightness."

The way Erina spoke of my mother sounded like how I spoke of Alaric and our mating bond.

She must have been able to read my thoughts from the look on my face because she added, "It wasn't like that. Your mother was my best friend and the bonds of friendship can be equally strong to that of a mating bond. It didn't happen overnight, but your mother and I became friends and I changed my wicked ways. I renounced my father and Hel, pledged myself as a servant to the Fates, and came to live in Fiah. I have upheld the Fates desire to maintain the balance, not just to aid them, but to ensure that I never am banished back to Hel."

It explained why Erina was always so tight-lipped with answers, but babbling about balance when Alaric and I first returned. But lately, it seemed like Erina was definitely living where black and white meets – the grey area where right and wrong sometimes get blurred.

Erina continued, shifting me from my thoughts. "Then, as you know, your mother came to me to put the spell in place. As I told you, Scarlet hadn't been conceived when this happened, so we had no way of knowing her existence would create a magical loophole. Once the spell was set, I began spreading word of the prophecy because prophecies give people hope. And people who hope have wishes. The purpose of the Endless Forest Trials was never just about granting wishes... it was always to find you. "

"But how? How were the trials going to aid you in that endeavor? I still don't understand their purpose."

Erina smiled knowingly at me. "The trials brought together masses of fae and humans every decade, allowing us to search for the qualities that we were looking for... two specifically."

"And those would be...?"

"The first was an affinity for fire. We knew that your fire magic, although dormant, would stay with your soul and show in your aura. All of the contestants showed some sort of affinity for fire."

"I don't understand. Scarlet had fire magic, so that makes sense. But what about Alaric?" I asked. My head felt like it was already spinning and I didn't know how much more of this I could take.

"Can your husband not control the sun? Can he not control the lightning? Those are all sources of fire."

I had never thought about it like that. She was right, of course. There had been many times that I had watched Alaric wield lightning that created fires.

"One contestant was a very talented blacksmith. Another was a candlemaker in their town. One way or another, there was a connection to fire tied to who they were."

"What was the other quality you were looking for?" I leaned in closer.

"Well, that wasn't something that we could entirely see during the selection process at the gates. It was something we were looking for that could change during the competition."

"But during the selection, your apprentices called Scarlet 'Firebird,'" I stated, but it was more of a question.

"They never *called* her 'Firebird.' Once they saw Scarlet and knew that she carried Remis' blood, they thought there was finally a chance to free you. The princess had always been sheltered inside the castle walls or heavily guarded the few times she was permitted to leave the gates. But if we were fortunate enough to find you during these trials, we finally had the opportunity we needed. And the Fates were on our side."

Upon thinking about it, the apprentices *didn't* call Scarlet the Firebird. We all just made an assumption based on their reaction. "What was the second quality?"

"It was white light." Erina gave me that knowing look again as Beau's words from earlier in the day hit me like a ton of bricks. Light magic was the key to killing Remis and his dark magic and Erina had known this all along.

She continued before I could interject. "Someone with white light is needed to kill a black magic user who has succumbed to the level of madness that turns their organs to dust. White light shows in a person's aura when they are pure of heart. When they're willing to make sacrifices for the greater good. Your mother had this white light... and so do you, Astoria."

I couldn't help but wonder if what I had read about fae hearts and the abnormality in royal bloodlines had anything to do with this. It seemed like too big of a coincidence.

"Four of you showed the white light in your auras and maintained it throughout the trials. You, Alaric – "

"Scarlet," I interrupted, realization dawning on me.

"And Beau," Erina added.

"But Scarlet – Why did she... did you..."

"Scarlet had the white light, but she also had Remis' blood. When the spell was originally cast, it was our hope that Remis would be killed and you would eventually be released. But over time, Remis was not only growing madder, but also getting stronger and better at keeping his onyx shield in place. We knew the only one that would be strong enough to defeat him would be you. So we needed to break the spell quickly. Scarlet was our only chance – the only way we had any chance at killing him was to bring you back then and there. Unfortunately, it also meant Scarlet's demise. It was our one shot and we took it."

"But why am I our best chance? What makes my white light stronger than anyone else's?"

"You have a heart of gold, Your Majesty."

Erina said it so matter-of-factly, but I suddenly felt like all of the air had been sucked out of the room. Those were the words my mother had said before I left the After Realm.

"Erina..." My voice was barely a whisper, but the plea was heard.

"You are the only one that can defeat Remis."

28

CHAPTER TWENTY-EIGHT

The more questions that were answered, the more questions that needed answers.

"My mother said that I have a heart of gold. What does that mean?" I asked, tears welling in my eyes and spilling down my cheeks.

"When did she tell you this?" Erina was the one to look confused now.

"I... saw her. When Alaric was poisoned and you turned me back into the Firebird, I somehow ended up in the After Realm with my mother. Did you know that she is one of the Fates now?" I sighed realizing that Erina and I were literally just asking each other questions now and resolving nothing.

"I suspected as much. There have been a few times after I pledged myself to the Fates that I've received messages from them."

"Messages?"

"More like the visions you have. They put them in my head and talk to me in my dreams. Very infrequently. But once, I saw your mother and believed that it was a message and not just a dream."

I choked on a sob. How many times have I had obscure visions? Were the Fates trying to tell me something? Was my mother?

"So Yrsula told you that you have a heart of gold, but didn't explain what that meant? How very Fates-like of her." Erina rolled her eyes and a giggle escaped me. I couldn't help it.

"It wasn't her fault," I began to explain. "A portal leading back here opened. She said it as I was saying goodbye to her. I didn't realize that it meant anything more than just 'you have a good heart.' But I read in this book about abnormalities in certain faes' hearts." I held up the book to show her and then found the reference. "Specifically in royal bloodlines."

Erina scanned the page, using her finger to read each line. She took the book off of the table and placed it directly in front of her, turning back to the beginning of the chapter and settling in her seat to read it in full.

"Do you think this part regarding the royal bloodlines is referring to the white light?" I asked, hopeful.

Erina shook her head slowly, as if unsure, but considering. "No... no, I don't think so. White light is more about someone's goodness and whether or not they place the well-being of others before themself. So earlier, when I told you that four of you displayed the white light while competing, that wasn't the full truth. As a healer, Shaelyte had the white light, but once she made the decision to not help Charlie, it dulled to a shade of grey."

Erina gave me a hard look and I realized that I had started snarling when she mentioned Charlie's name. I reeled my temper back in. I needed Erina to help me and taking my fury out on her would not serve me well.

Erina continued staring at me. "I told you once before that Charlie's soul was black. There was no good in him, Your Majesty. I need you to trust that."

Erina had proven herself time and time again. It really was time I let that loss go.

"I trust you, Erina. I apologize for my outburst."

Erina gave a curt nod of her head and redirected her attention back to *The Fates Are Black and White.* "Your mother had an uncanny ability to always put others before herself. She never prioritized her happiness over the kingdom's. Sometimes I would just watch her when she thought no one was and I could see that she was different from anyone else. Her white light shone so bright, but there was something more. Something that I could never quite put my finger on. I remember having a conversation with her when you were much younger and she told me that she thought you had a heart of gold. It seemed like she was just fond of you and since I was fond of her, I accepted the statement for what I thought it was. But one day, your mother confided in me and told me that she had this abnormality that she believed enhanced her inherent powers. I knew that she didn't have any Fates-given magic, but then she showed me what she was able to do with what she had.

She wasn't just fast... She was so fast that it would look like she momentarily blinked out of existence. And her strength was inconceivable. I witnessed her push down a tree that had existed for hundreds of years. Publicly, your mother often held back when it came to her magic, but she was definitely one of the more powerful fae that I had ever met, Fates-given magic or not. And she also believed that you were the same..." She trailed off and I tried to accept what she was saying.

Since my mother didn't have any Fates-given abilities, I always believed that her true power was being a great leader – A queen who was able to maintain a peaceful kingdom. But my mother was more powerful than I ever realized.

And I could be just as much. But how?

"Erina, if I can somehow figure out how to tap into this magic – and that's a big if – what will happen to Fiah after I've defeated Remis? If Alaric is tied to me and I die, who will rule Fiah after we're gone?"

Erina took my hands in hers and placed them on my lap. "Astoria," she began and the use of my given name made my heart squeeze. "I don't think you will both die."

"But Beau said – "

She raised her hand to silence me. "There is so much that we don't know about the realm and the lives we live. We put our faith in the Fates and do the best we can. And if there is a Fate that I would put all of my faith in, it's your mother. If she knew that you had this heart of gold and did everything to ensure you would be around to defeat Remis, why would she further bond you to Alaric if she thought you were going to die? She loved this kingdom as much as she loved you. She would never take that chance."

"So you think that Remis' onyx sword and my white light combined with my heart of gold are enough to defeat him?"

Erina smiled at me. "I think it's time you trust the balance, Astoria."

* * * * *

I spent the next few days holed up in the library, only leaving to get a few hours of rest each night. Brick was a gem and made me what he referred to as "brain food" while I poured over page after page, book after book. Malisande would deliver each meal to me in the library where I mindlessly would take a few bites to keep fueling myself enough to get to the next book. There had to be something here. Something that would help me to figure out how to tap into my superpowers. Because I did, in fact, trust Erina and more than that, I trusted my mother. She had been orchestrating everything from the very beginning. How could I ever believe that she would allow me to leave this kingdom unprotected?

Another question plagued my mind. It was written in *The Fates Are Black and White* that fae with the abnormality had heightened abilities. Were those powers equal to or greater than those of the macarong? I wasn't sure if it really mattered, but I wanted to know. If I could somehow protect them, too, I wanted to. If I could prevent any further deaths, I needed to know how my potential strength compared. But since the macarong were a new creation, there were no books in the Fiah library that could help me answer this. Then again, who said they *were* a new creation? How did the first macarong come to be?

Without taking my eyes off of my current book, I reached over for a glass of water and felt a piece of paper appear in my hand. I thought I had just messaged Alaric not too long ago to tell him I'd be busy again today, but I quickly realized that the sun was no longer shining outside my window. I had been in the library since breakfast and it was now dark. I'd lost a whole day. I scratched my head and wondered when I had turned a lamp on.

I opened the note and Alaric's voice filled the library. "I have a surprise for you."

A surprise? I wrote, suddenly feeling giddy. Alaric always had the best surprises. In fact, it was one of the things I loved most about him: his thoughtfulness.

Another note appeared. "Yes, a surprise, but you need to head back to our bed chamber. And quickly."

My heart was racing. I was hoping that the surprise would be Alaric, standing in our room, but I didn't want to be too hopeful. He had left Gelu after Elix's coronation, but I didn't think he'd make it back so fast.

I closed my book, turned off the lamp and walked as fast as I could towards our suite without looking insane or inciting fear in anyone walking around the castle. I got to the doors and tried to steady my breathing. Whatever awaited me on the other side would make me happy, even if it wasn't yet my husband. I threw the doors open and almost sobbed when I saw Alaric standing in front of me, arms wide and waiting for me to jump into them.

I practically flew across the room and leapt into his embrace, wrapping my legs around his waist. I kissed him hard on the lips and then peppered kisses all along his jawline and neck. I was so grateful to have him home and in one piece. It had been less than a fortnight, but when he wasn't close, the mating bond made the separation feel like a lifetime.

"I missed you, too," Alaric chuckled as he turned towards the bed. He took a few steps before climbing on top of it, my body still wrapped around his like I was a monkey climbing a tree. He gently placed me down and I pulled him to me. I needed him closer. I needed him inside me. The bond was demanding it and I wanted nothing more than to give the bond what it wanted.

Alaric kissed me and I moaned into his mouth when he pressed his hardness into my center. Fates, I had missed this. He pulled back and I whimpered, but was relieved when I realized that he was just making room to pull off his tunic. I ran my fingers down his chest and across the planes of his stomach, digging my nails in just slightly. I could see the bulge in his pants twitch and my stomach immediately warmed, pooling wet heat to my core.

Once Alaric's tunic was on the floor, I sat up and lifted my arms so that he could remove my tunic. Then I placed my hands around his neck and pulled him back towards me, his weight feeling so satisfying against my body. But I needed more.

Sensing my urgency, Alaric pulled at the waistband of my pants and I shimmied out of them. He then removed my undergarments and I was left naked and fully exposed, desperate to feel his cock inside me. I reached for his pants, but he stopped me.

"Let me play first," he insisted as he teased my center with his finger. I was already so wet that this foreplay felt unnecessary. He could easily slide into me and make me scream with one good thrust. But who was I to deny my husband his fun? Not that it wasn't fun for me, as well, but I wanted to feel him filling me. I wanted to feel as full of him as possible.

He plunged a finger inside of me and a filthy moan escaped my lips as I arched into him. "There's my girl," he crooned, adding another finger as he pumped in and out of me, my arousal coating each digit.

"More!" I demanded, a breathy command that made Alaric flash that stunning smile of his.

"I aim to please you, my queen," he replied with a grin before he bit my inner thigh and then sucked on the bundle of nerves at the apex.

"Holy Fates!" I screamed as I practically dug my fingers into his scalp to pull him closer. "Alaric, fuck!" I could feel him chuckle against me, the vibration bringing me closer to the edge. He continued to work me, using both his fingers and tongue to wring such pleasure from me, my legs were already shaking. It wasn't long before I crested over the precipice, seeing stars as I clenched around Alaric's fingers.

I stared into his eyes as he removed his fingers and placed both in his mouth, sucking them clean. Fates, that was sexy!

Alaric leaned over me, but I shifted my weight and rolled him onto his back. He looked surprised, but delighted. I kissed my way down his neck and then chest before reaching for his pants, springing his enormous cock free, liquid already gathering at the tip. I removed his pants entirely and my mouth went dry at the sight of him. He reached for me, but I shoved him back down onto his back. I wanted him inside of me so badly, but I could delay my further satisfaction for a little while longer.

"Now it's my turn to play," I said, eyeing him with hunger as I settled between his legs and dropped my head to his cock. I licked from the base to the tip and then swirled my tongue around the crown, loving the taste of him on my lips. Using my hand, I gripped his shaft and began pumping up and down as I took him fully in my mouth.

His moans spurred me on and I hollowed out my cheeks to increase the sensation. Alaric placed his hands on my head and I could feel that he was holding himself back from thrusting his cock down my throat.

"Astoria," he groaned, my name sounding like both a warning and a prayer. "I need to be inside of you."

"Thank the Fates," I shouted as I climbed on top of him, his erection still in my hand, and guided him towards my entrance. He looked lovingly into my eyes as I impaled myself on him, my back arching at the same time that he bucked his hips. Feeling him so deep inside of me, the mating bond purred with satisfaction.

With my hands on Alaric's chest, I rode him with abandon, pleasing him while also chasing my release. Without warning, Alaric shifted his body so quickly and effortlessly that he was suddenly on top of me.

"Hey! You used my trick against me!" I huffed a laugh. I bit my lip and then said, "Now what are you going to do with me?"

"Fates, help me..." he growled as he pushed in to the hilt and I saw stars. "When you bite your lip like that, all I can think about is fucking you until I can't breathe."

"I'd like to see you try," I challenged him, but then he pulled out of me and I whimpered. Practically pouted, in fact.

"Get on your hands and knees," Alaric demanded gruffly and the sound instantly made me wetter than I already was.

"Yes, my king," I replied and did as he instructed.

He reached over me and grabbed my wrists, pulling them out from under me, but holding me steady. He placed my hands on the headboard and with one hand, held them in place. His other grabbed his cock, which he slid between my legs and I waited with bated breath for him to press into me. Instead, he released his erection from his hand and reached around my hips, his fingers grazing that perfect spot. I gasped and then Alaric slammed into me from behind. I couldn't help from screaming and knew the whole castle could probably hear me.

I didn't care.

Nothing mattered in this moment.

As Alaric pistoned in and out of me, I could feel my legs getting weaker and then his grip on my waist tightened. He pulled me closer to him and his thrusting became more erratic. Two more pumps and I came hard on his cock as he spilled his release inside of me.

We were both slick with sweat and breathing heavily as we collapsed on to the bed, both of our bodies perfectly spent. We remained like that for several moments, trying to catch our breaths and steady our hearts that were pounding simultaneously.

"That was a good surprise," I breathed, feeling fully sated. I brought my hand to my head to brush off the damp locks from my face.

"Oh, that wasn't the surprise!" Alaric exclaimed as he suddenly jumped out of the bed. The male's stamina was incredible. He quickly pulled pants on and then hurried into the bathing chamber. I watched as he leaned down into the tub and pulled out something small and furry.

My eyes went wide. "A corgi!" I squealed as I pulled the covers off of me and grabbed the robe that was hanging by my bedside, wrapping it around my body, before I bounded towards the bathing chamber to greet this new friend. Alaric held him out to me and I practically jumped for joy when I saw his tan fur and that he had a little patch of white on his head that looked like a heart. I pulled him into my arms, snuggling him against me. "Where did you find him?"

Alaric chuckled as the corgi puppy sniffed my nose. "At a magic shop in Gelu. I was walking by and saw him and his siblings playing in the shop. I remembered your corgi,

Jasper, from when we were Jessina and Maverick and I was feeling nostalgic, so I went inside. Did you know that there's an ancient legend that fairies used to ride corgis into battle?"

The puppy licked my chin and I giggled as I shook my head. "I didn't know that," I replied, still giggling.

"Neither did I. The shop owner told me all about the folklore and how corgis are believed to have their own magical powers. It seemed appropriate for you to have one in your real life."

My heart felt like it was swelling with joy. I sat down on the floor and put my magical friend down. He bit down on the rope that tied my robe together and began tugging. With a gasp and then a laugh, I closed my robe before it could open any further and picked the puppy back up. "Does he have a name?"

Alaric joined me on the floor. "I figured you'd want to name him, so I've been calling him 'Good Boy.' But you can call him whatever you like."

I pursed my lips and said the first name that came to mind when I looked at him. "Winchester. Prince Winchester of Fiah," I declared. "Winny or Win for short." I looked at Alaric and smiled which made him smile. He placed a hand on my cheek and leaned it to kiss me softly. Winchester barked and it was the funniest sound I had heard in a long time.

"Hey!" Alaric scolded him. "I'm allowed!" Winchester jumped down from my arms and nipped Alaric's finger before running back to me. Already, he was protecting his queen.

"Boys, boys… Settle down."

Alaric stood up and then helped me off the floor, leading me back into our room as I cradled Winny in my arms. "So, now that I'm home, I want to hear all about Beau's unannounced visit." His lip curled for a brief moment, but he reined his anger in before it rained unexpectedly in Fiah.

I carried Win to the bed and carefully climbed into the center, spreading my legs open and placing him gently on the blanket between them. "And I want to hear all about your time with your mother and Elix," I added on.

Alaric shot me a contemptuous look. "Don't change the subject, dear." He reached into a sack that was sitting on the floor near the nightstand and dug around until he found a small toy that was shaped like a bone. He tossed it onto the bed and Winny snatched it, growling a soft puppy growl and shaking his head from side to side. He then settled down to chew on his new toy and I leaned back on the bed using my hands to support me.

"Where do I begin? Well, what Remis had said was true: He had hired Beau to kill Scarlet. But what Remis hadn't anticipated was that Beau would fall in love with her. Beau was initially very upset with us, which I'm sure is no surprise. He has so much anger in regards to Scarlet's death and the how and why of it all. But after some talking, it seems that he's on our side. He's been playing double agent, gathering intel on Remis while he pretends to be a member of Tellus' military."

A look of confusion spread across Alaric's face. "A double agent for who?"

"Oh!" I exclaimed. I was still coming down from the incredible sex Alaric and I just had, as well as the excitement over my new dog, and details were escaping my brain. "For Spirare. Beau is from Spirare and knows all about the macarong."

"Okay..." Alaric drawled. "So what else?"

With my mouth set in a straight line, I sat up. "Beau is a scholar. He's been researching black magic and he said that the only way to kill Remis is with the sword."

"The words sound good, but your face and tone say otherwise," Alaric stated.

"Only a wielder with white light can use the sword to kill him. Erina and I talked after Beau left and she said that you, Beau and I all have this white light – it was something they were looking for within us during the trials."

Alaric clapped his hands. "Great! So that's three people who have the power to end this. One of us needs to get the sword and – "

"Alaric," I cut him off. "Whoever wields the sword might die. It's what Beau believes, but Erina isn't sure." Despite ending on a more positive note, Alaric's face still fell. "And furthermore, Erina doesn't believe the white light is enough. Do you remember when you were poisoned?"

Alaric's lip curled. "How could I forget?"

"When I became the Firebird again and saw my mother, she said that I had a heart of gold. I didn't think much of it at the time, but while you were away, I did some research of my own and found something about fae with this abnormality of the heart. It makes them incredibly powerful. Erina thinks my mother was telling me that I have this abnormality."

Alaric collapsed onto the bed and rubbed his eyes with the heels of his hands. "Okay, and how do you access this power that you may or may not have? That may or may not be the thing that ends this... that kills you? That kills me."

"Do you see now why I didn't want to discuss this on enchanted stationary?" I smiled and winked at him.

"Don't make jokes, Astoria." I could tell he wasn't angry with me – just defeated. "This is serious," he whispered and I could feel my heart break. The one of gold in my chest.

"Alaric," I brushed his arm and tried to get him to look at me, his intentions clear that he didn't want to make eye contact with me in this moment. "I trust that my mother wouldn't set us up for failure. I think the Fates, despite their seeming disinterest in this situation, have a plan. And if not them, then definitely my mother. Alaric, I can feel it. Call me silly, but I feel it in my chest as if my heart is trying to agree with my mind."

He looked at me then, mouth slightly agape. I took his face in my hands and kissed him. "Trust me."

"I do," he sighed. "I just – I just hate all of this."

"I know," I agreed as he pulled me to his side. I wrapped my arm around his waist and rested my head on his chest.

"Promise me something?" Alaric ventured. I bobbed my head against his skin. "When this is over, we get away from here."

"What?" I asked, startled. I lifted my head off of his chest to stare at him. "What do you mean?"

Alaric chuckled and pulled me back towards him. "Not forever. Just for a while. I want to take you somewhere where it's only the two of us – "

Winchester sneezed, as if he was indignant to not be included.

"Fine!" Alaric laughed. "The three of us. And we can just be us. Not Queen Astoria. Not King Alaric. Just two fae, incredibly happy and desperately in love... with a dog that we should have named Trouble."

"Deal," I told him. "But it would be Prince Trouble."

Winny barked and then curled up against my back, soon falling asleep.

"Good," Alaric whispered as we drifted off to sleep, as well.

29

CHAPTER
TWENTY-NINE

I awoke early the next morning to the sound of Alaric snoring in my ear. He sounded like a bear and I had to stifle a laugh. I opened my eyes and saw Winny at the foot of the bed. For a puppy, he sure was a good sleeper. Maybe he really was magical.

At some point during the night, Alaric and I had rolled over so that he was now at my back. Wrapped around me, I could feel his erection pressing into my behind. I arched my back ever so slightly into it, eliciting the exact reaction I was looking for. The snoring stopped and Alaric groaned softly. I wiggled a little bit and his grip on my waist tightened, bringing me closer to him so that my back was flush against his chest.

Alaric's hand parted my robe and drifted between my legs causing me to arch again – involuntarily this time – and both of us to moan. He kissed my neck and then gently bit down on the flesh of my shoulder. Wordlessly, I turned over and rolled onto my back, Alaric shifting his weight on top of me. He kissed my neck and then shoulder and traveled further down to place a kiss over my heart.

"My Fireheart," he whispered.

I made eye contact with him as he took off his pants, but my gaze quickly shifted to his erection. It didn't matter how many times we did this, I knew I could never get enough of him.

Alaric buried himself inside of me and it wasn't long before our quiet moans and soft pants were the only sounds in our otherwise silent room. This coupling was not hurried – quite the contrary. Alaric pushed himself in and out of me so slowly that I felt like our souls were dancing.

And I wanted them to dance forever.

After Alaric and I were both pleasantly sated and resting in each other's arms again, Leeza came to our bed chamber to bring us breakfast. Brick had even gone as far as to add a plate of dog food consisting of meat scraps, carrots and rice.

We enjoyed our meal out on the balcony, taking advantage of the beautiful day set out before us.

"How is your mother?" I asked, sipping my coffee. I was genuinely worried about her. Not only was she grieving, but she now faced the reality of a war with her son as king. "Do you think that after this is over, she might want to stay with us for an extended period of time?"

"Maybe," Alaric replied. "It would be a while before she would feel comfortable leaving Elix to the affairs of the castle, but I'm sure she'd like to spend some time here. Get out of the cold. She told me her secret, by the way," he added casually.

"Did she now?" I asked, just as casually, as I took another sip of coffee. I wasn't about to get tricked into telling him, if that's what he was doing.

"She did. And it wasn't as surprising as it probably should have been. I remember as a kid, seeing her look like she was having conversations with the family dog or the woodland creatures that would come looking for food. I thought she was just talking to them the way anyone would talk to an animal... not expecting a response. But, apparently they *were* responding. It's kind of whimsical if you ask me."

I smiled into my mug. "I agree."

"And she said to tell you 'thank you.'"

Thanks weren't necessary. I would never betray her trust. "And how was your brother's coronation?"

Alaric put a piece of ham in his mouth and shrugged. "It was very Elix. Ostentatious. I left as soon as the actual ceremony took place, so I didn't see any of the debauchery that followed." He stabbed his fork into the slice of ham and sawed off another piece. "I was able to talk with him briefly about our alliance. He's still with us. Or rather, I think he's all for himself, but knows that he can't win this war alone. He told me that he had been warned that several civilians within the town were secretly holding rebel meetings. I'm unsure what they would be rebelling against. If Remis wins, they would be forced to give up their magic to him."

"Malisande heard the same of some folks in Fiah. She said that they were humans who had been promised magic if they joined forces with Tellus."

Alaric blanched. "Like Remis would really share his magic! It's absurd!" I could tell he was getting angry and immediately noticed clouds forming in the sky overhead. I grabbed his hand and used my thumb to rub circles against it.

"It's okay," I told him. "You can never make everyone happy."

The storm clouds started to dissipate, but I could see in Alaric's eyes that he wasn't happy. He was just more in control of his anger.

"It's treason, Astoria. Your mother... you... have worked so hard to keep the peace in Fiah and they have the audacity to rebel against you?"

I wanted to assure him that it was okay. To tell him that these things happened during wartime. Fae and humans... all creatures... were fallible. Erina further showed me that when she explained the white light and how Shaelyte's dimmed after she refused to heal Charlie. But I was also fully aware that Alaric already knew this – he just needed to feel his feelings.

"Regardless, they should not be punished. They're being manipulated and we both know what that's like."

There he is, I thought to myself. I knew he'd get there sooner rather than later.

I looked into Alaric's eyes and they were clear once again. Settling back into my chair, I took a deep breath of fresh air. There was something about the crispness in the air that made me feel calm today. Until I felt a tug at my robe and realized that Prince Trouble needed to relieve himself.

"I'm going to take Winny down to the courtyard for a bit. I will be back soon." I scooped Winchester into my arms and leaned down to give Alaric a quick kiss. I pulled away, but his hand shot up to my head and gripping my hair, he pressed me towards him for a harder and deeper kiss.

"I love you," he told me.

"Good! I was kind of hoping you did!" I winked at my mate and headed down the hall and towards the stairs where Erina was standing.

"Good morning, Your Majesty. Who is this?" she asked, pointing at Winny.

I held him up for the witch to assess. "This is Win," I told her, dangling his chubby body so that it looked like his short, little legs were dancing.

"That's what I wanted to talk to you about," she replied with a firm nod.

My face contorted in confusion. "You wanted to talk about the dog you didn't know I got?"

Erina rolled her eyes and shook her head, but her lips were curling into a smile. "No, your win. The war."

Huh. I hadn't realized that I nicknamed Winchester 'Win.' Maybe I was manifesting what I desired. "Go on," I drawled. "But please follow me. Little Win is about to burst and I don't think you'll appreciate urine squirting on your dress."

Erina rolled her eyes again and sighed. It really was astounding that she stuck around and continued to help me. Then again, she likely felt she owed it to my mother.

"I've been doing some further research and I have an idea – a way to maybe coax your magic out of you."

My heart sped up as we stepped into the courtyard. "I'm listening."

Out of nowhere, Marcus popped out of a bush and came barreling at me, a blast of some kind of power erupting from the palms of his hands. Above me, I heard Alaric shout.

"Fucking Fates!" I screamed as I tucked Winchester to my body and rolled onto the ground and out of the path of Marcus' magic. "What the Hel was that?"

Marcus had stopped running and was now standing next to Erina, looking quite pleased with himself which really pissed me off. "I think that if we orchestrate a few attacks on you, you might be able to tap into your power."

"So you ambushed me and my dog?" I stood up and brushed grass off of me as I checked Winchester over for any cuts or scrapes.

"Sorry, Your Majesty," Marcus stated with a grin.

"Your Majesty, with all due respect, you've never fought in any real battles. You've trained your magic your whole life and you've recently reacquainted yourself with sword fighting, but you've never actually been attacked before – never had to embrace all of your abilities to your full potential."

She was right. While I felt prepared for my first battle, if I wanted to entice my true power to show itself, this was likely the best plan.

Alaric leaned over the balcony and shouted, "I'm coming down! Don't do that again, Erina!" He then disappeared out of view.

"Don't you ever tire of him?" Erina asked and when I snapped my head towards her, her lips twitched.

"What was that magic that Marcus used just now?" I inquired, ignoring her previous question.

Alaric joined me at my side, wrapping an arm around my waist. It felt territorial and I knew it was because he still didn't trust Erina.

"I'll share that with you after our test," she replied. "King Alaric, if you wouldn't mind standing over there?" She gestured to a place about one hundred feet away. "And please, for the love of the Fates, don't try to help her. Your assistance will only hinder the goal we're trying to achieve."

Alaric gritted his teeth, but nodded. He released his grip from my waist and turned to me before placing a kiss on my cheek. "If you truly feel endangered, you tell me," he whispered into my ear. I nodded, but I knew I needed to do this on my own.

I handed Winchester over to Alaric and he stepped away as Francois and Gebert joined us in the courtyard. The three apprentices circled around me as if sizing up their prey. My heart started pounding and I could feel perspiration gather on my forehead. I wanted to believe that they couldn't hurt me, but this very much felt like an attack. I worried my lip as I watched them continue to circle.

"I've told you about that lip!" Alaric called out from the sidelines. I quickly glanced over at him and he winked at me, a devilish grin spread across his face.

It's all going to be okay, I reminded myself. *This is the only way.*

And that's when Gebert launched his attack, a blast of power shooting out of his palm. It was similar to what I had just seen Marcus do, but slightly different. Marcus' blast had looked more like wind coming towards me, but this looked more like purple light. I used my fae strength to run out of the path and then threw up a wall of fire around me to give myself a second to think.

But it was no use. Suddenly the flames started to bend away from me, creating a sun-shaped inferno around me. When I looked up, Francois' hands were moving as if manipulating my fire – shaping it to his will.

I was now facing off against all three apprentices and I could feel my pulse pick up. I didn't want to hurt them – that wasn't the point of all of this. I could easily shoot out a blaze of fire and end this all in an instant, but they were trying to help me.

Their help made me feel helpless.

They stepped closer and closer to me and I found myself slowly retreating, getting backed up against one of the walls that surrounded the castle. Suddenly, Winny started running across the field towards me.

"No!" Alaric shouted. All three apprentices turned towards the disruption. They gave each other knowing looks and then held their hands out in front of them.

Directly at Win.

"*Noooooooooo!*" I screamed. Fear for Winny overtaking the fear I felt for myself. I dropped to my knees and screamed again. The sound was so loud, I closed my eyes and covered my ears. Suddenly I felt a stillness inside of me. I dropped my hands to my sides at the same time that I opened my eyes and that's when I saw it...

All three apprentices were laid out on the ground, slowly coming back to consciousness.

Winchester was licking Marcus' face.

And Alaric's eyes were wider than I had ever seen them. "What *was* that?" he shouted at Erina who gave a knowing smile.

"That, Your Majesty, was a fraction of your mate's true power."

* * * * *

After my... display... we headed back inside the castle and into the throne room, closing the door for privacy. There were so many emotions flowing through my body. I felt scared, but I also felt... powerful. Like something had awakened inside of me. I could feel it like I could feel the mating bond. It was purring, but not like a cat. It purred like a tiger.

"Erina, what happened?" I needed to understand this. If I could understand it, I could harness it.

"The magic that my apprentices wielded never would have hurt you, but you didn't know that. They can bend reality – take what's already there – and use it as power. Marcus gathered the air to blast power at you, while Gebert refracted the light. Francois then took the flames that you provided and was able to bend them to his will. They were never going to actually cause you any harm, but they wanted you to think that. And you did. But you were choosing to risk your own safety for theirs instead of just attacking them. You take after your mother in that way. It wasn't until your dog was in harm's way that you let some of your power out."

Alaric turned to me. "Your love for Winchester triggered it..." He trailed off. "You sent a blast of power out that knocked them over and out so that they couldn't touch Win. It was incredible, Astoria!"

"You have a heart of gold, Your Majesty. It is the only thing that can defeat the magic of the soulless Remis."

"Why do you think that's only a fraction of what I can do?" I found myself asking.

"With all due respect, if you could send that much power out for a dog that you just fell in love with, imagine what you can do if it's your kingdom at stake?"

I thought back to when Remis stabbed Alaric. It had all happened so fast, I didn't process it until after Alaric was on the ground. Even Renfred hadn't been able to do anything. So if this was going to work, I needed to be strategic about it. See the bigger picture and know when to attack before it was too late.

I could do this.

My heart beat in agreement.

30

CHAPTER THIRTY

A week passed and we tried to elicit my powers out again, but it was no use. Now that I knew there wasn't any actual threat to myself or my loved ones, I couldn't seem to get my heart power to come out and play. I was growing more and more frustrated as time went on because the more time that passed, the closer I knew we were to facing off against Remis.

Renfred and I were out training in the courtyard when Malisande approached with a letter in her hand. I immediately recognized the seal.

Spirare.

My stomach sank as I reached out with a trembling hand and took the message from Malisande. I cracked open the seal and unfolded the letter. Alaric must have seen Malisande's approach because he was suddenly behind me, looking over my shoulder at the letter from Beau.

It is time.

Meet in Spirare.
- B

That was it. With six simple words, we were about to embark on the journey that would lead us back to Tellus. To end this once and for all.

"I'll send an enchanted letter to my mother and Elix right away. They'll prepare the troops and have them meet us in Spirare," Alaric stated, his voice rough, but firm. He turned to Renfred. "We should leave immediately."

"As you wish, Your Majesty," Renfred replied with a bow. And with that, he was off to rally our army. I could feel the tension radiating off of him as he walked away. It was evident that I wasn't the only one on edge. How could I be?

Alaric took my hand in his, the feel of it grounding me a bit. "Let's go," he said as he guided me towards the castle and up to our chambers. We packed light – a few changes of clothes, toiletries and, of course, weapons. As many weapons as we could fit to our bodies without restricting movement.

"Are we... I mean, can we... take Winchester with us?" I asked, my voice raspy.

"It won't be safe for him," Alaric warned.

I knew he was right. I knew what he'd say before I even asked the question, but my gut was telling me not to leave him behind. Win was the only being to ever draw out my golden heart magic and he was named after our ultimate goal. To win. I tried to push down the feeling of uneasiness that I felt thinking about leaving him in Fiah, but it refused to be kept down.

"Alaric, I really think he needs to come with us."

My husband turned to me with furrowed brows. "Okay… Why? Let's talk it through."

I huffed a heavy breath and sat on the bed. "I can't explain it. I just feel like he needs to come."

"But you know that you could be putting him in danger, right?"

I shook my head. "I really don't think so." I bit my lip, deep in thought, and saw Alaric's gaze darken. I quickly released the hold my teeth had. We didn't have time. There wasn't enough time. "Alaric, I have to trust my gut."

He walked over to me and kneeled between my legs, taking my face in his hands. "Then I have to trust it, too."

I dropped my head to his and we sat there for a moment, our breaths in sync with one another's. One way or another, this would be over soon. Either we would kill Remis and free Tellus, as well as save the rest of the kingdoms from being conquered, or Alaric and I wouldn't be returning to Fiah. I needed to believe that the latter was impossible – that there was no way we couldn't win.

Win.

* * * * *

At the last moment, I second guessed myself and left Winny in Fiah under Malisande's care. I truly believed that he was meant to stay with us, but I couldn't risk him getting hurt – or worse – without solid reasoning. And while my gut had never failed me before, I wasn't willing to take a chance this time.

Riding on Priscilla's back, we made it to the capitol of Spirare in two nights. I was pleased to see that Gelu's forces had already arrived. Since there was only so much room at the castle, the militaries camped out just outside the gates, but Alaric and I were offered guest rooms in the palace.

After we settled in, we met with Spirare's king and queen who informed us that Beau was in Tellus. While Remis had no idea that we were coming, Beau was ensuring that the army there was as ill-prepared as possible.

Good. We needed all the help we could get.

That night, we dined with the king and queen, as well as the Generals of each army. Conversation felt somewhat forced, but we mostly discussed battle strategies. Each army had been training and preparing to work with the other kingdom's militaries, but there were still fine details that needed to be worked out.

"I'm scared," I admitted to Alaric late in the middle of the night. My voice was so quiet, I wasn't even sure if he could hear me. Honestly, I didn't even know if he was awake to hear me. I just needed to say the words out loud.

Alaric pulled me towards him. "I know," he replied, his voice rough with sleep. "I'm scared, too."

"What if we fail?" I asked. It was a useless question, but I needed Alaric to keep talking to me. To keep my mind occupied.

He rolled me onto my back and cupped my face with one hand, his eyes glistening with love as the moonlight that streamed through the windows reflected off of them. "Darling, if we fail, then I will meet you in the After Realm."

We made love, slowly at first, but it quickly turned into frenzied passion. If this was the last time we would be together like this, then I wanted to make it count. I wanted the bond to feel how strongly I would fight for this male if the Fates threatened to tear us apart after death.

* * * * *

We spent the next day traveling with the armies, thousands upon thousands of soldiers, to Tellus and arrived hours after the sun had gone down. It was eerily quiet, which unsettled me. I expected to hear raucous sounds coming from the local taverns, but there was nothing. A chill crept up my spine.

We approached the gates under the cover of night and I immediately noticed that there wasn't a guard in sight. Something didn't feel right. I let a small amount of my fire magic out to test the wards, shocked to find that there were none.

"Of course," I groaned. Who needs guards or wards when they think they're unkillable? Who needs guards or wards when there's no concern for the innocents that lie beyond these gates? "Harm as few civilians as possible!" I shouted to the armies behind me.

And then we burst through the gates of Tellus.

It didn't take long for the screaming to begin. Fae and humans, seeing our entrance onto their land, yelled and ran for their lives into their homes, barring the doors. I shook my head. With Remis draining the fae's magic, they were defenseless. Sitting ducks.

"Keep going!" I yelled as we continued marching towards the castle. I needed to keep the momentum going to ensure that no one got any ideas and touched any civilians.

That's when the first arrow was shot at us. It narrowly missed Renfred, who was leading the charge, General Grinroff by his side. Almost immediately, storm clouds rolled overhead, shooting lighting that lit up the sky. I looked at Alaric's stoic face – my mate was ready for battle.

Now, fully aware of our presence, Tellus' army began to fight back. Arrows soared through the air, but were mostly deflected by a few Gelu fae at the front lines who used their magic to move them out of their intended path. Lightning cracked the sky as we approached Remis' courtyard which was already ablaze with magic.

And that magic was coming directly from The Six.

"Hello, sisters!" Erina called out in a taunting tone. "It's so good to see you! We would like an audience with your king if you'd be so kind as to take us to him."

All six witches sneered at the sister who defected from them.

"I'll take that as a no then?" She shrugged and then Erina began murmuring words that didn't sound like our language. An incantation in the old tongue? The ground began to shake and it felt all too familiar. The sensation brought me back to the trials.

"Erina, what are you doing?" I shouted at her, but I already knew the answer.

The ground erupted in front of us, spraying dirt, rocks and debris, and six shadowborgs emerged!

Shit! I had forgotten about those!

Looking at them again, they were just as vile as I remembered them to be. They turned to Erina and she simply pointed a finger at her sisters. That simple gesture was all it took for the shadowborgs to turn their attention towards The Six and blast shadows at them. But just as quickly as they acted, The Six reacted, putting up an invisible shield in front of them that the shadows bounced off of.

Tellus soldiers began to file out of the castle, but it wasn't long before we were surrounded on all sides. Wasn't Beau supposed to be keeping them distracted? How were they so prepared as to be edging us? Fortunately, we placed the macarong soldiers along the perimeter, seeing as they were the strongest and fastest. Our formation was like that of an onion, layered first by the macarong, then the fae, and in the center, the humans that insisted on fighting for their kingdom. Their loyalty was admirable and I needed to keep them as protected as possible.

I jumped off of Priscilla and patted her. "You know what to do! I love you!" I shouted to her before she flapped her wings and took off into the sky. I wanted her far, far away from danger.

Tellus' soldiers closed in and at Grinroff's word, the battle finally broke out.

Sound exploded as swords clashed and magic blasted through the air, both sides giving it all that they had. Alaric and I flanked one another. We knew that we were stronger together and agreed that separating would mean certain death – for both of us. We had trained our magic together for so long, that it was like a synchronized dance. Alaric would use the lightning to strike down soldiers and I would use the electricity to strengthen my flames. Power was being sent in every direction.

Alaric and I used our swords to take down a group of Tellus soldiers in close range, their blood spilling to the ground before their bodies followed. My attention snagged on a Spirare soldier that I hadn't noticed before. He had blonde hair and blue eyes and was most certainly human. Why was he on the outer perimeter? He fought well, but humans were supposed to stay in the center. What was he thinking?

I shook my head and directed my gaze back to the approaching group of Tellus soldiers who were closing in on us quickly. I let my fire magic free, flames roaring towards them, as nearby soldiers jumped out of the way of the scorching heat. But before the flames reached their target, in the blink of an eye, the soldiers disappeared and the flames instead hit several of the buildings that should have been behind them.

Illusion magic.

The shops were engulfed in flames and the soldiers were gone from sight. I looked to Alaric, pleading with my eyes for him to use rain to extinguish the flames, but he wasn't looking at me. I directed my eyes to where his gaze fell and that's when I saw him.

Remis.

The fire was spreading to homes and the residents were screaming as they ran out and away from the fighting going on just outside. My heart sank, but there was nothing that I could do because our target had finally made an appearance.

"It's nice to see you, again," Remis declared with a smile. He looked to Alaric. "I had thought you'd be dead by now, but... well, here you are! Destroying my kingdom." He clapped his hands like a raving lunatic.

"*You* are destroying your kingdom, Remis! And we won't let it continue," Alaric fired back. There was now so much lightning lighting up the sky that it almost appeared to be daytime.

"Is that so? You're going to stop me?" he replied with a sneer before directing his attention to me. "Hello, Little Queen. Just as my own daughter, I should have killed you as a babe."

A growl escaped me. Not at his empty and too-late threat, but at the mention of Scarlet. I would kill him for her and hope that wherever she was in the After Realm that she was watching and smiling down at me.

Shadowborgs continued to attack at The Six's invisible shield. Erina and her apprentices were desperately fighting to take it down with their magic, knowing full well that Remis would be less powerful without The Six's magic.

The Six began swaying, their black hair looking like sweeping curtains. Like Erina had been doing, they were also mumbling something inaudible. Suddenly, they grasped hands in unison and a strange power erupted from them. It was black and should have looked more like shadows, but it somehow had an iridescent quality about it that reflected the light around us. It hit Erina directly in the chest, her mouth forming an O as she froze for a moment. The power recoiled and Erina's knees buckled.

"Nooooooooo!" Alaric and I screamed in unison, running towards her as fast as our legs and magic would take us.

The Six smiled, even as the shadowborgs continued to attack their shield.

"Erina," I sobbed, dropping to her side.

The witch who had become a matronly figure in my life gave me a sad smile. "Looks like I'll be paying my father a visit," she said softly, her gaze fixed on the sky.

"No, Erina! No!" I cried, taking her hands in mine. "What can I do?"

She tried to take a breath, but wheezed and began coughing uncontrollably. When the fit ceased, her eyes met mine. "Kill them all."

"No. No, no, no, no," I kept saying in disbelief. This couldn't be happening.

"Tell my sisters I'll see them again in Hel." She smiled and it wasn't a kind smile. It looked sadistic. "Kill them all, Astoria. You're the only one that can." And then she was gone.

Alaric took his hands and brushed them over her face to close her eyes. "Astoria," he breathed. "We have to keep fighting."

I was shaking. With grief and with rage. Remis took from me *again*. Now I was going to take his life.

Alaric stood up and placed his hands around my arms, lifting me to my feet. My knees wanted to buckle, but I stood strong. A Tellus soldier ran up to us, his sword raised in the air and waiting to come down on one of us. I blasted him with a deluge of flames and when I dropped my hand, he was nothing but dust drifting away in the wind.

I didn't have time to think as more soldiers came at us relentlessly. They continued to come at us from all angles, but Alaric and I were more in sync than ever before, taking each one down one by one with ease.

I then felt true fear as I saw Winchester trot onto the battlefield. How the Hel did he get here? And was he... *glowing*? A soldier swung his sword at me and I ducked before slicing mine through his abdomen. Fuck him. He wasn't going to stop me from saving Winchester. Blood quickly saturated his tunic and I kicked his body off of my sword just as two white snow foxes approached Winny. He kept glowing as I ran towards him, the foxes eying him and his glow. They didn't seem to think he was a threat, though. They sniffed the air and then both healed, as if Winchester had commanded them to.

Something scratched at the back of my mind. A memory of something that I couldn't quite place.

"Winchester!" I called and he looked at me with a happy, little puppy smile on his face, his tongue wagging in time with his breathing. "Go! Get out of here!" I waved at him in a direction away from the fighting.

Still glowing, Winchester barked at the foxes and took off with his two new furry friends jogging behind him. They ducked off into an alley and I breathed a sigh of relief that, at least for a moment, Winchester appeared safe. And he apparently *did* have magic! That was just another thing I would have to deal with later – if I had a "later."

My moment of relief was short-lived as I looked around, my stomach plummeting again when I saw Alaric fighting with Remis. When had he left my side? We promised each other to stay together! Remis had his onyx sword in hand as steel met steel in a thunderous clang. I needed to figure out how to get that sword.

This was the moment that I had been waiting for. The moment that I needed to quickly assess the situation and send out my heart power. I watched as Alaric battled the mad king, sparks flying as their blades clashed again and again, and I tried to tug at that place in my chest. But something was wrong. Why was it not working? My husband – my *mate* – was in danger. I was terrified. But nothing was happening. Was it because I trusted that Alaric could handle himself?

Not knowing what else to do, I shot flaming hot lava at Remis, but the deluge of fire just recoiled off of his body and died in a puff of smoke that polluted the air. Remis turned to me, fighting Alaric without even looking and I realized that he had been toying with him the whole time. Their swords clashed and sparked. Alaric pressed forward, raining a flurry of blows at Remis, each strike more powerful than the last. Remis blocked each one and then sliced his sword in an arc, taking Alaric's down with his. So fast that my eyes barely registered the movement, Remis twisted so that he was behind Alaric, his sword digging into the flesh of his neck and drawing a thin line of blood. It began to drip towards his collarbone, a viscous red trickle.

That's when I felt it. At the sight of Alaric's blood being drawn, it was like something snapped inside of me and wanted to be let out so that it could tear the world apart. For him.

"Oh, Little Queen," Remis taunted me in a sing-song voice.

Suddenly, someone grabbed my hand and while my instincts should have told me to pull away, my chest warmed in a soothing way. It felt familiar.

So familiar.

I quickly turned my head...

And there was my mother beside me.

She wasn't corporeal, but I could still see her as if she was a mirage. And I could feel her hand against mine.

"Mom?" I squeaked out with wide eyes that were fighting back tears.

"Do you feel that, Astoria? That feeling in your chest?" Her voice was music to my ears.

Without thinking, I nodded. Because I could feel it. Something in my chest that felt hot like my fire, but that wanted to be let out more desperately than my fire magic ever had. It thrashed against my ribs so hard that I was forced to take a shuddering breath.

"Lean into that feeling, Astoria. Feel its warmth and the steady beat and let it out. *Let it out, Astoria!*" She screamed, but suddenly, I was screaming, too, as white light flooded out of me, exploding from my chest. I looked over at my mother and that same light was pouring out of her! Despite the fact that I knew she wasn't entirely here, that white light definitely was. It created a blast of power that shook the realm.

Out of the corner of my eyes, I saw all of our enemy soldiers get blown backward, many of them knocked out like the apprentices had been. Even The Six were down. But the blast hadn't been enough to deter Remis, though. It had jostled him enough to release his grasp on Alaric, who was able to extricate himself and get far enough away. Now rid of the sword at his neck, his fae abilities were already healing his wound. Remis turned his head to survey the damage, and once he did, Alaric retreated as far from Remis as he could get in a matter of seconds. He knew exactly what I was planning, although I wondered if he could see my mother, too.

She tightened her grip on my hand and we blasted Remis with pure, raw power. He flew through the air, his body tumbling as if he were rolling, until his head hit the ground with a sickening thud. His sword landed away from him, hidden somewhere in the shadows. Alaric was already on the move, frantically searching for it. Blood was pooling around Remis' head, but I could tell he was still alive. My power wasn't enough. We needed the sword. And fast.

I looked up at my mother and she smiled at me. She then squeezed my hand reassuringly and vanished as if she had never been there at all. I didn't know why the Fates allowed her to intervene, but they did and I was more grateful than they could ever know.

Beyond where my mother had just been standing, I saw the blonde-haired boy running away from the skirmish. I was glad to see him still alive, but where was he going?

And where the Hel was Beau?

Realizing I had been distracted at a crucial moment, I quickly turned my attention back towards Remis just as his fingers twitched and his body jerked. Alaric was still looking for the sword. It had to be somewhere close by. It couldn't just disappear.

Remis placed his hands on the ground to steady him and then slowly stood up. He laughed cynically and then looked at me, a sneer on his bloodied face. He lifted his hands towards the sky, looking like he was summoning power from somewhere. "You bitch," Remis snarled. "You think you can kill me? You can't!" the mad king roared, laughing maniacally.

But the sound was cut off as a sword shot through Remis' chest. Confused, I searched for Alaric. After all of my research and the discussions we'd had, he knew better than to try to take the killing blow. But then I saw him. He panted as his eyes met mine, questioningly. We looked back towards Remis. Slowly, the light in his eyes dimmed and his head slumped forward. When the sword was pulled away, the evil king crumbled to the ground...

Revealing Scarlet standing behind him.

Nonchalantly, she swiped the sword along her pants, ridding it of her father's blood and then pointed it at me.

Scarlet was alive!

And she was now the Queen of Tellus.

I gasped, bringing a hand to my mouth in utter surprise. All this time she had been alive? How was this possible?

Behind her, Beau approached – the bastard – and placed his hand on the small of Scarlet's back. He was joined by a female with long, dark hair whose face was all too familiar. Scarlet narrowed her eyes at Alaric and then turned to wink at me. "Hello, Cousin," she said, venom dripping off her words as she smiled, flashing a fang.

Scarlet was a macarong.

ABOUT THE AUTHOR

Kimberly is an avid reader of fantasy and romantasy. After a conversation with her sister, she was inspired to write her own romantasy, using her least favorite trope as inspiration and changing it so that it's less predictable. She wanted to write something that breaks the rules and leaves the reader in shock.

When she's not writing or reading, Kimberly is with her family, cooking, baking or selling homes in Orlando, FL.